Out of the Crash

by

Susan Poole

Cover Art by *Teddi Black*

The Wild Rose Press, Inc.
PO Box 708
Adams Basin, NY 14410-0708
Visit us at www.thewildrosepress.com

Publishing History
First Edition, 2025
Trade Paperback ISBN 978-1-5092-6051-5
Digital ISBN 978-1-5092-6052-2

Published in the United States of America

Dedication

To my children, who have shown me the true meaning of love, filling my life with endless joy and laughter. Thanks for inspiring me to never give up on my dreams. Cheers to our Poole Party of Five!

Pam Carlson: *Looks like paramedics carrying a stretcher. I'm heading over there now.*

Sammy Wells: *Watching from my front yard. Someone's lying in the road.*

Claire Brady: *Can't be good.*

Pam Carlson: *I see a bike in the bike path too. Looks like it was hit.*

Kendal Tenner: *I hate that bike path. Way too narrow.*

Cindy Leighton: *Oh, God. It might be a kid.*

Pam Carlson: *Nope. Looks like a woman. The police won't let me any closer.*

Sammy Wells: *Oh shit. I recognize her. Her son's in my daughter's grade. And she's not moving.*

August 15th–Saturday morning

SHAWNEE SPRINGS ONLINE PARENT PAGE

Claire Brady: *Anyone know what's happening on Lakeshore Road? I'm driving to the high school to set up concessions for the girls 'soccer game. Both lanes are closed. Not much traffic but I can see flashing lights ahead. Worries me.*

REPLIES:

Tina Cole: *I heard sirens. Must be an accident.*

Kendal Tenner: *Glad my kids are still in bed.*

Karri Craig: *Checking on mine now. I fell asleep watching TV last night. Not sure my son made it home from the bonfire.*

Lucy McDuff: *An ambulance whizzed by my house.*

Cindy Leighton: *I have a bad feeling about this.*

Mick Nally: *Don't you people have anything better to do?*

Jo Williams: *Agreed. Could be a drill. Stop trying to stir up drama.*

Claire Brady: *Not trying to stir up anything. Just concerned.*

Gary York: *My daughter is at the high school taking the ACT. When does that let out?*

Jo Williams: *Whenever they finish. Duh.*

Mindy Grace: *Can anyone on that end of town what's going on?*

Chapter One

Three days earlier

Caroline Beasley sprinted toward the Las Vegas convention center, hoping to arrive on time for her speaking engagement. A flight delay had put her behind schedule. She charged through the lobby's glass door and stopped briefly to admire the bright lights reflecting off the white marble floor. A faint lemony smell hung in the air, welcoming her to another hectic day in the life of a popular yet reluctant public figure.

Alongside the registration desk, an oversized poster with an image of Caroline's younger self caught her eye. She walked toward it slowly and cringed. She hated that picture, always had. Why hadn't she listened to her press agent and agreed to another photoshoot? Stubborn was one thing. But agreeing to display that ridiculous photo of herself in an obnoxiously bright pink headscarf and matching sports bra was just plain stupid.

In the poster, she held a copy of her book in one hand while clenching the other in a tight fist. She wore a pair of satin boxer shorts and a pitiful scowl on her face. At least her crow's feet weren't visible. The picture had been photoshopped, right down to the digitally enhanced boobs that hid her botched implants.

She'd been barely forty when that picture was taken, and she'd come a long way over the last five years— from sharing her story with a small support group to eventually accepting advocacy as her calling and turning it into a speaking career. Initially, that branded image empowered her. But today, it made her cheeks burn hot with regret. Before she could analyze the past publicity mistake any further, a young woman in a meticulously pressed suit raced toward her.

"Ms. Beasley, Ms. Beasley!" Even in a hurry, the woman walked with perfect posture, effortlessly balanced on a flaming red pair of six-inch heels. She extended her arm toward Caroline for a shake long before they were close enough to touch.

Caroline stood still and smiled, recognizing the woman from her LinkedIn profile but almost forgetting her name. "Hi, um, Ms. Anderson?"

The woman nodded aggressively and yanked Caroline's hand from alongside her hip, shaking it with the same enthusiasm Tanner, Caroline's Labrador retriever, used on his favorite pull toy.

"It's a pleasure to meet you, Ms. Beasley."

"Please. Call me Caroline."

"Oh, good. Carol it is."

She clenched her jaw at the annoying abbreviation of her name. Even if the woman hadn't read her book, she should be able to read the name on the poster. "No. I said Caroline."

"Oops! Sorry." Her voice hitched nervously. "You can call me Kira. Excellent. Now we're on a first-name basis." Kira smoothed her skirt and turned toward the dreadful poster. "I love, love, *love* this picture of you, Ms. Beasley—I mean Caroline. It's so badass. Makes you look invincible, which you are. My mom died of breast cancer when I was in high school. I wish she would have been around to read your book. Maybe she would have fought a little harder."

Kira's eyes widened as she flipped her wrist to reveal a tattoo of the pink breast cancer awareness ribbon. She stared at Caroline as if waiting for a response.

"I'm sorry about your mother. That must have been tough."

Tears welled in Kira's eyes as her head bobbed up and down.

Caroline gently squeezed Kira's hand, hesitant to change the subject, but the clock was ticking. She needed to put her game face on and prepare for her speech. "If you'd like to talk about it, I can stick around after my presentation."

"Seriously?" Kira said. "You'd do that? For me?"

"Of course." And she meant it.

"Oh, gosh, I'd love that." Kira blew out a breath. "Unfortunately, I've got to head home after the conference. My husband works nights, and we take turns watching our two-year-old."

"I understand. I've got teenagers. My husband Jordan helps at home a lot, too."

Who was she kidding? Jordan handled most of the kids 'stuff these days. He had since she got sick and afterward when her career exploded. Caroline looked at her watch. "Shit! Today's their first day of school. I forgot to call home to wish them luck."

"Go! We've still got a few minutes before you're on."

"No point. It's three hours later back in Shawnee Springs. By now, they're in class." Caroline checked her phone and found several missed texts in their family group chat. Her heart sank, reminded again of the constant struggle to balance motherhood with a demanding career. To make matters worse, Kira released a slight gasp. *She must think I'm a terrible parent*, Caroline thought.

She stood tall and forced a smile. "Oh, well. Let's head to the auditorium so I can set up."

Kira smoothed her skirt again and silently led the way to the elevator.

Despite the ambivalence Caroline felt about using her voice in such a visible way, she thrived in front of an audience. When her tour first launched, nerves presented a problem. Her palms would sweat, and when she opened her mouth, her words often cracked like an adolescent boy's. She once blanked for several awkward seconds in the middle of a television appearance, thankfully recapturing her train of thought before it fled for good. But over time, the opening jitters became manageable, and once she got going, she never felt more alive than from behind a podium.

Standing in front of the sold-out Vegas crowd, Caroline anticipated her introduction. Kira spoke too loudly into the microphone, and a high-pitched squeal erupted from the speakers, ringing throughout the room. She glanced at Caroline apologetically before continuing.

"I'm honored to introduce our keynote speaker, Ms. Caroline Beasley. As you know, Ms. Beasley is the author of *I'll Kill You First: One Woman's Journey to Beat Cancer Before It Beat Her*. After stepping away from her law practice to fight breast cancer, she's become a champion for the cancer community, inspiring women throughout the country to follow their instincts and demand the absolute best from their healthcare providers.

USA Today referred to Ms. Beasley as 'a modern-day hero who never stops pounding the drum of self-care.' *The New York Times* called her book 'every woman's guide to taking control of her body. 'And in her hometown of Shawnee Springs, a suburb of Buffalo, New York, she's been heralded for fiercely defying the medical industry and humanizing the overall treatment of cancer patients."

Caroline had listened to the bio over a hundred times—175 to be exact, including today—but it never got old. The words served as her warm-up song, energizing her to share her story.

Another shrill sound screeched through the speaker as Kira waltzed across the stage to hand over the microphone. "Without further ado, I give you Caroline Beasley."

Caroline took a deep breath; thankful she'd worn flats. "Thank you, everyone." She grabbed the mic with her right hand and waved her left hand high in the air. "I'm happy to be here, but wowzah, it's hot! Could someone please turn up the air conditioning?" She swiped her free arm across her forehead. "I don't know about any of you, but chemo didn't rid me of these damn hot flashes, and I'm roasting up here!"

The audience erupted in laughter and applause, immediately putting Caroline at ease. After requesting someone dim the spotlight blinding her from overhead, she launched into the speech she'd given repeatedly across the United States. No matter where she spoke, the faces staring up at her bore a strong resemblance to one another. Their stories varied, but their expressions universally declared that the dreaded "C-word" had altered their lives forever.

As Caroline paced the stage, she examined the people who had paid good money to hear her—mostly women, with a few men in the mix. She admired the rainbow of wigs and bandanas and mentally high-fived the women who dared to go bald, something she'd never been brave enough to do in public. She spotted the women whose hair struggled to grow back after chemo and empathized with those who'd lost their eyebrows and eyelashes, maybe their fingernails and toenails, too—some of the trade-offs treatment offered in exchange for saving a life.

Caroline's wrist vibrated as her watch sounded an alarm—almost time for the Q & A, the part of her presentation that should have sparked relief. But turning the conversation over to the audience terrified her.

She wrapped things up with her signature tagline—
Be Brave, Stay Strong, and Fight Like Hell—then opened the floor for questions.

Hands flew into the air. Caroline scanned the crowd before pointing to a woman in the third row waving an arm wildly as if swatting flies.

"You, there. In the green dress."

The woman stood and cleared her throat as a crew member hurried toward her with a portable mic. "How did you find the time or energy to gather so many second opinions? It's hard enough to keep up with my regular appointments. I can't imagine starting over with new doctors like you did just because you weren't satisfied with what they were saying."

Caroline nodded. "It was time-consuming. And exhausting. I'd be lying if I said my quest to find the right doctors didn't come with sacrifices—often personal ones." Her mind jumped to her son and daughter who were most likely eating lunch in the school cafeteria by now. They'd be angry she had failed to call home, but hopefully, they'd forgive her when she returned.

Stifling her fears, Caroline answered more questions, some specifically about where she found the motivation to fight and others regarding how and when to challenge the so-called experts. The toughest question came from a man holding hands with a woman in a pale pink turban, who said, "I'm sure you had people to lean on when the going got tough. What are some things they did to help during your treatment?"

"Great question." Caroline smiled. "You obviously understand how important it is for cancer patients to have support from their loved ones. Is that your wife beside you?"

The man nodded.

"You're a lucky woman." Caroline's mouth turned dry. She took a giant step toward the podium and leaned in hard to brace herself against an impending doom. "So am I. Nothing specific comes to mind, but my husband helped by making sure the kids and house were cared for, so I only had to worry about myself."

The man frowned as if he'd been hoping for a different answer. Perhaps he expected Caroline to say her husband accompanied her to every appointment. Or how Jordan was actively involved in determining her treatment plan. Those would have been lies. Caroline took pride in her self-sufficiency. She went alone to most of her doctor visits and only engaged Jordan in the decision-making when she got genuinely stumped about how to proceed.

All marriages differ. Hers stood solid, but mostly

because she and Jordan didn't rely on each other for too much. At least that's the story she told—to everyone, including herself. Too bad Jordan didn't always agree with her version of how married life should be.

Caroline turned abruptly to the other side of the room. "There's only time for one last question. Let's see, you there in the baseball cap on the end."

The woman in the cap pointed at her chest and mouthed, "Me?"

"Yes. What's your name?"

The woman popped up from her seat and grabbed the mic from a crew member as soon as he came close. "My name's Paula. Oh my gosh, I'm starstruck and forgot my question. You're my idol. I've read your book from cover to cover and keep a copy on my nightstand."

Paula shifted the mic back and forth from one hand to the other. "I remember now. You seem so courageous and strong. Never afraid. But facing mortality is terrifying. There must have been times when you curled up in the fetal position and surrendered to a good, long cry. Would you mind telling us about one of those?"

A sour taste rose in Caroline's throat. She bit her lip and prayed no one could see the sweat dripping down her temples.

This time, she had to lie. No one would believe her if she didn't.

"Of course. I cried plenty."

****

Ethan Shawver ducked into the bathroom for a quick hit on his vape before entering the school cafeteria, careful not to step on any cracks in the floor to avoid "breaking his mother's back." He stopped to look around and caught a whiff of the familiar stench. No matter what they served, it always smelled like a mix of greasy food, bleach, and B.O. He sure wouldn't miss that stink once he graduated. Senior year. Three down, one to go.

Plopping down at the lunch table across from his best friend and next-door neighbor Cole, Ethan wrinkled his nose at Cole's plate. "Gross. Couldn't they give us something better on the first day back at school?"

"What?" Cole said. "I love chicken nuggets."

"Me too," Ethan said. "But not when they look like breaded turds."

"Screw you." Cole dipped a nugget into a plastic cup of mystery sauce and shoved it in his mouth. "Not everyone's mommy packs his lunch every day. Got anything good in there?"

Cole grabbed for Ethan's brown bag, but he wasn't quick enough. Ethan hugged the bag to his chest, slowly unfolding the top and snatching the napkin from inside. No doubt his mom had scribbled a note on the napkin like she always did, something his friends would totally tease him about if they noticed. He pretended to wipe his nose with it, then jammed it inside his shirt pocket.

"Let's see," Ethan said with a grin. One by one, he revealed the remaining contents of the bag. "One ham and cheese sandwich. One cheese stick. One bag of pretzels. And three homemade chocolate chip cookies."

"Sweet!" Cole elbowed their friend Theo, who was sitting directly to his left. "Looks like Mrs. Shawver didn't forget about us."

Ethan doled out the cookies, bit into his sandwich, then surveyed the cafeteria. "Here we go again. Same shit, different year."

"At least it's our last one," Theo said. "I can't believe we're seniors."

"Pretty sick," Cole said with a mouthful of chicken. "I'm retaking the ACT this Saturday. Either of you gonna be there?"

"I will," Ethan said. "Let's hope the fifth time's a charm."

Theo stole a nugget from Cole's tray before leaning toward Ethan. "You've taken that stupid test four times?"

"Yup. My dad keeps insisting. I got a twenty-eight last time—good enough to get into the University of Utah. But he's not sold on me going there. Says video game design is a dumb profession and thinks I should become a lawyer like him."

"It's your life, man," Theo said. "Tell him to fuck off."

Cole snapped. "Wow. A little harsh. Be happy you have a dad who gives a shit about your future. I'd kill to have mine around once in a while, even if it's not always great." Turning to Ethan, Cole said, "What does your mom think?"

"I dunno. She's caught in the middle. She wants me to be happy, but I don't think she's crazy about me going out of state. She'd probably like me to go to the University of Buffalo and commute. Fat chance I'm living at home while I'm in college. I'm getting as far away from here as possible."

"I'm with you, dude," Theo said.

Suddenly, the good-looking lunch monitor approached their table. Wearing clear plastic gloves and a hairnet, she still looked like she could've been a supermodel back in the day. "You boys finished?"

"Yes, Ma'am," Ethan and Cole said in unison. Theo sat mute with his lips slightly parted.

"Then clear your trays and get to class. Lunch period is almost over."

As soon as she walked away, Theo puckered his lips and made an obnoxious kissing noise. "Ms. Nelson's such a MILF."

"Cut it out," Ethan interjected. "She lives across the street from us." He hated when Theo talked like that. They'd been friends a long time, but Theo could be annoyingly cocky because his dad was the high school athletic director, and like it or not, *nothing* mattered more than sports at Shawnee High—nothing besides sports victories, of course.

Theo winked. "Cool, then you can watch us through your front window."

"You're creepy." Ethan threw Cole's last chicken nugget across the table, hitting Theo in the forehead. Theo stood up and got in Ethan's face but twisted his head sideways and sat back down. Staring at a group of girls walking by their table, Theo said, "Whoa! Who's that chick in the miniskirt?"

Ethan followed Theo's gaze and immediately understood why he was asking. "OMG. That's Grace Beasley. She sure has changed."

"You know that girl?" Breadcrumbs stuck to Cole's lips.

"You do too, dumbass," Ethan said. "That's Kyle Beasley's little sister. She must be a freshman."

"Holy shit." Cole wiped his mouth with his sleeve. "I remember her from when we played baseball on Mr. Beasley's team. She was just a little shit running around the dugout back then. She's definitely grown up—in more ways than one."

They all laughed, staring at Grace until she

11

disappeared from the cafeteria.

"What's going on with Kyle anyway?" Cole said. "I heard he got a baseball scholarship somewhere."

"Geez, where've you been?" Ethan said. "He signed last year with Niagara University."

Cole said, "Is that Division One?"

"Sure is," said Ethan. "Good for him."

"Are you two friends?" Theo said to Ethan.

"Kinda. We used to be. Like Cole said, we played baseball with him when we were younger."

"And athletic." Cole laughed.

"He's an okay guy," Ethan said. "Doesn't really give me the time of day anymore, but at least he's not a prick."

"I think he's a prick," said Theo. "And not just because he's a jock, and my dad worships the ground he walks on."

Suddenly, music blared through the school's new sound system, thanks to someone's dumb idea to replace the morning bell with songs only their grandparents would have enjoyed. At least Ethan recognized this "oldie but goodie" from one of his video games. It was repetitive as hell but still kinda catchy, reminding him to *hustle* to class. The earworm would make it hard to forget.

Theo rose from his seat, gathered his books, and left his tray on the table for Ethan and Cole to take care of. "Gotta run. I've got some dirt on Kyle. Maybe someday I'll tell you about it."

The rest of the school day lagged until Ethan got called to the principal's office in the middle of math class. Mrs. Duncan, the school secretary, told him to wait in the chair directly across from her desk. She kept peering over her glasses to scowl at him as the second hand on the wall clock ticked like a time bomb. He distracted himself by counting the hairs on his arm.

Ethan had no clue why the principal wanted to see him, but Mr. Leandry scared the shit out of him. He'd worked at Shawnee High since Ethan's dad attended school there—back when it was okay to paddle kids for getting in trouble. There were rumors Mr. Leandry used to swat students with an eight-foot boat oar if they got sent to his office. Maybe he still kept it in his closet.

Another lame song blared through the sound system, muffling the sudden rush of students in the hallway as they hurried to and from class. Good thing he had a study hall next period, so he wouldn't miss anything important. Ethan jerked in his seat when the door flew open, and Kyle Beasley blew in like a tornado.

"Hey, Shawver," Kyle said. "What's up?"

"Hey, Kyle," Ethan muttered.

"Have a seat, Mr. Beasley," said Mrs. Duncan. She removed her glasses and pointed them toward the chair next to Ethan.

"What are you in for, Shawver?" Kyle flashed a Hollywood smile, revealing his perfectly white teeth. No wonder the girls loved him.

"Not sure. You?"

"I guess I've got to take the ACT this Saturday, but I never registered. Gonna see if good ol 'Mr. Leandry can pull some strings for me."

"Why would *you* have to take the ACT? I thought you already committed to Niagara."

Kyle rocked in his chair and ran his hands through his hair. "Exactly. But I got an email asking why I hadn't submitted my scores. It's probably a mix-up, but my old man thought I should take it to be safe. The test is only offered here at Shawnee High one more time." Kyle chewed his fingernails, bit off a sliver, and spit it across the room.

"Hey, I saw your little sister today," Ethan said.

"Yeah. So what?"

"The fellas were checking her out in the cafeteria."

Kyle's face turned red, and his eyes practically bulged from their sockets. "What the hell do you mean by that?"

"Um, nothing, man, it's just that she's, you know…kinda good lookin 'now."

Kyle glanced sideways at Mrs. Duncan before jumping to his feet and getting in Ethan's face. "Don't make me have to kick your ass."

Ethan shrank into his seat. "Relax, man. Just an observation among friends."

Kyle sat back down before Mrs. Duncan could say a thing. "Doesn't matter. Don't mess with my family. Grace is off-limits. Remember that. Tell all your buddies, too."

Ugh. Ethan should have kept his mouth shut about Grace. He hadn't meant to piss Kyle off. They used to be good friends, and so were their families. But somewhere along the line, they grew apart, finding different interests and joining new friend groups. He wasn't exactly sure when things had changed, probably around the time Kyle's mom got cancer. None of the Beasleys were around much then. Or maybe Theo was right, and Kyle had grown into a selfish prick, so full of himself after becoming a baseball phenom that he couldn't be bothered with kids like Ethan anymore.

But some of his best memories involved playing

baseball on Mr. Beasley's team—when Mom packed a cooler with enough snacks to feed half the town, and Dad cheered him on from the bleachers as if they were playing major league ball and every game was part of the World Series.

Back when his father was proud of him.

The office phone buzzed, and Mrs. Duncan picked it up right away. "Yes, he's here. Uh huh. Uh huh. Uh huh. Sure." She hung up and frantically pecked at the keyboard on her desk. Another five minutes passed before she finally looked up from her computer and gave Ethan another scowl.

"Mr. Leandry will see you now, Mr. Shawver. Leave your belongings with me, including your cell phone."

What the heck was going on here? He looked at Kyle just in time to see him spit another fingernail from his mouth, almost hitting Mrs. Duncan in the face. Surprisingly, she didn't seem to notice. She just kept glaring at Ethan until he parked his backpack at her feet and walked toward the principal's office.

"Hello, young man," Mr. Leandry said as Ethan entered the room. "Have a seat."

Ethan did as he was told and folded his hands in his lap. The wait was killing him. Let's get this over with.

"This isn't how to begin the school year," Mr. Leandry said. "Especially your senior year." The principal's eyes rolled back in his head until his pupils completely disappeared, reminding Ethan of the hardboiled egg he'd had for breakfast. "Do you know why you're here?"

"Um, no."

Mr. Leandry blinked, thankfully revealing his pupils

again. "That's trouble in itself that you don't know when you're breaking a school rule."

Ethan looked down and examined his outfit. His black button-down contained no swear words, and his shorts fell well below his knees without being overly baggy. Plus, he'd worn the same sneakers last year. It couldn't be a dress code violation.

His heart pounded, and he could feel the blood rushing to his cheeks. He stared into Mr. Leandry's eyes, hoping for an answer, but he was baffled. He must have looked pathetic as he sat there poker-faced, waiting for something to happen.

Mr. Leandry cleared his throat. "We have a strict policy against vaping on school premises, Mr. Shawver. Are you aware of that?"

"Yes."

"Did you bring a vape pen to school today?"

Ethan shifted in his seat and averted his gaze toward the ground. One of Mr. Leandry's orthopedic shoes tapped from side to side. He obviously knew the answer, but Ethan had no idea how.

"Careful how you respond, son."

Ethan nodded but kept watching the principal's foot.

"Okay, then. I appreciate your honesty. Please spread the word among your peers that we installed closed-circuit cameras over the summer in all the restrooms—not in the stalls, but in the common areas. We won't tolerate smoking or vaping anywhere on school property, and your first offense requires a note sent home to your parents. Mrs. Duncan is preparing a memo now. You're to return it by Friday—with both their signatures."

"But—"

"Stop, Mr. Shawver. There's no use arguing."

"But, what if one of my parents, um—is unavailable? Is it okay if only one of them signs it?"

Mr. Leandry rolled his eyeballs back inside his head. Yuck. Ethan looked away.

"If that's the case, have your mom or dad confirm that in a note. You're a good kid, Mr. Shawver. I'd hate to see you get derailed senior year."

"Thank you." Ethan stood and walked out of the office, almost tripping over Kyle's extended legs, which obstructed his path. "Excuse me," he said without making eye contact. As he approached Mrs. Duncan's desk, she held out her hand, clutching a sealed envelope addressed to his parents. He grabbed it quickly, retrieved his backpack from the floor, and reentered the hallway— but not before catching one last scowl.

Ethan crinkled the envelope and tried to stuff it in his shirt pocket. Something got in the way. He dug inside and pulled out his lunch napkin, unfolding it to read Mom's message.

"Today's a big day, honey! The start of your senior year. I hope you know how proud I am of you and everything you've accomplished. I can't wait to see what comes next. Love you to the moon and back, Mom."

Dang it. Getting busted for vaping was definitely *not* what she meant. Senior year was off to a terrible start. He sure hoped he could convince Mom to sign that note without telling Dad.

Chapter Two

Ahh...the kitchen! The heart of every home—precisely like the plaque above the pantry door read. It felt good to be back, and even better that Kyle and Grace never said a word about Caroline forgetting to acknowledge their first day of school.

She pressed the power button on the coffeemaker to brew a cup of dark roast and leaned against the center island. She looked around the room, impressed at how clean Jordan and the kids kept everything while she was away. The sink was empty, counters wiped clean. It even looked as if the floors had been swept. Her friends often complained about how sloppy their husbands could be. She was lucky hers was such a neat freak, and he kept on top of Kyle and Grace about their chores.

Breathing in the sweet smell of hazelnut, she grabbed her steaming hot mug and paused in front of the refrigerator. The creamer inside tempted her, but she'd been trying to drink her coffee black, so she passed right by and sat at the kitchen table. The silence invited an avalanche of family history. She glanced back at the fridge, suddenly recalling how photos, crayon drawings, and gold-star papers once cluttered the door. That was before they replaced their old fridge with a fancier model, a stainless-steel side-by-side without magnetic doors. Now it was just a blank slate.

But endless memories lingered within those kitchen

walls. Grace falling out of her highchair when she was eighteen months old, requiring a trip to the emergency room and a forehead full of stitches. Kyle standing on the dishwasher door as a toddler, jumping on it every chance he got until the supports finally gave way and the door broke right off. Preparing daily lunches and weekend breakfasts. Helping with homework and watching the nightly news. Baking cookies and stuffing turkeys. A lifetime of meaningful events—big and small—centered around one modest but well-equipped room.

Caroline also drew strength from that kitchen. It's where she first declared war against the tumor growing inside her. Feeling nauseous one morning after chemo earlier in the week, she'd found herself in a predicament. The toilet in the powder room off the kitchen needed repair, and she couldn't make it upstairs. She'd had no choice but to throw up in the kitchen sink. No one else was around, but it was humiliating all the same. She remembered hanging her head over the cast iron basin, breathing in the sour smell wafting from the garbage disposal, and praying the uncontrollable retching would stop before anyone else got home. At that moment, she felt so sorry for herself—a helpless victim surrendering to an invasive disease.

But something had clicked inside her that morning. After cleaning herself up, she sat at the kitchen table and started writing, a pastime she'd always enjoyed but rarely made time for anymore. Unable to pinpoint why her creative side had diminished with age, she found it almost impossible to believe she'd entered college as an English major. She first pivoted when switching to Criminal Justice, and her writing became much more mechanical during law school. After that, she barely had the time or opportunity to compose her full name. Motherhood and cancer took over, consuming every available brain cell until she found herself there—at the kitchen table—wondering how her life had strayed so far off course.

It felt good to revisit the right side of her brain, kickstarting her dormant artistic abilities as her fingers frantically attacked the keyboard one stroke at a time. She grew stronger with every word…every paragraph…every page. That's when she knew the secret to her healing was in expressing herself, not yielding to individual challenges but speaking out about her experience and sharing it with others fighting the same fight.

If it hadn't been for her epiphany in the kitchen that morning, she never would have interjected herself into cancer support groups, donated her time as a patient advocate, or written a book that became a bestseller. The enormousness of what she once faced could have crushed her if she hadn't learned how to channel her energy into safe and small-scale spaces. From that point forward, no matter how terrified she became about dying, the kitchen served as *command central*—the "war room"—where she wrote day and night as she battled her way back to health like a beast.

The sound of flushing water overhead signaled someone else was awake. A few minutes later, Tanner bounded down the stairs with white tufts of hair spraying from his coat. He wagged his tail and whined at the sliding glass door to go out. Caroline started rising from the table, but Kyle was right behind the dog. "I'll get him, Mom. Stay put."

"Good morning, honey." She stood anyway. "What

are you doing up so early?"

"Taking the ACT today, remember?"

"Oh yeah, of course." A little white lie never hurt anyone. She stared at her boy as he gazed out the window, watching the dog in the yard. Damn, he was handsome, just like his father without the thinning salt-and-pepper hair. Kyle's dark brown locks were a mess, thick and wavy, and past his shoulders—way too long, but she knew better than to suggest a haircut. His skin was a dark shade of brown, matching his eyes. Nobody in the family tanned like Kyle, and the standing joke was he must belong to one of the umpteen delivery drivers who frequented their front porch. And when had Kyle grown so tall? Caroline had only been gone three days, but her son looked like he'd shot up a few inches since she'd last seen him.

"You making breakfast?" he said.

"Sure, what would you like?" She walked to Kyle and hugged him, pausing to rub his arms and shoulders. "You've been working out, haven't you?"

He flashed his smile, flexed his muscles, and planted a kiss on his right bicep.

She laughed. *Humble* was not an adjective she ever used to describe her son.

Kyle opened the cupboard and rummaged around. "Never mind. I'll grab a doughnut."

Caroline groaned. "That's not very nutritious. Let me make some eggs."

He glanced at the microwave clock. "No time. Can I take your car? It's behind mine in the driveway."

Before she could answer, Jordan and Grace walked into the kitchen together. Grace wore her soccer uniform, and Jordan looked ready for a round of golf in his polo

21

shirt and khaki shorts.

"Good morning, you two." Caroline shuffled toward them in slippered feet. Grace leaned in and allowed Caroline to give her a peck on the forehead, but Jordan scurried in the opposite direction before disappearing into the walk-in pantry. By the time he emerged, Caroline had lost interest in greeting him with a kiss, instantly struck by the hot and cold of a long-term marriage.

Unwrapping a granola bar, Jordan said, "I've got a patient coming in this morning for an emergency root canal, but I can drop Grace at her game on my way into the office."

Grace pulled a scrunchie from around her wrist and wrapped her long, thick hair into a ponytail. "Are you coming to watch, Mom? It's my first high school game."

"Of course. What time is kickoff? I'll run to the dry cleaners first. I'm headed out of town on Monday and need to have a few things pressed."

"You're leaving again?" Grace whined before stomping to the cupboard and plucking the last doughnut from its box.

"I told you this was a busy month. Just a quick trip to Pittsburgh and back this time. I've got to take the bookings when they come."

"Funny how you travel more during soccer season than baseball season. Plus, you already missed the first day of school, and Open House is next week. You gonna miss that, too?"

Jordan, who had been fixing a cup of coffee with a heaping spoon of sugar and a splash of vanilla creamer, spoke up. "I can go to the open house if your mom's not around."

"Whatever." Grace yanked at the scrunchie and let her hair fall back over her shoulders. "I'll be waiting outside."

"Oh, good. Perfect timing." Kyle glanced again at the clock. "Dad, can you take Mom's car so I can get mine out?"

Jordan paused as if considering the idea. "I'd rather drive my car," he eventually said. "Plus, Grace's soccer bag and cleats are already in my trunk."

"Geez, the never-ending game of musical cars in this house drives me crazy," said Caroline. "Grab your car keys, men, and let's get moving."

Tanner barked at the back door, but no one budged to let him in. They were all too busy scampering for their keys.

Caroline snatched hers first and waited while Kyle and Jordan hunted for theirs. "If you two would ever take the time to put them on the hook where they belong, we'd get out of here a lot faster, now wouldn't we?"

As expected, Jordan and Kyle ignored her. She couldn't blame them. She sounded like a broken record.

Once everyone cleared out, Caroline welcomed Tanner back inside, resettled at the kitchen table, and breathed a sigh of relief. Considering a second cup of coffee, she decided against it. She was jittery enough after the morning's chaos and needed to relax a few more minutes before getting ready for the game.

A short time later, a car door slammed in the driveway. Who could that be? She'd watched Jordan's BMW and Kyle's Jeep drive away from the house.

The back door flew open, and Kyle raced into the kitchen with a panicked look in his eyes. Tanner turned toward him without a care in the world.

"Forget your Number Two pencils?" Caroline smiled.

"No, I need your credit card. I'm almost out of gas. Hurry, please. If I'm late, I won't be allowed to take the test."

Caroline resisted the urge to make another nagging comment. She grabbed her wallet from her purse and handed it to Kyle.

"Good luck today." She kissed him gently on the cheek. "And please, drive carefully."

"Yes, Mom. I will."

The door slammed shut. Kyle's tires squealed as he sped away from the house, and Caroline cringed at his total disregard for her warning.

****

Ethan woke to the sound of his mom's whisper. "Sweetie, wake up. Time to get ready for the ACT. And please shut off your alarm. I don't know how you sleep through that racket."

He opened one eye to see Mom standing over his bed. Rolling over, he grabbed his cell phone to silence the loud clanging noise that never did its job. His feet hung over the end of the bed, and the top sheet wrapped around his ankles. The smell of breakfast coming from the kitchen drifted into his room.

"Did you make pancakes?"

"Sure did. Bacon, too. Do you promise not to fall back asleep if I go downstairs?"

He grunted. "Promise."

Moments later, he sat at the kitchen table. Mom prepared his plate with her back turned toward him. As soon as she spun around, her eyebrows raised, and she shook her head.

"Oh, no. No, you don't. Get back upstairs and change. You can't leave the house in the same clothes you slept in."

Ethan slumped in his chair. "I'll change after I eat."

"Nope. Now." She pointed a finger toward the stairs. "And wash your face and brush your hair while you're at it. Maybe even your teeth—to make sure they get done."

Ethan did what he was told—with warp speed—and settled back at the table in no time. Seconds later, his dad joined him.

"Morning, Amy. Morning, Ethan." Dad looked down at his plate of pancakes and bacon. "This looks delicious. Big breakfast for a big day."

Mom poured two glasses of orange juice and set them on the table. Ethan grabbed one, guzzled it down, and then shoveled a massive bite of pancake into his mouth.

"So, Ethan. You ready this time?" Dad slathered his pancakes with a knife full of butter. "Have you put in enough effort to raise your score?"

"Oh, Dan," Mom said. "Let him eat his breakfast."

"I'm not stopping him from eating. Just making sure he knows how important it is to do well today."

Oh, shit. Here comes the lecture. Ethan took another bite of his pancakes before stretching his arm across the table. "Please pass the syrup."

His dad passed the sticky glass bottle and met Ethan's gaze. "This is your last shot at raising your score. We all know you're capable of getting a thirty or higher. The question is whether you're taking this seriously enough."

"Dan! Stop it! You're putting too much pressure on him. You wanna upset him right before the test?"

"If lighting a fire under his ass helps him live up to his potential, then yes."

Mom shot Dad the stink eye before filling Ethan's juice glass, slamming it down on the table before turning away to hide her face.

Geez. Why couldn't they back off and let him eat in peace? The glob of pancakes in Ethan's stomach threatened to travel back up his esophagus.

"It's okay, Mom. And I'm ready, Dad. All I need to do is raise my math score. Most of the schools I'm applying to super-score, and that's the subject that keeps tripping me up."

"There you go again." Dad raised his voice. "Always looking for a shortcut. Why not just try to do well on the entire exam?"

Mom stomped her foot. "Damnit, Dan! That's enough."

A knock at the door interrupted his parents' bickering.

With a mouthful of bacon, his dad said, "Who could that be this early on a Saturday?"

"Probably Cole," Mom said. "I ran into him yesterday and invited him to breakfast." She turned and looked at Ethan. "You two are riding together today, right?"

Ethan nodded. "Come on in!"

Within seconds, Cole was seated between Ethan and his dad, digging into the stack of pancakes before him. "These are delicious, Mrs. Shawver. Thanks for the invite."

"Of course," she said. "You boys need to carb up before the test."

Seriously, not that stupid test again. Ethan couldn't

stand hearing Dad's ACT sermon any longer and needed to move on. "Hey, Cole, did I leave my backpack in your car yesterday?"

Ethan already knew the answer. He purposely left it in Cole's backseat because he still hadn't shown Mr. Leandry's note to his mom. He needed to catch her alone to explain about the vaping but was still waiting for the chance. Or the courage. She would not be happy. Hopefully, she'd sign the memo without telling Dad and return it with an excuse for only one signature. Mom hated to lie, but maybe she'd take pity on him after this morning's nag-fest.

"You did," Cole said. "I dropped it in your back hallway when I came in."

"Thanks. Hurry up and finish eating. It's time to go." Ethan cleared his plate from the table, put it in the dishwasher, and turned toward his parents. "What are you two doing today?"

His mom grabbed Cole's empty plate and placed it in the sink before finally sitting down to eat the last pancake.

Dad passed her the butter and syrup. "I'll start the yard work but could use a hand before Ethan's available if you're not busy, Amy."

"Give me an hour, okay? It's already heating up outside, so I'd like to get my bike ride in early." Glancing at Ethan, she said. "Good luck on the exam."

"Thanks." Ethan dashed toward the table and kissed his mom on the cheek. "Have fun on your ride—and don't forget to wear a helmet."

She smiled. "You sound like me now."

His dad shot them both a look—as if he wanted to say one last thing. Ethan didn't give him a chance. He and Cole raced out the door and headed toward the high school.

****

"Wow! What a game!" Caroline called out to anyone within earshot as she and Grace walked through the parking lot after the soccer match. Grace had scored two goals; the last one in overtime secured the win. Thankfully, Caroline had been there to watch, especially since Jordan never made it. His root canal patient took longer than expected.

But Grace was much more forgiving of her father. Her daughter's earlier insinuation that Caroline attended more of Kyle's games than hers was hard to hear. She shook off the guilt it triggered by recapping the game during the drive home from the high school. Grace chimed in with an occasional comment, but she was mostly quiet and clearly exhausted. When her stomach growled loud enough to stop traffic, Grace said, "I'm starving. Wanna try that new diner for lunch?"

The invitation warmed Caroline's heart. She would have agreed to lunch in Paris if Grace had suggested it. "Great choice—let's do it. You deserve a celebration."

"Yay! Let's stop home first so I can change out of this smelly uniform."

While Grace showered, Caroline eagerly awaited the long overdue mother-daughter lunch, trying to avoid dwelling on how much she missed when she was on the road. At least she was more involved in her kids 'lives than her own mother had ever been. That should count for something. Caroline sat on the couch, killing time and diverting her attention to her laptop. Tanner snored like an overtired trucker on the floor by her feet.

After several minutes of scrolling through some of

her favorite online shopping sites, the garage door opened. Who else was home? The ACT exam would be over by now, so maybe it was Kyle. But Jordan was expected any minute, too. They'd both be hungry. She feared their girls 'lunch could be in jeopardy. A car stopped inside the garage, which usually meant Jordan. Kyle typically parked in the driveway.

But suddenly, Kyle appeared in the kitchen. He ran right past her, up the stairs, and into his bedroom. She'd only caught a quick glimpse of his face. He looked pale, white as a death mask, and his eyes were swollen red as if he'd been crying. The door slammed shut overhead, so hard a picture hanging in the family room shifted sideways. Seconds later, the crashing of unidentified objects against the upstairs walls frightened her.

Caroline waffled between going to Kyle immediately or giving him some time. Something had obviously upset him, but he didn't stop to tell her about it. If she questioned him too soon, he might not appreciate her concern. Maybe she should hold tight and mind her own business.

Grace ran downstairs, still in her underwear. "What's wrong? Kyle's throwing things around in his room. I tried to go in, but the door's locked."

Tanner raced past Caroline and up the stairs. The banging overhead grew louder, more threatening. What the hell? Kyle never lost his temper. He'd always been so cool under pressure, even as a young boy. Something terrible must have set him off, and the ACT didn't make sense. He'd secured his spot at Niagara University, and taking the standardized test was supposed to be a formality. He'd barely mentioned it until this morning. There must be something he wasn't telling them, like maybe he screwed up by not taking it earlier. Maybe his baseball scholarship was in jeopardy.

With zero confidence in her ability to diffuse the situation, Caroline sprang from the sofa and sprinted toward the bottom of the stairwell to stand beside Grace. She desperately needed Jordan but couldn't avoid her son's tantrum one more second.

"Mom!" Grace screamed. "Do something!"

"I'm going!" She placed her fingers on her temples and squeezed. Think, Caroline, think. The ruckus upstairs wasn't coming from a stranger. It emanated from her son, her baby, the gentle soul she'd raised since birth, who'd grown into a nice young man with a bright future. Comforting him shouldn't be rocket science. She needed to find out what happened and figure out how she could help.

She made it to the landing, which separated their two short sets of stairs, and stopped abruptly at the sound of Jordan's voice.

"Caroline! Kyle! Is everyone okay?"

Holding a palm to her heart, she hurried back downstairs and met Jordan in the family room. "How did you know? Did Grace text you?"

"Know what?" he said. "I haven't looked at my phone, but have you seen Kyle's car?"

Dumbfounded by the chaos, Caroline paused until her husband's question registered. She raised her hands to her face and closed her eyes, trying to stop herself from imagining the worst. "Well, no. I didn't think of looking in the garage when he got home. Why? What's wrong with it?"

"Come see." Jordan led her out toward the garage. Grace followed them a few steps but turned and ran back upstairs, presumably to put some pants on.

As Caroline stood in the mudroom doorway, she stared into the garage at Kyle's Jeep and saw the smashed windshield. The thick glass was shattered from one side to the other, resembling Lake Erie during the late winter months when huge pressure cracks break out in the ice for miles. Something obviously struck the vehicle directly in front of the driver's seat—something big and heavy, like a boulder. The giant dent must have made it impossible for Kyle to see. It's a miracle he made it home safely.

"Oh my God," she cried. "What the hell happened?"

Jordan opened the Jeep door and looked inside. "Hmm. The airbag didn't deploy."

"Why is that? Could that mean he wasn't going too fast or whatever hit him didn't strike hard enough? What if he's hurt?"

"It definitely hit hard enough," Jordan snapped. "Where is he?"

Grace appeared fully dressed beside her mom. "Still in his room. It's quiet in there now."

Jordan brushed by them both quickly. "Stay downstairs, you two. Let me handle this."

Caroline didn't argue. She was relieved to have Jordan take the lead and confident Kyle would rather talk to him anyway. A familiar sense of denial washed over her as her mind wandered back to when she first learned about her cancer diagnosis. Instead of thoroughly digesting the detailed booklet from her doctor about HER2-positive breast cancer, Caroline skimmed the table of contents and put the information aside for another day. Over time, she gently faced reality in bite-sized pieces—a page here, a chapter there—always shielding herself from the complete picture as if peering through a protective screen.

Sometimes, ignoring the truth, or at least easing into it slowly, was the only way she knew how to survive.

****

Ethan and Cole stopped for Mexican food after the exam and took it back to Ethan's house. His parents weren't home, but lawn equipment littered the front yard. The grass had already been mowed, and clippings covered the driveway. Ethan spotted the electric blower propped next to the weed whacker and wondered which job was meant for him—probably both.

"Let's hurry and eat," he said. "Looks like my afternoon chores are waiting."

They rushed inside and sat at the kitchen table to find a note from Dad. "Ethan, I ran to the store, but don't go anywhere. I can't wait to hear about the test. Get started in the front yard until I'm back."

No *please*. No *thank you*. No respect.

Ethan ripped the note in half before inhaling one of his steak tacos. His stomach gurgled ferociously, either because he ate way too fast or because he could predict exactly how his conversation with Dad would go. Hopefully, Mom would get home first, but only after he and Cole finished eating. If she had planned something for lunch to celebrate the completion of the ACT, which wouldn't be a stretch, catching them with takeout would bum her out.

Cole unwrapped his second oversized burrito, pulling it toward his mouth with both hands as a mess of rice and beans fell from inside the tortilla. "My mom's probably still in bed. She didn't even get up this morning to wish me luck."

"Did she work late last night?" Ethan was looking for an excuse to make his friend feel better. Mrs. Kerns was hard to figure out. She may have tried hard, but being a single mother couldn't be easy, especially in Shawnee Springs, where most households still had two parents.

Cole shrugged. The bite he'd taken from his burrito interfered with his ability to speak.

Suddenly, the doorbell rang. They both jerked in their seats. Ethan got up to see who was there while Cole kept chewing.

"Oh, shit!" Ethan called back from the living room as he peered out the front window. "It's Officer Raines."

It seemed strange seeing the school resource officer outside school grounds, where he typically clowned around with most students and cracked jokes about his cushy job supervising the cafeteria. Was he even a legit police officer? Some kids called him "Mall Cop" and insisted he was only a security guard. But he sure looked official today, standing on Ethan's doorstep in full uniform, complete with a gun and badge.

Cole muttered, "What's he doing here on a Saturday afternoon?"

Ethan's heart raced. Unfuckingbelievable. How ridiculous that Mr. Leandry sent someone to his house to track down that stupid note. Ethan should have forged his parents 'signatures and turned the memo in on time.

Tempted to ignore the bell, Ethan preferred dealing with Officer Raines without his dad hovering nearby. He opened the door, smiled, and played dumb. "Hey. Fancy meetin 'you here. What's up?"

The officer didn't smile back. He looked miserable, as if needing to get something serious off his chest. "Hi,

Ethan. Is your dad home?"

"My dad? Uh, no. Neither is my mom. Can I help you with something?" The sound of Cole in the kitchen crinkling his burrito wrappers and throwing them in the trash distracted him. Officer Raines strained his neck, peered over Ethan's shoulder, and called out. "Hey there, Cole. I thought I saw your car out front."

Cole walked into the living room. "Yeah, I live next door. We just took the ACT."

Ethan looked at Cole, then back again at Officer Raines. Awkward.

"So, listen, Officer Raines," Ethan said. "I know what this is about. I promise to turn that memo in on Monday. First thing. Before the homeroom bell. Cut me some slack, would ya? It's the first week of school and I completely forgot about it." He tented his hands together before his chest and pleaded with his eyes.

Officer Raines frowned. "I'm not sure what you're talking about. But I need to speak with your dad. You boys finish your lunch. I'll wait in my car."

Just then, Dad's car pulled into the driveway. He must have noticed the police cruiser out front because he stopped before driving into the garage and walked around to the front door. Confusion distorted his face.

"Hello, Officer. I'm Dan Shawver." He offered his right hand for a shake. "What can I do for you?"

Officer Raines shook his dad's hand. "Mind if I come in, Mr. Shawver?"

"Please, call me Dan." His dad walked up the steps, opened the front door, and gestured for the officer to enter. "After you."

Officer Raines looked back over his shoulder. "You boys stay here for a minute."

Go figure Dad would be the one home to greet Officer Raines instead of Mom. Ethan almost gagged on the lump in his throat. "Just my luck." Sitting down on the front steps with the bright sun on his face, he told Cole about the trip to Mr. Leandry's office and how he'd avoided showing the note to his parents.

"You think that's what this is about?" Cole said. "That seems weird."

"I know. But what else could it be?"

Moments later, the front door opened again, and Officer Raines motioned for Ethan to join them inside. "Your dad wants you to hear this from me," he said.

Nervously, Ethan glanced over at Cole. "I'll text you later." He followed the officer into the house and immediately noticed his dad seated at the kitchen table with his head hung low and his hands covering his face. His shoulders violently shook as he struggled to breathe.

"Is everything okay?" This obviously wasn't about the note.

"Sit down, son." Dad's voice croaked as he lifted his head to reveal a face flushed with pain. He patted the chair directly beside him. "Please continue, Officer Raines." His dad's words were barely audible as if each syllable fought to get out.

Officer Raines sat across from Dad and folded his hands on the table, looking at Ethan. "I'm so sorry to be the one to tell you this. I just informed your father there's been an accident. On Lakeshore Road. Your mom got hit by a car while riding her bike in the bike lane."

Ethan's brain stopped processing after hearing "hit by a car." The words chimed repetitively in his head while the officer's lips moved, and Dad vigorously nodded as if suffering from convulsions. Ethan's mind raced to remember every hospital he'd ever been to—the Urgent Care behind the baseball field when he got hit by a line drive; Strong Memorial, where he had his tonsils removed; and Sisters of Mercy, where he'd once dropped off toys for sick kids with his mom. Clamping a hand over his mouth, Ethan blinked as his eyes burned with tears. "Mom? Where is she?" His body trembled. His stomach lurched. "She shouldn't be alone. What are we waiting for?"

Dad and Officer Raines remained still as statues at the table, filling Ethan with rage and a desperate need to flee. Without warning, a harrowing scream tore through the silence in the room. Coming from his father, the cry sounded like an animal injured in the wild.

Anger exploded in Ethan's chest. He leaped up and started for the door, spinning wildly in circles, searching for the car keys. "Come on, let's get going! Mom needs us!"

"Sit back down," Dad said with a tortured look on his face, underscoring the seriousness of the situation. Ethan wanted to run but suddenly lost all control over his arms and legs. Falling into the chair, he threw himself into Dad's lap, face down into his thighs, where he could block out the light and blindly scream into the darkness. The touch of his father's fingers as they raked back and forth across his head reminded Ethan of how Mom used to wash his hair when he was little. The memory angered him even more.

He popped up and screamed, "Don't just sit there, Dad! Let's go!" They needed to go, didn't they? Ethan's cheeks caught fire. He felt the urge to hit something—or someone—so he lunged toward Officer Raines and took a swing. But the officer was quick, wrapping his arms around Ethan and pulling him close. Ethan fought to get away, but his body wouldn't cooperate. He felt weak and helpless and eventually gave in, allowing the officer to support him as he fell limp in his hold.

"I'm sorry, Ethan. But your mom didn't make it."

Chapter Three

"Open up, Kyle!" Caroline pleaded after finally following Jordan upstairs, leaving Grace burrowed beneath a blanket on the family room couch. "He's been in there alone long enough. Maybe we should bust down the door."

Seconds later, the click of the lock offered access to the bedroom, and the stiffness in Caroline's chest became slightly more bearable. At least Kyle was still conscious. She grabbed Jordan's hand, holding on tight as he squeezed hers back. They listened to their son scuffing his feet across the carpet, waited several moments until it got quiet again, and walked inside.

His room looked like a crime scene. Every drawer had been pulled from the dresser and turned upside down. The bookshelf stood empty—every book, picture frame, trophy, and trinket scattered across the room. The bed had been stripped of all its blankets, revealing the bare mattress he'd slept on since he was a young boy. His "big boy bed," they once called it. Why hadn't they ever replaced it with a larger one?

Careful not to step on anything, Caroline made her way toward the closet, bending down to pick up the pieces of Kyle's MVP award from last season, a beautifully etched piece of glass with his name and jersey number—now broken beyond repair. Tears formed behind her eyes, but she wouldn't let them fall.

Instead, she clenched her fists and followed Jordan into the closet, discovering Kyle curled on the floor behind a mound of dirty clothes.

The stench of pain and fear overpowered the teenage boy smell that typically plagued Kyle's closet. Everything about her son's presence screamed for help. The way he buried his face beneath a musty bath towel. How he gathered his long muscular legs into his chest and wrapped his arms around them. His deep, irregular breaths and the grumbling sounds of his stomach ready to explode.

Jordan approached Kyle slowly, as if their son was fragile enough to break. Moving an empty laundry basket aside, he sat down and gently placed a hand on Kyle's head. "Talk to us. You can tell us anything. Anything at all," he whispered.

Caroline stood still, staring at Kyle from against the closet wall. She felt paralyzed, unable to move closer or find the right words to comfort him. Memories flooded her mind, reminding her of her own mother's silence during difficult times, like immediately after her father had died and Mom failed to offer any solace. After learning she was pregnant with Kyle, Caroline promised herself to be a better mother to her son, but now she felt the hefty weight of her failure. Her heart ached for him, as if his pain had become her own.

"We saw the Jeep," Jordan said. "Tell us what happened."

Kyle's face emerged from underneath the towel. He mumbled into the carpeting without uncurling himself from the fetal position. "I had an accident. Everything happened so fast, and I don't remember much."

"It's okay," Jordan said. "Take a few deep breaths.

We're here to help."

"Why don't we get out of this closet?" Caroline trudged to the other side of the bedroom and patted the bare mattress. "Come sit on the bed."

Surprisingly, Kyle heeded her instructions, moving like a zombie and sitting in the exact spot she suggested. Rug burns speckled the skin beneath his swollen and bloodshot eyes. Caroline folded her arms and waited for someone else to say something.

Jordan spoke up first. "What did you hit, son?"

"I don't know." Kyle sighed.

"What do you mean you don't know?" Caroline said. "That's a big impression on your windshield." Her patience waned, but she needed to proceed slowly. "It's okay. Take your time. Think it through. Start by telling us where you were going."

Kyle straightened his spine and perched on the very edge of his mattress. He looked ready to talk, so she and Jordan waited until the words flowed from his mouth.

"I was coming home from the ACT but stopped to grab lunch. I took Lakeshore to avoid the stoplights, and I was going to cut up one of those side streets on the other end of town."

He paused long enough for Caroline to interject. "I hate the Lakeshore bike lane. It's too narrow. Haven't I told you never to take that way?" She drew her hands to her mouth to stop from saying anything more.

Kyle bit his fingernails.

"I'm sorry," she said. "Keep going."

"Anyway," Kyle continued. "I was listening to music, squinting a little because the sun was so bright and I'd forgotten my sunglasses, and suddenly I looked into my rearview mirror and saw flashing red lights. I thought I was getting pulled over, so I looked at my speedometer. I wasn't even speeding. Then I realized an ambulance was coming right up my ass. I never heard a siren until I veered over to let it pass. All I remember after that is not being able to see, um, I guess from the sun, and then there was a giant thud against my windshield." Tears streamed down his face. He paused to wipe them away.

So far, Kyle's story lacked the detail Caroline wanted, but she bit her tongue to avoid making things worse with an all-out interrogation.

"What was it?" Jordan said. "Was there anyone driving in front of you? Did something fall off the back of another vehicle? Did you hit a deer or something?"

As Kyle's eyelids twitched, he stuttered, "I guess I may have seen something in my rearview mirror. It must have been a deer. It could have been anything, but um, yeah, I'm pretty sure it was a deer."

"So, after you stopped, what did you see?" Caroline said. "Was the deer dead? Injured? What happened to the deer?" So much for not peppering him with questions.

Kyle screamed. "I don't know! I can't remember!" His chest heaved as he gasped for breath. He threw himself on the bed and curled back into a ball. Turning away from Caroline and Jordan to face the wall, he cried harder—a cry so filled with sadness and confusion that it pierced right through her.

A quiet tap at the bedroom door broke Caroline's concentration. Reluctant to take her gaze off Kyle, even for a second, she rushed to the door and opened it a crack. Grace was lying in the hallway, her face turned to the side with one cheek flattened into the carpet. She had obviously been listening, but hopefully she hadn't been

41

there long. She didn't need to hear any of this until Kyle calmed down.

"What's happening? I'm worried." Grace sniffled.

"Everything's fine." Caroline's white lie dropped easily. The same way she'd misrepresented the facts in Las Vegas when that audience member asked her to share a vulnerable moment in front of the sold-out crowd. When had she become such a master at masking the truth?

Grace pulled herself onto her hands and knees. "Can I see him?"

"Not yet." Caroline stroked her daughter's hair and whispered, "I'll come get you soon. Go to your room for now." She closed the door gently and turned back toward Kyle and Jordan. They hadn't shifted an inch. All that changed was Kyle looked more fearful than he had mere seconds before.

She wished she could put an end to her son's misery. Take away his hurt and bear the brunt of his suffering. After everything she'd been through and all the words of encouragement she'd shared with others, nothing compared to the fear she felt right now. She was at a complete and utter loss for words, immobilized by his sorrow and the helplessness settling in her gut.

Jordan sat on Kyle's bed and rubbed his shoulders until the crying finally stopped. Calmly, he said, "So, after the ambulance passed, what happened? Did you get out of the car to check on the deer? Call the police to report the incident?"

Still facing the wall, Kyle whispered faintly, "Um, no. I pulled back onto the road and drove home."

Confused by his assertion, Caroline had more questions and concerns. But Kyle had finally settled down, crashing after his adrenaline rush. She studied his backside for over an hour as it trembled beneath her husband's touch, slowly waning until his breath finally signaled a deep sleep. Feeling confident he'd be out for a while, she tapped Jordan on the shoulder and motioned for him to follow her as they quietly left the room.

They spent the remainder of the day and night trying to make sense of their son's account of the accident. Kyle stayed in his room, and when Caroline checked on him around midnight, the door was locked again. There was no noise coming from inside. Afraid to knock, she tiptoed to her own room to rest.

After a night of fitful sleep, Caroline woke to find Jordan lying on his back beside her with his mouth wide open. She slowly removed the bed covers while thrusting herself into a seated position. Grabbing her phone from the nightstand, she was annoyed to find the battery nearly dead. There was a lot to do today—getting the Jeep to a body shop topping the list—but she plugged the phone into its charger and allowed herself a slight delay to scroll mindlessly through her apps.

The news of a local woman's death caused Caroline to sit up straighter and search social media. Reports of Amy Shawver's death flooded the internet. Countless people in town knew and loved her, which didn't surprise Caroline. She remembered when Amy's son, Ethan, played Little League baseball with Kyle. Jordan coached the team back then, and Amy volunteered as the parent helper in charge of the snack schedule and email reminders about the games.

Amy had treated that job like a paid position, always going the extra mile. If it was hot outside, she packed the boys a cooler of ice chips. If someone forgot their socks, she always had an extra pair. And if anyone needed a ride to the field, she didn't hesitate to add more kids to her minivan. Caroline didn't have much in common with Amy—whom she and Jordan nicknamed "Super Mom"—but they'd shared a few memorable moments over the years.

Learning about Amy's passing saddened Caroline. As she read through a long list of online tributes, she wondered about the circumstances of the beloved mom's death. She couldn't recall hearing that Amy had been sick, and the only information she could find was a comment about her death being sudden, with no further details. Amy had been an ultra-competitive triathlete, and it wasn't unusual for seemingly healthy people to die suddenly because of unknown underlying conditions. Maybe it was something like that.

She scrolled further to find the Shawnee Springs Online Parent Page and searched for more information. Post after post, community members expressed their outrage about reckless driving and bike lane safety.

And then, the answer appeared.

Amy had died in an accident while riding her bike.

Oh, God.

Caroline's chest tightened. Her breathing stopped. The gravity of the situation suffocated her as the pieces clicked together in her mind.

Frantically, she continued scrolling until she found a link shared by the local police department. They were looking for help identifying the owner of a vehicle involved in a hit-and-run collision on Lakeshore Road. The accident occurred shortly after noon on Saturday.

The bottom of the post read:

Witnesses to the crime or anyone with information

about a dark gray Jeep Liberty with a New York license plate beginning with the letters "KEA" are asked to call the precinct.

Caroline grabbed hold of her throat with both hands, praying not to hurl. She would never reach the bathroom, so she closed her mouth and swallowed hard.

No. It couldn't be. But she knew damn well they were referring to Kyle's Jeep. KEA 9326. Last week, she'd written that exact letter-number combination on Kyle's high school parking pass application.

Kyle's cracked windshield.

The large dent in front of his driver's seat.

A make-believe deer.

The imprint of Amy Shawver's body took shape, threatening to crush Caroline's entire existence. Her face burned hot at how gullible she and Jordan had been by quickly accepting Kyle's explanation. They should have known better and looked beyond what they wanted to hear—that his story made sense.

What now? Should they come forward and hope the police understood Kyle's mistake, or sit tight and see how this played out? Her brain kicked into survival mode as random ideas on how to save their son raided her thoughts.

If only she knew where to start.

What had Kyle been thinking? He hit a person and just kept driving. And with such force that she died.

Whirling around to face Jordan, she shook him by the shoulders. "Wake up! Wake up!"

Jordan groaned and turned his back toward her. She shook him again, harder, almost knocking him over the side of the bed.

"Geez, Caroline." Jordan tucked the covers under

his chin. "Where's the fire?"

"No fire. But it's an emergency. Sit up!" She yanked her phone from its charger and shoved it in his face. "Read this."

Jordan hurried to grab a pair of readers from his nightstand, holding them to the bridge of his nose as he stared at the screen. The corners of his mouth turned downward as he pursed his lips. His Adam's apple rolled slowly underneath his skin, and Caroline could feel his suffering with every swallow. "Our boy killed someone." His voice cracked, and tears pooled in his eyes. "What do we do?"

"Go get him out of bed," she replied. "Now."

****

Word traveled fast in a town like Shawnee Springs, where everyone knew everyone or at least someone else who knew everyone. That's precisely who showed up at Ethan's house the following morning—everyone. People from the neighborhood, the school, and who knows where else rang the doorbell, carrying casseroles and baked goods as if homemade food had the power to resurrect his mom.

Ethan hated how everyone treated him like a little kid, especially his father. College could not come soon enough. Yesterday, Dad wouldn't let him come along when he identified Mom's body. "It's for your own good. No son should see his mom in that condition."

Fuck that. He could have handled it. Today, Uncle Dave stayed at their house while Dad went to make the funeral arrangements, as if Ethan needed a babysitter. How dumb.

All three of his uncles were just like Dad. They loved hunting and fishing, and they'd gone camping together once a year since long before Ethan was born—the annual "Shawver Boys" weekend in Canada. Ethan used to look forward to those trips but stopped going when he started high school, and not for the reason his dad believed—that he'd rather be sitting in his room playing video games. He had friends, a social life, and things he didn't want to miss out on. Not wanting to hang out with a bunch of middle-aged Boy Scouts didn't make him a bad kid.

But that's how his father made him feel—that Uncle Dave, Uncle Brett, and Uncle Tom agreed with Dad that Ethan was a loser. They'd even offered his season ticket to the Buffalo football games to one of his younger cousins last year. That sucked. Unlike the rest of the Shawver boys, he might not have wanted to attend *every* home game sporting an oversized jersey and painting his face blue and red, but an occasional game would've been nice. He couldn't remember when they'd last asked him to come along, so he stopped waiting for an invitation.

Ethan didn't plan on hanging out with Uncle Dave for one minute. As soon as Dad left for the funeral home, he plodded to his room and searched his phone for information about the accident. After Officer Raines delivered the news about Mom's death, he tried explaining what he knew about the crash. An ambulance on its way to another emergency had phoned it in, calling another pair of paramedics to the scene, but not soon enough. She didn't even make it to the hospital alive.

Multiple witnesses had come forward, including members of a landscaping crew who were nearby at the time and the nurse who tended to his mom's injuries at the scene. The nurse had been riding his bike that morning, too, and happened to be near the intersection where his mom got hit.

Ethan couldn't recall much of what Officer Raines told him, but he distinctly remembered a promise that it shouldn't take long to uncover who was driving the vehicle that fled the scene. Maybe that's where he could help—by scouring social media and looking for clues. But he could only take so much. Reading the never-ending comments about how wonderful his mom had been made him too sad. All he wanted to do was sleep, so he threw himself on the bed and buried his face in his pillow.

Long stretches of silence enticed him to slip into oblivion. He wished for an escape—the ability to stop thinking, feeling, and hurting. But random interruptions kept him teetering on the edge of consciousness. Birds chirping in the backyard trees. Cars driving into and around their cul-de-sac. The roar of an occasional airplane high in the sky.

Frustrated that his mind kept spinning, Ethan slunk out of bed to close his bedroom window, returning to hide beneath the covers. He squeezed his eyes shut but couldn't find the darkness he craved, and the noises kept coming. Chatter from the downstairs television. The ring of the doorbell. Voices in the hallway until the door slammed shut again. Even the slightest of sounds amplified in magnitude, storming his brain at high-level decibels and preventing him from getting any peace.

Grasping for something more constructive to think about, he anticipated the arrival of his half-brother George from California. Dad called him after Officer Raines left their house because Ethan couldn't find the strength to deliver the news himself. Although Ethan and George talked regularly, the last time they saw each other was last Christmas. After hearing enough stories from Ethan over the years, George was the only one who might truly understand how difficult Dad could be. As his stepson, George treated Dad kindly but held him at arms-length. Even if he agreed Dad was a pain-in-the-ass, George was the type of guy who'd always bit his tongue out of respect for Mom. But he'd be a good buffer for Ethan during the funeral services.

A muffled voice from beyond his bedroom door cut his game of mental hopscotch short. Uncle Dave yelled. "Ethan! Buddy! You ready to eat something yet?"

Ethan ignored the question and finally gave up trying to sleep. He wandered across the hall to his parents 'bedroom, where the faint smell of Mom's perfume still welcomed him inside. Dad bought her the same fragrance every Mother's Day, and the newest bottle sat barely used on her dresser. Ethan lifted the pale purple dispenser, sprayed it a few times, and inhaled so deeply he started sneezing. His eyes watered, but he let them be. He'd already grown tired of wiping away tears.

Ethan paced the room, dragging his bare feet across the thick, pile carpet and searching aimlessly for remnants of his mom's presence. He put a light hand on the neat stack of workout clothes on her dresser, ready to be put away. He gently tossed her running shoes from beside the bed into the closet and returned a pair of silver hoop earrings from the nightstand to her jewelry box.

Yesterday, she'd been so alive, eager to start the day doing something she enjoyed—riding her bike and training for her next triathlon. Mom thrived on a good challenge, big or small. Always bringing her "A-game," she was just as competitive participating in a race as entering the annual high school chili cook-off. Ethan remembered how she organized a collection for a family who lost everything in a fire one Christmas Eve. She relentlessly solicited donations from everyone she knew, determined to make sure the three young kids had a magical holiday despite spending Christmas in a crisis shelter. Things like this shouldn't happen to such a good person. It made no sense.

Ethan's stomach hardened as he continued to scan the room. Mom's pink bathrobe hung on the doorknob, hiding a stash of ponytail holders she kept there so they'd always be handy, which drove Dad crazy. A hamper filled with unmatched socks sat beneath the back window, waiting for her to pair them up. A souvenir glass from an amusement park, half full of loose change, sat on a hanging shelf, perpetuating Mom's dreams of their next family vacation.

Returning to her dresser with no real purpose, Ethan opened each drawer this time. He stopped to thumb through a pocket-sized Bible tucked in the back of the deepest drawer. Between the pages, he found a half-sheet of paper where she'd handwritten her favorite prayer. *God, grant me the serenity to accept the things I cannot change, the courage to change the things I can, and the wisdom to know the difference.*

Alongside the Bible, he discovered a tiny mesh bag filled with colorful metal coins—too small to be poker chips, but definitely not jewelry. He'd never seen them before and suddenly felt like he was invading her privacy. A wave of guilt washed over him, so he gently closed the drawer and fell into the comfy chair-and-a-half wedged in the corner where he often sat seeking Mom's advice. She'd keep busy making the bed or folding laundry while he'd unload enough teenage angst to top off the landfill in the next town over.

Ethan yawned. His eyes grew heavy, and he got up to grab Mom's robe to use as a blanket before sinking deeper into the chair. He must have drifted off until a loud crash from inside his parents' walk-in closet startled him. "Shit!" He jumped to his feet and raced across the room to find his dad kneeling on the closet floor with a pile of open shoeboxes, lids, and miscellaneous shoes cluttered around him. "Dad, when did you get home? Are you okay?"

Dad pointed to the metal shelf that had come unattached from the wall. "Sorry if I scared you. I got home an hour ago and was looking for something inside one of those boxes. I lost my footing and put too much weight on the damn shelf. Your mom's entire shoe collection crashed on top of me."

Still groggy from his catnap, Ethan wiped his eyes and laughed. "Let me help you up." He grabbed hold of Dad's big, firm hand. As soon as their skin touched, Ethan felt the irony in how he reacted to seeing his father so vulnerable. For all the times he wanted to create distance from Dad, he could never break free entirely. Maybe his impulse to lend a hand was a sign their relationship deserved another chance. Now that Mom was gone, that seemed more like a lost cause.

Dad stroked his chin as he walked through the closet door and toward the bed. "I need some help choosing an outfit for your mom to be—" His voice croaked. He covered his face with his hands and collapsed onto the bed.

Oh no. What should he do? Ethan waffled between feeling awkward, confused, and terribly sad. Mom would have encouraged him to take the high road, to try

making a difference for someone obviously hurting—
like when she convinced him to skip the class trip after
Cole broke his leg and couldn't go. His best friend would
have been the only eighth-grader in school that week if
Ethan hadn't volunteered to stay behind with him.

Sitting beside his father as if Mom guided him there,
Ethan held his breath. Nervously, he smoothed the
bedspread and waited for Dad to move, bouncing his
knees up and down and trying to muster up enough
courage to make a fast exit. "Want me to leave you
alone?"

After a long pause, his dad said, "No." Sitting back
up and revealing a face masked with grief, he walked
back toward the closet. "Help me put these shoes back
where they belong, then we can decide on that outfit.
Any ideas?"

Ethan had already thought about it. Mom's favorite
color was green. She looked pretty in that color because
it matched her eyes. "How about that dark green dress
she wore to Uncle Dave's wedding last year?"

The frown lines on his dad's face softened. "Perfect.
But I can't believe you remember that. Have I ever told
you what an old soul you are?"

"Plenty." Ethan half-smiled. "What were you
looking for in the closet, anyway?"

"A necklace I gave your mom for our tenth wedding
anniversary. I want her to wear that, too."

"Wouldn't it be in her jewelry box?"

"You'd think so." Dad chuckled with a slight
twinkle in his eye. "But you know your mom, always
hiding things in odd places. She'd say if we ever got
robbed, a burglar would go straight for the jewelry box,
so she kept her valuables somewhere inconspicuous. I

never understood that, and I'm sure it's one reason she often forgot where she put things."

"She did spend a ton of time looking for stuff," Ethan said flatly. Memory Lane could be a scary place. He couldn't go there anymore today. "So, did you find the necklace?"

"Not yet. But I did find this." Dad walked to the dresser and picked up a small package wrapped in Christmas paper. "No surprise she already started her holiday shopping."

"Who's it for?" Ethan said. "It looks like there's a tag on the bottom."

Dad flipped the package over and read the name written in red magic marker. "George. It's for your brother." His dad glanced at his watch. "Uh oh. His flight lands in less than an hour. Do you mind picking him up? I need to head back to the funeral home."

Without thinking, Ethan said "yes." It wasn't until he left the bedroom that he realized how uncomfortable he felt about driving, especially Mom's minivan. He'd been a passenger in that van countless times, rarely the driver. This wasn't how things were supposed to be. He wanted his mom back where she belonged. In the driver's seat. Alive and well. Organizing their lives and keeping the peace. Everything was off-kilter now, and nothing would ever be the same.

Chapter Four

Jordan hurried to summon Kyle from his room while Caroline threw on a bathrobe, tore downstairs, and began pacing the first floor. Her hands trembled as she squeezed them together, nervously expecting a confrontation to unfold. They might catch Kyle off guard in revealing what they knew about the crash, or maybe he suspected they'd already learned the truth. Either way, Kyle had some explaining to do.

As soon as her husband and son entered the kitchen, Caroline gasped. Still wearing the same t-shirt and shorts from the day before when he'd taken the ACT, Kyle looked like a vampire. Chalky skin. Oily hair. Eyes so red they could have been bleeding. With Tanner at his heels, he walked slowly. Emotionless. As if someone had sucked all the life out of him.

The slight sound of raindrops drew Caroline's attention outside. A cluster of dark clouds was rolling in as if Mother Nature wanted to weigh in on the storm brewing inside their house.

Moving to shut the kitchen window, Caroline brushed by Kyle and caught his wrist. His skin was cold and clammy. She wanted to swoop him up and wrap him in her arms like a baby, hold him so tight, and make the shock of yesterday's tragedy disappear. But he winced at her touch and wandered to the other side of the room.

"Have a seat, son," Jordan said. The tremor in his

voice matched the quiver in her gut.

Expressionless, Kyle grabbed an energy drink from the refrigerator before dragging a chair from the table to sit down. Interlacing his fingers, he placed them on top of his head, elbows flared out wide. He stared at Tanner, who had plunked down at his feet.

After a long pause, Jordan sat across from him. "Anything to say for yourself?"

Without moving, Kyle said, "No."

Caroline remained standing and bit down on her lower lip. "We know what really happened. Regardless of whether you don't remember much about the accident, we assume by now you realize you didn't hit a deer."

"Yes." Kyle dropped his face onto the kitchen table and buried it beneath his folded arms. His back and shoulders shook. A few short sobs broke free from deep inside his throat.

Caroline snatched a crinkled tissue from inside her robe pocket and handed it to Kyle. "Can you tell us more about what happened?"

Kyle sat up again. Tears streamed from his eyes while a bubble of mucus popped from under his nose. "I already told you what I remember. I was driving along Lakeshore when an ambulance appeared out of nowhere. The sun blocked my vision, and music blasted in my car, so when I finally noticed the siren, it scared me. That ambulance would have barreled right into me if I hadn't swerved into the bike lane."

"Wait," Caroline interrupted. "I thought you said the flashing lights startled you, and you didn't hear the siren until after you veered to the side. Which is it?"

"I dunno. Everything happened so fast. Either way, it surprised me, and I swung over." Kyle shifted in his seat and blew his nose in the tissue, startling Tanner, who jumped to all fours and rested his chin on Kyle's thigh. "I almost got hit from behind, so I was rattled by the time something crashed into the windshield."

Jordan piped in a bit too aggressively. "That *something* was a *someone*. And not just *anyone*. It was Mrs. Shawver."

"I know! I know! It's everywhere on social media. I can't believe it."

"But you're not denying it, right?" Caroline said.

"Of course not. But I honestly don't know where she came from."

"Is there a chance she hit you after you stopped? That would make sense to me," Caroline whispered, searching for any sliver of hope Kyle wasn't in the wrong.

"Maybe." Kyle blew his nose again as a fresh round of tears spilled down his cheeks. "She showed up out of the blue."

"So, you did see her?" Jordan said.

"No. I mean…I don't know." He tugged at his hair with both hands.

Caroline cleared her throat and spoke softly, suddenly conscious of Grace listening from the furthest corner of the family room but not bothering to shoo her away. "Where was your cell phone?" She had to know.

Kyle's face turned beet red, matching his bloodshot eyes. "Are you fucking kidding me? I *wasn't* texting and driving!" He shoved Tanner aside, got up from the table, and patrolled the kitchen. The dog stood still as a statue, looking dazed and confused.

"Settle down, Kyle," Jordan said. "And don't use foul language with your mother. No one's accusing you of anything."

"Bullshit!" he yelled.

"It's a natural question," Caroline said. "I see plenty of kids with their noses buried in phones while they're behind the wheel of a car."

"Whatever," Kyle scoffed.

Jordan pointed a sharp finger at their son. "We've got more important things to talk about here. We can't be fighting."

"Agreed." Caroline nodded before detecting a mysterious glance pass between Jordan and Kyle, as if they were keeping something from her. "I'm sorry, Kyle. I shouldn't have said that. Let's talk about what to do next." A well-worn switch flipped inside her brain. She was ready to think and act like a skillful lawyer again instead of a heartsick mom. Her professional role often came easier. More logic. Less emotion.

Caroline shot Grace a look suggesting she shouldn't be hearing any of this and then continued. "Let's start with why you left the scene, Kyle. Why didn't you stop the car and get out to see what you'd hit?"

Careful not to make things worse, Caroline abstained from adding he may have been able to save Amy Shawver's life if he had stopped and called for help. Truth. But Kyle obviously felt terrible about what he'd done. She'd never seen him so distraught and couldn't bear to pile on any more hurt.

"I honestly don't know."

"What do you mean you don't know?" Jordan said.

"I guess I kinda freaked out. I wasn't thinking clearly. I didn't realize how serious the accident was until I got home and inspected my car."

Caroline wanted to believe him with all her heart,

but something didn't seem right. The windshield was completely smashed. Driving home would have been difficult. Also, if Kyle was truly dazed and unaware of how serious the crash had been, why had he parked inside the garage when he usually parked in the driveway?

"I'm going to call Jim Doughman, a colleague at my old firm. He's one of Buffalo's best criminal defense attorneys. He'll know exactly what to do."

Jordan's eyebrows shot up. "Wait a second. Maybe we should call the police first. Kyle made an honest mistake. Anyone with a teenager would understand how he panicked."

"Agreed," she said. "But let's make sure we're not missing anything. As Kyle's parents, it's impossible to be objective. We need outside counsel, so all our ducks are in a row first."

Leaning over the kitchen island, Kyle alternated his attention back and forth between his mom and dad, not quite as quickly as a spectator watching a ping-pong match, but close.

Jordan said, "I'm no lawyer, but I know what 'time is of the essence 'means. What if you can't get a hold of Jim? The authorities have Kyle's license plate. They're already looking for the owner of his Jeep. If Kyle doesn't turn himself in soon—as a showing of good faith—waiting even another second to talk with a lawyer could backfire."

"So could confessing to a crime without having a lawyer present," she said. "And one that's not your mom. Legally, if they're going to charge him with hit-and-run, the damage occurred as soon as he fled the scene. Coming forward now or a week from now won't make a difference. But you have a good point. The optics would be bad if they identified him before he had a chance to come clean. Let's see if I can reach Jim."

Caroline left the table to call her former colleague but only got his voicemail.

Seconds later, the doorbell rang, and she peeked through the sidelight while Tanner barked at her heels. The rain had stopped, and two uniformed police officers stood on the front stoop alongside a woman in plain clothes wearing a badge. The officer on the left looked familiar and friendlier than the other two.

Caroline hesitated and gestured for Grace to get Tanner out of the way. When she finally opened the door to let the police inside, the woman with the badge inched forward. "Mrs. Beasley?"

Caroline nodded.

"I'm Detective Hightower. I'm here with Officer Burgess and Officer Raines. Is your son home?"

Kyle stepped out from inside the kitchen and tilted his head toward the friendly-looking officer, who she now knew was Officer Raines, the school resource officer.

After confirming the license plate on the Jeep in the garage started with the letters KEA and that the vehicle was registered in Jordan's name but regularly driven by Kyle, Detective Hightower wasted no time reading their son his rights as she hurried toward him with handcuffs.

Officer Raines edged forward and said, "Are those really necessary?"

Detective Hightower scowled. "Among other offenses, this young man is being charged with vehicular homicide, a crime he committed before fleeing the scene, leaving a mother to die in the street."

The words "vehicular homicide" struck like lightning, leaving Caroline speechless, her body frozen in shock.

Kyle bowed his head and surrendered his wrists to the handcuffs. Tanner growled from behind them and pulled to break free from Grace as she tightened her grip and dabbed at her eyes before leading the dog out of sight.

"Can one of us ride with him?" Jordan said.

"He's eighteen, so no. But you can meet us at the courthouse and visit him after he's booked. Since it's Sunday, his bail hearing will be tomorrow," Detective Hightower said.

Caroline rushed to Kyle's side before they escorted him away, cautiously pulling him into her arms and exhaling when he accepted her this time. The thought of her son spending the night alone in a jail cell was unfathomable, but arguing with the detective about the process was pointless. They'd post bail first thing in the morning and have him home by noon. In the meantime, she'd learn everything she could about the accident, the witnesses, the charges being filed against him, and how she could best help her son.

"Don't worry." She kissed Kyle on the cheek. "Everything will be okay."

If only she believed that herself.

****

After agreeing to pick George up from the airport, Ethan wouldn't dare change his mind, even though he wanted to. Getting out of the house for a while felt good, but he drove white-knuckled the whole way there, overwhelmed by a new and strange sense of anxiety behind the wheel.

Thankfully, the Buffalo airport wasn't too far from home, and traffic was light. Pulling up in front of the "Arrivals" sign, Ethan parked curbside and waited inside the minivan for George.

Ethan loved coming to the airport when he was younger, watching the planes taxi the runways, and daydreaming about where they were traveling to or from. At one time, he wanted to be a pilot. The lifestyle intrigued him, getting to go anywhere in the world with long stretches of time off between trips. Although his interest in flying as a profession faded after he discovered video games, he still hoped to travel someday. He'd only flown once in his life and never even had the chance to visit George in California. Maybe he should book a trip out West to visit the University of Utah before the deadline for fall semester applications. His mom had promised to take that tour with him, but he could go alone. And getting the hell out of Shawnee Springs sure sounded like a good idea now.

A sudden tap at the van window made him jump. He looked out to see his brother's smiling face mashed against the glass. At least, he presumed the man staring in at him was George. He looked different since they last saw each other.

Stepping out of the van, Ethan gave George a giant bear hug. "What's with the beard?"

George whimpered, squeezing him so tight Ethan could barely breathe. "Good to see you, bro," he said. "I can't believe it. When your dad called about Mom, I thought he was bluffing for a split second. What a sick joke that woulda been. How are you holding up?"

Ethan straightened his spine and broke away from the hug, holding back tears. He was tired of breaking down and didn't want his big brother to see him crying. "It sucks. What more can I say? Hey, let's get your bags loaded. Do you mind taking the wheel from here? I'm not feeling so great. Could use a breather."

George shot him a strange look. "Sure. But I have no idea where I'm going."

"Just follow the GPS. It's an easy route."

After throwing his stuff in the backseat, George hopped into the driver's seat. They picked up where they'd left off as soon as they hit the highway. Despite the ten-year age difference and the fact that they'd grown up in different households on opposite ends of the country, Ethan and George shared much more in common than their looks, starting with how much they both adored their mom.

"So, how did this happen?" George said. "Your dad was pretty shaken up when we spoke. A lot didn't make sense."

"Not everything makes sense to me, either. The story's half-baked, and I can tell Dad's holding stuff back. I'm sure it's no shock he and I still aren't getting along, so talking to him about this has been hard. We've had a few decent moments since Mom died, but most days we tiptoe around each other. All I've gotta do is stay out of his way until I graduate, and then I'm outta here."

"Cut him some slack. This is tough for him, too."

"I know. I just wish he'd stop treating me like a kid."

"Don't worry. I'm here now. We'll get through this together."

Ethan filled George in on everything he knew so far, including the recent announcement that Kyle had been the one behind the wheel of the car that hit their mother.

"What's this asshole Kyle Beasley like?" George

said.

"He's all right, I guess. A jock with a full-ride scholarship to play Division One baseball."

"How well do you know him?"

"We used to be pretty tight. Our families were friends when we were little, but we haven't hung out since starting high school. He got too cool for me, but we still say 'hey 'to each other in the halls and stuff."

Ethan didn't feel like talking about Kyle anymore. Learning someone he'd known most of his life was responsible for his mom's death bothered him, and he'd barely had time to process the news since it broke overnight. Desperate to change the subject, he said, "Did my dad tell you Mom donated her organs?"

"Yep. I'm sure she's smiling about that up in heaven," George said. "She sure loved to help other people."

"Was she always like that?" Ethan said. He often wondered about his mom's life when she was younger, trying to raise George as a single mom in California.

"I think so," George said. "I didn't have the same experience with Mom you did. She worked long hours when I was a kid, so I spent a lot of time with my grandma. But there was this one time when we were driving home, and we saw a homeless guy on the side of the road with a sign reading, 'WILL WORK FOR FOOD. 'Mom drove past him but made a quick U-turn in the middle of a busy street. Other drivers slammed on their brakes, and horns were honking everywhere. She almost got us killed. But she was determined to give that guy money—even though we didn't have much of our own."

"That sounds like Mom." Ethan grinned, but only

for an instant. "Wait a second. You mentioned your grandma. Did you mean Mom's mom? Grandma Packer? I thought she died when Mom was little."

"She did. I meant my dad's mom."

"Oh, wow. I always assumed Mom was raising you alone, that you and your dad didn't see each other much until you lived with him as a teenager."

"That's not right. Even though Mom and my dad never got hitched, he and his family were always in the picture. Until he got married last year and moved to Arizona."

"Is that why you stayed with him after she moved here? Because you liked living with him better?" Ethan couldn't relate. Choosing his own dad over Mom was unimaginable. George's father must have been way different.

The minivan's turn signal clicked as they veered to the right and exited the highway. They weren't far from home, and Ethan wished for George to take a wrong turn so they could keep talking.

"Nope. That wasn't it. My parents both fought hard to get full custody of me. In the end, Mom lost. I had no choice but to stay in California." George sighed.

"No way. How did that happen?" Ethan clenched his teeth and tried hiding the confusion in his gut.

"You really want to get into this before Mom's funeral?" George said.

"Absolutely. I'm starting to see there's a lot I don't know about her life. You could help fill in some blanks."

"Let me think about it. You caught me off guard with these questions. Sharing details about Mom's past might not be a good idea right now."

"Pleeease, George. Stories about Mom are all we

have left."

"I know. But some things are better left unsaid. Trust me on that."

But the tone of George's voice was anything but trustworthy. And how he nervously picked at his beard made Ethan wonder what secrets his big brother was keeping.

Chapter Five

Ethan's nose itched at the musty smell of the funeral home. He stood at the front of the receiving line counting the cabbage-like flowers in the faded maroon and gold carpeting, wondering how long before he could duck behind the heavy green curtains across the back window and disappear. He hated being so close to his mom's casket but gradually found the courage to look over at her body—longer and longer with every glance.

Despite the green dress he and Dad had agreed upon and the anniversary necklace that eventually surfaced, Ethan barely recognized Mom upon entering the room. She'd always worn her hair in a ponytail, but today, her long brown hair was big and wavy, draped over her neck and shoulders. Curious, he touched the top of her head. It felt so stiff he thought it might crack. Heavy makeup coated her face and lips, making her look like one of those figures he'd seen at the wax museum in Niagara Falls. This was not how he wanted to remember his mom.

She had so many friends in Shawnee Springs; they'd all come to pay their respects. The line to enter the private parlor wrapped around a wide corner and down a dimly lit hallway, snaking through the main entrance and extending far along the outside sidewalk. One by one, people approached him to say the most awkward things. If he got paid a dollar for every time someone said,

"Sorry for your loss" or "My deepest sympathies," he could buy a fancier gaming console by the end of the day. Some people didn't know what to say, so they just hugged him, squeezed him, or pinched his cheeks. A few women remarked about how tall he'd grown or how much he resembled his mother. The comments hit an all-time low when one of his neighbors insulted his ill-fitting outfit.

"Oh, Ethan," she'd said. "You should have let me take you shopping. Is that your dad's blazer you're wearing? And those pants—they're floods. Why didn't your father call me?"

Blood rushed to his face as he hurried to roll up his jacket sleeves and arrange his pants lower on his hips. That comment would have horrified Mom, and he suddenly felt self-conscious. He looked over at Dad and frowned. When Ethan asked if he looked ridiculous that morning while they were getting dressed, his father could have admitted it. He could have found something more appropriate, but Dad insisted he looked fine, saying, "No one will notice what you're wearing. Even if they do, the coat's only a tad oversized. That style's supposedly coming back. And if you wear black socks, they'll blend right in with the hem of your pants."

His father was oblivious. Or maybe he'd written Ethan off because he no longer cared, something Dad needed to be called out on. Not here. Not today. But Dad didn't deserve a pass for letting him go out looking like a bum in public, not to mention at his mom's funeral.

George arrived late and squeezed through the crowd to stand next to Ethan. His eyes were bloodshot, as if he'd just stepped out of a heavily chlorinated swimming pool. He moved them up and down Ethan's body, clearly agreeing with the outspoken neighbor about his outfit. Too bad his brother was nowhere to be found when Ethan and Dad were getting ready.

"Hey, brother," George said. "How's it going?"

"How do you think?"

George eyeballed the room. "Mom sure knew a lot of people. Do you know everyone here?"

"Not really."

"And look at all those flowers. Outside of California, I've never seen so many poppies in one place."

"They were Mom's favorite. She tried like crazy to get them to grow here."

"Huh. Maybe that's cuz they reminded her of where she was from. When I was little, we had a garden full of them, every shade of orange, pink, and red you could imagine."

The hum of increased chatter down the line caught Ethan's attention. People were staring at George and whispering. It appeared not everyone in town knew about Ethan's half-brother.

It's not like Mom hid the fact she had another son, but no one talked much about her life before she married Dad. Ethan's version of the story lacked detail itself. All he knew was Mom had a kid when she was twenty years old, and they lived out West, where she'd been born and raised. She met Dad when he was in California for a legal conference. They fell in love and dated long distance before Dad finally convinced her to move to Buffalo. Unless someone saw George during his less-than-regular Christmas or summer visits, it made sense people might not know he existed.

After enduring a few more cringy comments, Ethan

watched a woman who smelled like she'd bathed in lavender grab hold of George's forearm. In her best outside voice, she said, "Who is this handsome young man?"

Ethan recognized the woman from the local library, but he didn't know her name. "This is my brother, George. He lives in California."

"Nice to meet you, George. It's a shame what happened to your mother. I hope they catch whoever did this." She stepped sideways and gave Ethan a peck on the cheek. "Any news on the owner of that Jeep?"

Ethan clenched his teeth, surprised at how someone who worked in a library could be so clueless about the latest breaking local news. Lavender Lady must be living under a rock. Everyone else in town seemed to know Kyle Beasley was under arrest by now. Ethan refused to be the one to explain, barely able to think about Kyle, let alone say his name out loud.

"I'll be right back. I need to find my friends." Ethan stepped abruptly out of the receiving line, pretending to look for Theo and Cole despite knowing they hadn't arrived yet.

Passing by the spot where Dad had been standing most of the afternoon, Ethan noticed his father's absence. Worried about where he could have gone, Ethan checked the restroom, glancing briefly at himself in the mirror and rolling his eyes at his outfit. *Let it go*, he thought. Not finding Dad there, he looked toward the picture displays they'd stayed up most of the night finishing. He spotted his father in front of his wedding portrait, talking with Uncle Tom and Aunt Sally. Even from afar, Dad's eyes appeared swollen and anguished.

Maybe he wasn't being fair to his father. They'd

shared a few good memories while sifting through photo albums together. The conversation had been minimal, but Ethan could sense how deeply his dad was hurting. He never doubted that Dad loved and adored Mom, and sometimes Ethan felt guilty for creating a wedge between them. He knew how uncomfortable Mom felt whenever he asked her to run interference. She wanted nothing more than the two of them to get along like they used to. He should have tried harder when she was alive.

His dad turned around and joined eyes with Ethan, gesturing toward him while mouthing, "Come here." As soon as Ethan neared the picture table, Dad grabbed his hands. "Thanks for helping with these. They turned out great. Your mother would have been pleased."

"She would have." Ethan took a slight step toward his father, contemplating a half-assed hug but stopping short at the sudden surge of conversation throughout the room. Heads appeared collectively turned toward the back of the line, near the exit to the outside. What was everyone looking at? He and Dad both marched away from the table to investigate. Ethan figured it out first, leaned over, and whispered, "Mrs. Beasley's here. What the hell?"

By the looks on people's faces, Mrs. Beasley's presence shocked more than just him and his dad.

"Where does she get off showing up here like this?" Dad said. "Let's go together and tell her to leave."

Ethan puffed out his chest, eagerly joining forces with Dad to confront their unwanted guest. Mrs. Beasley looked as if she were alone, with no one else from her family in tow, and she stood tall in line as if she belonged there the same as anyone else. She didn't appear to notice either of them as they approached, greeting his dad with the warmest look of sympathy as soon as he said hello.

"Dan," she said. "I'm so sorry. I wasn't sure if I should come, but I couldn't stay away. This whole thing is such a terrible tragedy, for all of us. Amy was a wonderful woman, and it kills me to think my son was involved in—the accident."

Dark red blotches appeared on Dad's neck; a warning Ethan knew too well. Dad was about to lose his cool. "You've got some nerve coming here today, Caroline. Your son was more than *involved* in Amy's death. He caused it. One hundred percent. Kyle killed my wife, and he's going to pay for it."

"Please, not here, Dan. Let's get together privately and talk things through. Whenever you're ready." She gripped her fingers together, her knuckles turning white.

"Not happening. Never. Now, kindly leave before creating a bigger scene than you already have. Your son has not only robbed me of my one true love, but he's left our son without a mother. Think about that when you roll over and try to fall asleep tonight."

Mrs. Beasley remained stoic and emotionless, like a mannequin. She opened her mouth to say something to Ethan but paused and turned to walk away.

Before ducking into the restroom, she looked back over her shoulder, revealing a warm and mournful pair of eyes. "Ethan, one of your mom's favorite sayings was 'it takes a village to raise a child.' I'll always be here if you need me."

Her words angered and confused him. With a burst of nervous energy, Ethan charged through the funeral home and out into the parking lot. He stomped across the blacktop, paying little attention to where he was going and weaving recklessly between the parked cars until he almost collided with a black BMW. The car's engine was running, and the heavy bass of a rap song blasted from inside. The sight of Grace Beasley stretched out in the passenger's seat, tapping her feet on the dashboard, stirred a vicious anger inside him.

Ethan pounded both fists on the car window. "What the hell are you doing here?"

Grace jolted in her seat and pivoted toward the window. Her wide-eyed expression reminded Ethan of when he scared her back in sixth grade by taking a frog to the playground and dropping it down her shirt. The window opened slowly as her eyes grew even bigger. "Hi, Ethan," she stammered. "I'm, um, I'm waiting for my mom."

"I figured that." He shouted over the music. "But why are either of you here? Your mom's inside embarrassing herself and upsetting my dad. Just because she's some big celebrity doesn't mean she can show up like this."

"I'm sorry," Grace said. "I tried talking her out of it. But once my mom makes up her mind about something, there's no going back. Besides, she only wanted to tell you and your dad how sorry she is for your loss."

"Sorry? Sorry for our loss? Save the bullshit for someone else, Grace. Your family has a lot more to be sorry for than that!"

"It's not bullshit." Grace's nostrils flared as she turned down the radio. "You think this is easy for us? We're sad, too. We all loved your mom and feel terrible my brother was involved. My parents have no idea how to handle his arrest, and I'm just doing what I do best—living in Kyle's shadow and trying to pretend like everything's normal."

"Boo-hoo!" Ethan mocked. "Is that supposed to make me feel bad for you?"

Tears streamed down Grace's cheeks while her shoulders shuddered. She rolled up the window until Ethan grabbed hold of the glass. He needed to take one more jab and go for the jugular to make sure she knew how wrong it was for her and her mom to be there.

But when he opened his mouth, the words wouldn't come. Something about the way she peered out at him from inside the car calmed his temper. The anger he'd been so eager to unleash gave way to a strange connection with a girl he barely knew anymore— someone tangled in the same bad dream he and his dad were living but on the opposite side. All he could do was bow his head and walk away.

****

Wallowing in regret the day after Amy Shawver's wake, Caroline took Tanner for an early morning walk to try to shake it off. Wearing oversized sunglasses, a baseball cap, and a long raincoat with a hood pulled over the cap, she kept her chin down and avoided looking at the few people she passed on the sidewalk. It's not like she could have disguised her identity. Everyone in the neighborhood knew Tanner. She only hoped to emit her best "don't talk to me" vibe, especially after making a spectacle of herself at the funeral home.

What had she been thinking? Caroline wanted the Shawvers to know she hadn't forgotten what happened to their family. Heaven gained an angel the day Amy Shawver died, and Caroline mourned along with them.

Her mind flashed to the day she and Amy volunteered at the annual winter festival, selling hot chocolate together at an outdoor concession stand near the waterfall in the middle of town. The weather had been frigid, with temperatures below zero. Caroline had just finished chemo and wore a thick wool hat to cover her bald head. When a powerful gust of wind whisked behind the concession counter and blew the hat into the air, Caroline stood in front of the entire community, exposed and unprotected. Within seconds, Amy captured the hat and returned it to Caroline's head. Caroline could have sworn Amy possessed magical powers; she'd acted so fast. They resumed selling cocoa as if nothing had happened and never spoke of that moment. That was the last time Caroline ventured out in public without a wig until her hair grew back, and she never forgot Amy's kindness.

Despite Caroline's unconditional defense of Kyle for what he'd done, Amy's death left her immeasurably sad. But she should have known her presence at the funeral home would have exacerbated her family's grief. They'd suffered an unimaginable loss. She should have listened to Grace and stayed home.

A squirrel raced past her, and Tanner tugged at his leash, forcing Caroline to pick up the pace. She made it around the block without making eye contact with any of her neighbors, who were probably whispering about Kyle behind closed doors. She couldn't blame him for not leaving the house since his release late Monday. She and Jordan had turned over a cashier's check for five thousand dollars to prevent Kyle from spending more than one night in jail—something their son claimed was "no big deal," although he wouldn't give more detail. Her former colleague Jim Doughman accompanied them to the courthouse to pick Kyle up, but she couldn't quite understand why. The whole ordeal went off without a hitch, taking less than half an hour. His bill would surely tell a different story, briefly making her question why she no longer practiced law.

Caroline led Tanner through the front door to avoid going through the garage. The absence of Kyle's Jeep made her heart hurt. At least she didn't have to stare at the shattered glass a moment longer. After a policeman and an insurance adjuster photographed the damage, a tow truck driver loaded the vehicle onto a flatbed and hauled it away. The emptiness tortured her, reminding her of what a wreck her son had made of their lives.

But nothing, of course, compared to the lives of Dan and Ethan Shawver.

Caroline entered the kitchen to find Jordan seated at the table, staring blankly across from her spot where a glass of orange juice and a plate of cinnamon toast waited.

"Good morning," she said. "Thanks for the breakfast. You're so sweet." Jordan's thoughtfulness was rarely overlooked, but she often forgot to voice her appreciation. She promised herself to try harder. The months ahead would be difficult.

Jordan's slight smile couldn't curtail the worry on his face. "You're welcome."

"How long have you been up?" Caroline said.

"Pfft. I'm not sure I ever slept."

She removed Tanner's leash so he could greet Jordan. "Me neither. Is Kyle still hiding in his room?"

Jordan nodded while Tanner beat his tail against the leg of the table, signaling for someone to feed him. As soon as Caroline filled his bowl, he gobbled up the kibble and whined for more. "Enough, big boy," she said. "We're going to need to put you on a diet." She patted

Tanner's head and sat across from Jordan. "Any movement from Grace yet?"

Jordan leaned back in his chair and glanced at the ceiling. "I thought I heard her alarm go off, but no footsteps or running water yet. By this time on a school morning, the kids are usually fighting for the bathroom up there. I don't like how quiet it is."

"Me neither. It's kinda spooky."

But right on cue, the shuffle of feet across the upstairs floorboards announced Grace was awake. Less than ten minutes later, she ran downstairs wearing a pair of yoga pants and a baggy sweatshirt with her hair a mess on top of her head.

"Who's driving me today since Kyle's staying home?"

"Good morning to you too, Grace," Caroline snapped without thinking. "You're wearing that to school?"

"What's wrong with it?" Grace grabbed a banana from the bowl on the counter.

"You look like you're going to the gym, not school," Caroline said.

Her daughter shot a side-eye to Jordan. "Dad, help me out. Tell Mom to lay off."

"I'm right here, Grace. You can tell me yourself."

"Good. Then, yeah. Like, who's driving me to school?" Without giving either of them a chance to answer, Grace continued. "Oh, and no soccer practice today, so I'll need a ride home around 3:30."

"That might be a problem," Jordan said. "We're waiting to hear from our lawyer to see if we can meet this afternoon."

Grace peeled her banana and took a bite. "You both

need to be there for that?"

Caroline said, "Yes, Grace. Do you not understand what's happening in this house? Your brother was arrested. On some very serious charges." For once, their daughter could try thinking about someone other than herself. Parenting teenagers was hard, and Grace could shift Caroline's temperature gauge from *cold* to *hot* in a split second.

"Give me a break, Mom. I know what the Golden Boy did and how much trouble he's in. Don't get me wrong, it's awful. But I still need to get to and from school, don't I? Or should I just stay home and mope around the house?"

"I don't like your tone, young lady. And no, your father and I would prefer you go to school. All we're asking is you try to be flexible. Maybe see if you can get a ride from a friend or take the bus for a change."

With a toss of her messy bun, Grace marched into the mudroom and grabbed her backpack. "You two have no idea what it's like for me growing up in this family. For as long as I can remember, it's been Kyle this, Kyle that. Now that we're in school together, it's even worse. Every teacher. Every coach. Every damn lunch lady. They all ask me the same thing. Are you Kyle Beasley's little sister? It was already getting old, and now everyone's gonna know I'm the sister of the kid who killed Mrs. Shawver and tried to hide it. How'd ya like to start high school with *that* target on your back?"

Grace hit the button to open the garage door and stormed out. Caroline sighed, imagining how hard this situation would be for a teenage girl, especially one accustomed to taking a back seat to the limelight often surrounding her big brother. No matter how hard she and

Jordan had tried to treat their children equally, Kyle was just one of those kids who captured people's attention. He was cute, charismatic, and ultra-athletic, moving through life with a seemingly innate confidence and ease.

In contrast, Grace flew under the radar. She was an average student, a decent athlete, and moderately shy. Her fierce work ethic compensated for much of what she lacked in natural ability, but she still struggled to achieve anything close to what Kyle could with far less effort.

Caroline stood to go after Grace, but Jordan grabbed her by the wrist. "Let her go," he said. "She needs to blow off some steam."

"The morning bus already passed. She'll be late to school if she walks."

"My guess is one of the other parents going that way will pick her up."

Jordan was right. Caroline recalled a time when they told Kyle he had to walk to middle school because he'd missed the bus for the third time that week. They'd been trying to teach him a lesson and agreed neither one of them would drive him that morning. When he returned home at the end of the school day, he didn't seem the least bit upset about having to walk, later revealing he'd only gone four houses before a neighbor offered him a ride. Hopefully, someone would rescue Grace the same way today.

Finally making herself a cup of coffee, Caroline said, "Can we talk about Kyle for a minute? I'm struggling with so much of this, especially the lies."

"Me too. But that's what teenagers do. They lie. Usually to their parents to cover their butts."

"Are you excusing his behavior?"

"Not at all. But I remember being that age and not being completely forthcoming with my parents either."

"Sure, about trying a drink at a party or peeking at someone else's paper during a test," Caroline said. "But this is big stuff. Huge. He shouldn't have told us he hit a deer. I don't get the sense he ever really believed that."

"Me neither. But it's possible he didn't remember. I'm the one who first suggested he hit a deer. He just played along with it."

"I suppose. We need to sit him down and get more information about the accident. I understand how an ambulance suddenly on your ass could startle you, make you panic. That's happened to me before. It's petrifying. And maybe Amy Shawver was riding her bike outside the bike lane or wasn't visible because of the bright sun. What color clothes did she have on? Were they equipped with reflectors? We need to cover all the bases and look for a better reason why they collided."

Jordan nodded as she talked, interjecting an occasional "Mm. Hmm. Mm. Hmm." Then he added, "Let's not forget to explore what *he* was doing inside the car, too."

"Right." Caroline sat back down at the table with her coffee. "He got so mad when I asked where his cell phone was at the time of the accident. We need to carefully revisit whether he was texting while driving so he doesn't get defensive again."

"I'll handle that question." An odd look crossed over Jordan's face as if he felt guilty about something.

"What aren't you telling me?" She took a sip of coffee and burned her tongue.

"There is something you need to hear. And you're not going to like it."

She knew it. Caroline could always tell when Jordan was holding something back. "Go ahead." She clenched her jaw and waited for him to spill the beans.

"Last summer, Kyle hit a parked car in the high school lot because he was texting while driving."

Caroline flinched at what felt like a swift backhand to the face. "What? Why didn't anyone tell me about that?"

"No one got hurt, and there was no damage to our car. We didn't want to upset you because you were out of town, and you were already dealing with so much."

"Gee, thanks for protecting me. Next time, let *me* be the one to decide whether I can handle something or not."

Jordan let out an evil laugh. "Those words sound familiar. Isn't that what I said to you after you rang the bell at the cancer center without telling me about it? As if I wouldn't have wanted to be there to celebrate your final chemo treatment. Don't *you* dare lecture *me* about keeping things to myself."

"Oh, not that again. I've already apologized for that."

But Jordan was right. She'd been guilty of trying to shield her family from reality as best she could while undergoing treatment, choosing to carry the weight of the situation primarily on her own. Her inherent and stubborn self-reliance remained somewhat of a mystery. Caroline liked to blame it on her emotionless and fiercely independent mother—the oldest of five children raised in a strict German household who worked as a hospice nurse until she had kids. She'd passed away before Caroline and Jordan got married and wasn't around to defend herself.

Caroline's habit of shutting people out often backfired. Give her an auditorium filled with nameless people affected by cancer and she had no trouble opening up, at least partially. But offering those closest to her an intimate view of what scared her most had proved difficult. Almost impossible. Despite wanting to change, she couldn't quite figure out how. Over time, she'd learned to accept that about herself. But the stakes felt higher now. Even if she could be the best possible wife and mother, she couldn't predict whether Jordan and the kids would eventually let her back in. If not, she might never forgive herself for putting up that wall.

She continued, "Is there a record of Kyle's previous incident floating around?"

"The police never filed a report, and I paid cash for the repairs to the other kid's car to avoid an insurance claim. Kyle got off with a warning from the athletic director."

"But I assume there were witnesses. We better hope nobody steps forward to tell someone. If this information gets out, it won't look good for Kyle."

Chapter Six

Ten days had passed since their family nightmare began, but Caroline could barely remember transitioning from one day to the next. Random thoughts came and went, leaving her mind a scrambled mess. Today was sure to be rough. Kyle was scheduled for his arraignment, and they'd already hit a snag approaching the courthouse in Jordan's car. A small group of cyclists gathered in the parking lot. They'd shown up in support of Amy Shawver, holding signs reading things like "Hold Him Accountable" and "No Acceptable Pleas."

People had ruthlessly attacked Kyle on social media. Caroline read posts calling him a *punk*, a *liar*, and a *murderer*. While slinging hatred online was one thing, it took nerve to show up in person and confront a highly regarded young man about his mistake. His very bad mistake.

She turned to look at Kyle in the back seat. His chin was tucked into his chest, and his eyelids were shut tight. She stretched to place a hand on his knee, but he flinched at her touch.

Jordan's voice cut through the tension in the car. "Is Jim joining us again this morning?"

"No, he's in the middle of a big trial," Caroline said. "He's turning Kyle's case over to one of his partners. A woman named Valerie Saks."

"Did you practice with her?"

"No. She joined the firm as a partner long after I was gone, but Jim claims she and I will hit it off. Apparently, she volunteered to take this case."

"Do you think some of the local lawyers will support the Shawvers, at least privately? Dan's law practice is one of the best in the area, and isn't he president of the Erie County Bar Association?"

"He stepped down last year. But he's still well-liked and extremely connected. He and his brothers practically run Shawnee Springs."

Kyle, who hadn't made a sound the whole way over, groaned like a weary traveler after a long and difficult journey. "Can you please stop talking about Mr. Shawver?"

"Sorry," Caroline said. "I'm sure he's the last person you're thinking about right now, but his position in this community might work against you. We can't ignore what happened to him and his family."

Kyle groaned again. She looked over at Jordan, who stared at Kyle through the rearview mirror. Out of the corner of her eye, she noticed how close they were coming to the bright yellow parking block in front of them. "Jordan, watch where you're going!"

He slammed on the brakes and stopped abruptly, throwing the transmission in park and immediately exiting the car. "Let's get this over with," he huffed.

Caroline and Kyle followed Jordan from the car and through the parking lot, steering clear of the cyclists and keeping their heads hung low. Entering the lobby, Caroline said, "Let's wait here for our attorney."

"Is that her?" Jordan pointed at a short, thin woman—extremely thin—who was circling the courtroom door wildly. Her eyes bulged from their sockets beneath a thick pair of horned-rimmed glasses. She wore an oversized black jacket and a baggy pair of wide-legged pants that needed hemming. Her allover gray hair was in a messy knot with whisps of short, wiry strands circling her gaunt face.

Caroline sized up the woman rushing toward them. Not the image she would have expected from Jim's recommendation. She looked vaguely familiar, but Caroline couldn't place her. The woman greeted Kyle first, adjusting the large leather bag slung over her shoulder before extending her hand. "Nice to meet you, Kyle," the woman said. "I'm Valerie Saks. Feel free to call me Val."

Kyle nodded but kept his gaze directed at the ground.

"Hi, Valerie," Caroline said, placing a hand on her husband's forearm. "I'm Kyle's mom. And this is his father, Jordan."

"I know who you are," Valerie said. "You must not remember me. We've met before."

"We have? I'm sorry, I don't remember. Jim told me you joined the firm after I'd gone."

Valerie smiled. "We met at one of your discussion groups. Shortly after you published your book."

Oh, God. Now she remembered. No wonder Jim thought they'd hit it off. Valerie was a cancer survivor. The first time they met, Valerie talked to the group about living with metastatic breast cancer. That was several years ago, when Valerie wore her then-brown hair in a long braid. Good to see she was doing well.

"Oh, right," Caroline said. "Nice to see you."

"You, too. I wish the circumstances were different." They both looked over at Kyle.

Jordan said, "So, what's next, Ms. Saks?"

"Please, first names only. We'll be spending a lot of time together over the next several months. No need to be so formal." Valerie turned toward Kyle. "I'm sure your mom has explained much of this, so stop me if I'm telling you something you already know, okay?"

Kyle nodded again.

"Today, you'll be arraigned. Since the issue of bail has already been settled, all that happens this morning is the judge will officially inform you of the charges against you, and you'll state your plea out loud. Obviously, *not guilty*."

She paused, and Caroline felt a twinge of guilt, realizing how little she'd prepared her son for how this would go. Continuing, Valerie said, "Good with that, so far?"

Kyle chewed his fingernails and nodded.

"Okay, then. At that point, the judge will set a court date for a pre-trial hearing, which I'd recommend waiving. Because your case involves multiple felonies, it can't be tried here in Municipal Court. It'll be bound over to the County grand jury to determine whether there's enough evidence to take this to trial."

"How long before the grand jury convenes?" Jordan said.

"Depends on their caseload," Valerie said. "At least another week or so. That gives us time to decide whether Kyle should make a statement during that proceeding, and either way, prepare for the next step." She turned to look directly at Kyle. "Any questions so far?"

Kyle ripped a fingernail from his pinky. "When will I get my phone back?"

Valerie shot him a quick eyeroll. *Better her than me*,

Caroline thought. Where were Kyle's priorities?

"It won't be anytime soon," Valerie said. "At a minimum, the police will keep the phone as evidence until they determine whether you were texting while driving."

"I wasn't," he said. "I swear. My phone was in my backpack."

Caroline watched Kyle closely as he and Jordan exchanged glances. She had yet to tell Kyle she knew about his previous offense of texting and driving, as Jordan had asked her not to. Now, her husband's suspicious look suggested he, too, wondered if Kyle had been looking at his phone when he hit Amy Shawver.

Suddenly, the bailiff poked his head into the hallway. "The People versus Kyle Beasley," he called. "Judge Maureen McCaffrey presiding."

Caroline let out a sigh of relief upon recognizing the judge's name. A fair-skinned, red-haired woman in her late sixties, Judge McCaffrey was known for her no-nonsense approach to the law. She also had grown children. Caroline hoped she'd understand why Kyle had done what he'd done and go easy on him.

"Show time," Valerie sang. "Come with me, Kyle. Your parents won't be far."

Caroline and Jordan sat directly behind the defendants 'table, leaning shoulder-to-shoulder for support. The perspective from this side of the table differed drastically from what Caroline remembered from her time as a practicing lawyer. The most noticeable difference was her lack of any control over the situation. Valerie played the lead, while Caroline settled for a role in the supporting cast—a background member of the chorus. She was just an ordinary citizen, an interested bystander, a mother whose son was about to be charged with the murder of a beloved member of their community.

Had the crash been an accident? Of course. Did Kyle deserve to be punished? Arguably so. He'd left the scene of the crime and failed to come forward before the police showed up looking for him.

But the fact that he was a good kid should carry some weight—says his mom.

Caroline sucked in a breath to stop herself from shaking while Jordan placed a hand on her knee. If only the judge knew their son like they did, she'd have to see charging him was senseless. His initial willingness to hide the truth might plague Caroline forever, but at least he'd shown his true colors as soon as they confronted him about the fictitious deer. Either he was confused or didn't remember much, but she refused to accept her son was guilty of anything more than a lapse in judgment. Holding him accountable for that would not serve justice. No one felt worse about what happened than Kyle.

Except the Shawver family. No amount of justice could make them whole again.

Caroline's position might differ if the roles were reversed. She could easily be the one advocating for harsh consequences if someone had killed a member of her family. But drawing a hard line in the sand hardly seemed fair. Nothing would bring Amy Shawver back. Regardless of what the circumstances of the crash revealed, knowing he played a part in someone else's death would weigh heavily on Kyle for the rest of his life. As his mother, she had to believe that was punishment enough.

Although she hadn't attended church in ages, Caroline folded her hands and prayed the judge would agree. Arraignments rarely ended in a dismissal of charges, but crazier things had happened in criminal court.

It didn't take long to grasp the futility of her prayers. Kyle stood alongside Valerie as the judge charged him with criminally negligent homicide and leaving the scene of a fatal accident without reporting. A string of lesser-included crimes echoed throughout the room, but the judge's voice stopped making sense. Caroline magically descended into a cartoon classroom where she heard nothing more than the synthesized voice of a teacher spewing, "Wah, wah, wah, wah, wah."

She stared at the back of her son's head, admiring his long, wavy hair and wishing he'd turn around. Kyle had always been a respected member of the Shawnee Springs community, a rising baseball star who'd recently been the talk of the town, the subject of hometown pride. The chain of events leading to his arrest could crush him, ending the dream he'd been chasing since he was a young boy. Caroline needed to see his face and longed harder for him to glance back over his shoulder. She could at least send him a reassuring look or mouth the words, "It'll be okay." But his back remained toward her, blocking any view she might have of his deep brown eyes and preventing her from assessing his reaction to the devastating charges.

A disturbance coming from the back of the courtroom startled her. The picketing cyclists from outside had attended the proceeding and chattered among themselves. Turning in her seat, Caroline recognized one of them as a neighbor who often rode his bike up and down their street in the early morning. "Justice for Amy Shawver," the man fake whispered. "Put Kyle Beasley behind bars."

The hostility in his voice made Caroline's skin crawl, as if millions of tiny ants were marching all over her body. She turned back to the front of the room and inched closer to Jordan, suddenly struck by how cruel and vindictive people could be. People she'd coexisted with for decades, who watched her kids grow and became her friends. She'd never known Shawnee Springs to be the type of town that could split in two, but an accident like this could be divisive, prompting people to choose sides like they do when a couple gets divorced. Caroline had already isolated herself from much of the local community after she got cancer. Perhaps in an attempt at self-preservation, she became self-absorbed, initially focusing on her recovery and later on her advocacy for others. But in doing so, she had also turned her back on many of the friends she'd made when Kyle and Grace were younger.

The force of regret threatened to destroy her. Having people attack one of her children was far worse than hearing the words "You have cancer." And her withdrawal could hurt them. While Jordan's reputation as a well-respected dentist should help, it might not be enough. Like it or not, public opinion played a part in these cases. Kyle's actions would be tough enough to overcome, but he wouldn't stand a chance if the town turned against him.

****

Ethan hadn't been to school since Mom died two weeks ago, spending most of his time alone in his bedroom. Dad started getting on his case about it, but

Ethan didn't care. With the funeral behind them, he planned on avoiding Dad whenever possible. Spring couldn't come fast enough, and Ethan was ready to bust outta town after graduation.

His teachers didn't seem to mind his prolonged absence. Only the calculus teacher had emailed assignments to do from home, following up with a handwritten note delivered by Cole after Ethan deleted the email. "No pressure. Just thought you might like to keep up on your classwork to avoid falling behind," the message from Mr. Warren said. "Sorry about your mom. She was a special lady."

Ethan crumpled the note into a ball and threw it toward the trash in the corner of his room, raising his hands over his head in victory as the ball dropped into the can. "Two points!"

Ignoring the buzz of an incoming text, he sat on the edge of his bed and debated whether to take another nap. But he'd already promised Cole and Theo he'd go with them to the high school football game, which started soon. Shawnee Springs was playing Hudson Heights, their biggest rival. The whole school would be there. Probably the entire town.

Jumping back into real life made Ethan nervous. Another good thing about cocooning himself inside the house was he got to spend time with George, who decided to stay for a while since he could work remotely. Between his brother's conference calls and Zoom meetings, George would knock on Ethan's door to check on him or barge inside to deliver a stupid joke. They grabbed lunch together regularly, usually something delivered right to their door. Sometimes, they'd take a midday break to play a quick video game or watch an episode of a reality TV show. George was cool, and Ethan was surprised at how alike they were.

George was a great referee between Ethan and his dad, too. Just last night, when Dad yelled at him for spending too much time playing a war game, George stepped in and invited Dad to play with them. "It's lots of fun and a great escape from reality once in a while," he'd said. "Something we could all use right about now."

Dad, who usually agreed with whatever George said, sneered at the idea they could actually have fun together, but at least he backed off on the yelling.

When the phone buzzed again and again, Ethan finally looked at the screen.

Theo's text read,

—*You still in? I'm next door at Cole's. Can you drive to the game?*—

Even though Ethan now had full access to a car, his mom's minivan, the thought of taking over her seat behind the wheel still made him too sad. Another reason he had yet to return to school.

Ethan texted Theo back.

—*I'll see if George can take us.*—

Theo responded.

—*I didn't realize he was still here.*—

—*He works from home, so he can stay as long as he wants.*—

—*Cool. Think he'd buy us some beer before the game?*—

—*I'll ask. Walk over here when you're ready.*—

Less than half an hour later, Ethan entered the football stadium behind Theo and Cole, both of whom wreaked of alcohol and could barely walk a straight line. George had adamantly refused to buy them beer, but they'd obviously had no trouble getting it somewhere else and pre-gamed without Ethan before showing up at his house. George joined them for the game, walking alongside Ethan and laughing at how drunk his friends were.

Looking around, George said, "So this is what small-town Americana looks like, huh?"

Ethan scanned the bleachers, the overhead lights, and the hordes of young people scattered everywhere. Elementary-aged kids playing tag or tossing a football on the lawn behind the entryway fence. Middle-school boys wearing their football jerseys, hoping to impress the girls. Freshmen awkwardly finding their way and making new friends. And plenty of upperclassmen who smelled like Theo and Cole, some of whom remained in the bathroom hiding from the teachers and administrators because they'd had too much to drink.

"This is it," Ethan said. "I'm sure this same kinda thing goes on in California, right?"

"Sort of. But the vibe is different here," George said. "This is nice. Very quaint."

"Quaint?" Ethan raised an eyebrow. "I never thought of it that way."

Walking by the concession stand, Cole looked back and hollered, "Want somethin' to eat you two?"

George spoke up, but Ethan interrupted right away. "You go ahead. We'll grab some seats."

"You, okay?" George said. "You look like you're gonna puke, dude."

Ethan stuttered. "I just don't want to go by the concession stand."

George wrinkled his nose. "Why not?"

"Mom used to volunteer there during the games.

Another one of her pet projects. She was usually in charge of the kettle corn."

"That sounds delicious. Mind if I go with your friends? I'm hungry."

"Sure. They know where to find me."

George ran ahead to catch up with Theo and Cole, while Ethan made his way to the student section. Seniors typically claimed the first few rows of bleachers, standing instead of sitting throughout the game. Since it was the first home game of the season, Ethan wasn't exactly sure where to go. He approached slowly, looking for a familiar face.

Heads turned as he walked past. Chitchat spread throughout the crowd. Despite the blare of the marching band warming up near the visitors 'side end zone, Ethan could still tell people were talking about him. They wore pity, kindness, and concern on their faces. The showing of support should have made him feel good, but being the center of attention only made him uncomfortable. He put a hand over his stomach to stop it from rumbling.

Out of the blue, someone shoved past him, knocking him sideways into a group of elementary school kids approaching from the opposite direction.

Ethan quickly checked on the kids, then yelled ahead at the asshole who'd rammed into him. "Hey, watch where you're going!"

When the kid turned around, Ethan recognized him as Brad Sullivan, the catcher on the baseball team and one of Kyle Beasley's best friends. "What did you say?" Brad stopped in the middle of heavy foot traffic, groups of kids coming and going. Like a bully, he crossed his arms over his chest. From nowhere, two other baseball players appeared beside him.

Ethan straightened his spine and took a few steps to get in Brad's face. His heart was pounding. "I said watch where you're going. You could have hurt someone."

Without hesitating, Brad shot back. "Too bad your mom wasn't watching where *she* was going." His baseball buddies snickered as they wobbled on their feet, obviously wasted. One of them slapped Brad on the back. "Nice one, bro." They laughed in unison.

Ethan clenched his fist and got ready to deck Brad when a flock of freshmen swallowed him up as they fought through the crowd to claim their spots in the stands. "Low blow!" Ethan called after Brad. "Even for a dickhead like you!"

With Brad out of swinging distance, Ethan turned around and shot up the aisle, settling into Row Five after squeezing past a couple of younger students who weren't giving up their end seats. As he examined the row to make sure there was room for George and his friends, he spied Grace Beasley. Seated at the opposite end of his section, she stared in his direction. They locked eyes, and Ethan's cheeks smoldered. She must have witnessed his altercation with Brad and probably agreed with what Kyle's friend had said. How awkward. Quickly, he glanced down at his phone, hoping she'd look away so he could stop feeling so self-conscious. After what felt like an eternity, he couldn't shake the feeling he was still being watched.

Tempted to make eye contact with her again, he leaned sideways to peer down the bleachers. A tall kid had taken the seat next to Grace and blocked Ethan's view. Bending forward to get a better look, Ethan saw Theo and Cole walking toward him, carrying paper plates loaded with pizza and nachos. George followed behind with a cup carrier and four supersized drinks.

Almost tripping on his way up the concrete steps, Theo stood at the end of Row Five and shouted to Ethan while Cole and George remained at the bottom of the stairs. "Why are you sitting there? We get to be in front this year."

"I know," Ethan said. "Mind if we just stay here tonight? I'll explain later."

"Sure." Theo waved his free arm wildly at Cole and George. "Up here, guys!"

They all squeezed in just before kickoff. The buzz in the air shifted to the game, the biggest one of the season. Hudson Heights was the reigning conference champ, and winning tonight might give Shawnee Springs a shot at the title this year, maybe even a trip to the state championship game.

But Ethan couldn't focus on what was happening on the field, still pissed about Brad's nasty comment. It never occurred to him that anyone in this town, or *anywhere*, would talk smack about a hit-and-run victim, especially someone like his mom. The brotherhood of the baseball team must have distorted Brad's thinking, convincing him to believe Mom was somehow responsible for her own death. If that was possible, maybe others felt the same way.

Ethan leaned over to Theo. "Hey, are you hearing anything weird about my mom's accident?"

Theo bit his lip, then ripped off a hunk of pizza with his teeth, chewing it with his mouth open. "What do you mean? Like what?"

"I dunno. Anything. You look like you're not telling me something. Go on. Out with it!"

"I guess. Of course, kids have been talking about it

at school."

"What have they been saying?"

"Mostly how terrible it is your mom is gone."

"And?" Ethan scowled.

"I heard a few guys in the bathroom talking about how bad they feel for Kyle."

"Bad for Kyle?" Ethan's voice raised an octave.

"I guess because he got arrested. Like maybe the crash was just an accident, and he doesn't deserve to go to prison."

Ethan looked at Cole and George, who'd been listening to the conversation. "Is that what you think, Cole?"

"Of course not!"

"Me neither," Theo said, swallowing the pizza still in his mouth. "Besides, my guess is Kyle was texting when he hit your mom. That would definitely make it more than an accident."

George leaned closer and said, "Why do you think that?"

Theo paused, looking first to his right at George and Cole and then to his left at Ethan. "I wasn't supposed to say anything, but Kyle got busted for texting and driving before."

"When? And how do you know that?" Ethan said.

Theo set his empty paper plate beside his feet and stared at the ground. "Promise you won't tell anyone you heard this from me?"

Ethan and Cole nodded.

Theo continued. "Kyle and Mr. Beasley showed up at our house last summer to see my dad. They made me leave the room, but I eavesdropped from upstairs. I heard them talking about how Kyle hit a parked car in the school lot. A teacher witnessed the whole thing and told my dad Kyle never looked up from his phone until it was too late. He got off with a warning, but my dad said he could get kicked off the team if it happened again. And then bye-bye scholarship!"

"Holy shit. So, the Beasleys covered it up?" George said.

"Pretty much. Maybe he was doing the same shit when he hit your mom."

"Maybe," Ethan said as his eyes filled with tears.

Chapter Seven

Caroline and Kyle waited side-by-side inside the dreary conference room at Fleischmann, Russ, and Carrel, Attorneys at Law. The outdated office furniture nearly faded into the mahogany paneled walls and dark wood floor. A grainy portrait of the firm's founding partners hung askew next to the door, and an oriental rug in varying shades of deep red and hunter green offered the only pop of color in the predominantly monotonous space. The room had barely changed since Caroline worked there. The fact that the Old Boys 'Club had yet to spring for a makeover suggested they were still cheap or not as successful as they claimed.

The brass door handle rattled, and the well-dressed receptionist poked her head inside the room. "Would anyone care for coffee or water?"

"No thanks. What about you, honey?" Caroline touched Kyle's hand, but he jerked it away.

"I'm good." He nervously raised a hand to his mouth and nibbled on his fingernails.

The receptionist nodded. "Okay, but please holler if you change your mind. Ms. Saks is on her way." After she closed the door, the sound of bodies colliding resonated from the hallway, followed by the thump of something falling to the floor.

"Oh, shoot!" The receptionist's voice rang out. "Sorry, Ms. Saks. I'll get those for you."

"No, no. I've got them."

Valerie entered the room with a large leather briefcase over her shoulder and a mishmash of documents gathered in her arms. Her untethered gray hair fell haphazardly over her face, and her horn-rimmed glasses had slipped to the very end of her nose. Surprisingly, Jordan followed close behind carrying a few random sheets of paper she must have missed.

"Look who I found in the parking garage," Valerie announced without really acknowledging anyone, whirling across the room like a spinning top. "Did you two drive separately this morning?"

"We did." Jordan waited while Valerie shuffled through her stack of papers and assembled them on the conference table before setting his pieces on top. "Our daughter Grace needed a ride to school."

Caroline sighed and glared at her husband. Grace didn't *need* a ride to school. She just didn't want to walk or take the bus, and Jordan enabled her by driving her whenever she asked. Earlier in the week, they'd argued about it. Jordan had snapped, saying, "Let it go, Caroline. Kyle's arrest is affecting her, too. Her classmates treat her like a leper. She notices how they look at her differently and whisper behind her back when she walks past in the halls. Try to remember what being a teenager was like. If I can make things better by giving her a ride, I will."

Caroline knew how hard it was to be a teenager, especially since her father died when she was sixteen. Leave it to Jordan to overlook that. But she also remembered how her tough-as-nails mother taught her to be mentally strong. When things didn't go Caroline's way, her mom would simply say, "Deal with it." She left no room for debate in delivering her go-to advice in the most indifferent and unsympathetic way. Caroline rarely welcomed those early lessons. They hurt like mad. But later in life, they proved useful, especially when Caroline got cancer. She never could have endured those long, grueling months of treatment without the inner strength to persevere.

"Shall we get started?" Valerie adjusted her glasses back into place and continued sorting her papers—turning them front ways, back ways, and right side up, presumably to put them in order. Once again, Caroline questioned Jim Doughman's judgment. If Valerie was as scatterbrained as she appeared, she may not be the best person to represent Kyle.

Jordan sat on Kyle's other side and folded his hands in his lap. All three of them waited quietly until their attorney finished collecting herself. Finally, Valerie cleared space on the table, plopped a yellow legal pad in front of her as she sat down, and untangled a pencil from the nest of hair on her head. Her facial expression changed dramatically, from one customary of a dimwitted airhead to that of a hungry barracuda ready to draw blood, reminding Caroline of Dr. Jekyll's transformation into Mr. Hyde.

"So," Val said. "We've got our work cut out for us, with two major obstacles to overcome. The most serious offenses you're currently facing are criminally negligent homicide and leaving the scene of a fatal accident—both class E felonies. The grand jury *could* add a charge of manslaughter. I've seen some aggressive prosecutors try to set examples with these distracted driving cases, and there's precedent in New York State making that a possibility."

Kyle shifted in his seat. "I wasn't driving distracted."

"Good," Valerie said. "Then we should be able to prove that. Can you tell me anything about Mrs. Shawver's behavior?"

"Like what?" Kyle wrinkled his nose. "I told you. I barely saw her."

"I know. But we need to paint a picture that something was happening with *her* that afternoon. Can we show she was careless in any way? Riding her bike without a helmet or bright clothing? Maybe she was riding erratically, weaving in and out of traffic without using hand signals. I've ordered an autopsy to eliminate the possibility that a medical condition caused her to fall. That's a long-shot theory, but I never like to leave any stone unturned."

"I heard she donated her organs. Can they still perform an autopsy on an organ donor?" Caroline said.

"Of course," Valerie said directly to Caroline. "Only the organs removed for transplant are precluded from the autopsy. It may take weeks to get the report back, but again, it's a long shot."

Turning back to Kyle, Valerie continued. "If you didn't notice anything suspicious about Mrs. Shawver's actions that day, perhaps we can find people who might help us show a pattern of carelessness, who could testify to her erratic or negligent behavior on different occasions."

"I doubt you'll get very far trying to prove Amy caused the accident herself," Caroline said. "But that stretch of bike lane along Lakeshore is dangerously narrow. Maybe she was riding too close to the road. I wonder how many other accidents have occurred near that spot."

"It's all worth investigating," Valerie said. "The prosecution will depict Kyle as a reckless teenager who paid no attention to his surroundings that day. We could rebut that by insinuating Amy was also reckless or perhaps the road conditions were somehow unsafe. Even if we overcome our first hurdle by creating doubt regarding the accident's cause, we'll still have to face the charge of leaving the scene. That's the more difficult issue, in my opinion, but first things first. Let's start by trying to dethrone the otherwise perfect Amy Shawver—at least in terms of how well she followed the rules of the road. I'll also have someone dig into past police reports to see whether there've been similar incidents along Lakeshore Road."

Valerie's first strategy sounded intriguing. Caroline wasn't entirely comfortable portraying Amy as anything other than a victim. But, if that might help get her son acquitted so he could resume his college plans, she would try just about anything.

After Valerie finished outlining the remainder of her game plan and they'd scheduled their next session, Caroline, Jordan, and Kyle stood to leave. Quickly, Valerie grabbed hold of Caroline's wrist. "Would you mind hanging back for a second? I've got an unrelated question to ask you."

"Sure." Caroline nodded at Kyle. "Why don't you go home with Dad? I'll meet you two back at the house."

As soon as they left, Caroline settled again in her seat. Valerie walked around the table and sat in the chair directly beside her, turning it sideways until her knees dug into Caroline's thighs. Unnerved by the close proximity, Caroline inched her chair backward, attempting to create some much-needed personal space without being too obvious.

"Thanks for sticking around," Valerie said. "Please don't think this is strange, but I thought you might be a good person to talk to about something I'm dealing with right now."

"What's that?" Caroline said. "How can I help?"

"It's my cancer. It's getting more difficult to manage, and I don't know where to turn."

"What do you mean by difficult?"

"I've been living with metastatic breast cancer for almost ten years. That's a miracle in itself. But the medication I've been on has wreaked havoc on my body, and the side effects are catching up with me. I eat healthy. I exercise every day. But I'm always exhausted, and it's interfering with my work. Please don't take this the wrong way. I'll work like hell to advocate for your son. But you saw me today. And I don't know how much longer I can maintain this pace."

Caroline almost choked over Val's candor. "Have you considered getting a second opinion? I could give you a few referrals if you're interested."

"I've thought about consulting another physician but have yet to take the next step. I'm not lazy, just busy."

"I understand. But sometimes the only way to get different results is to switch providers. You should think about it more."

"I know. You're right. Especially since I may be running out of time."

Caroline chose her next words wisely. "Forgive me for asking, but how old are you?"

The ends of Valerie's mouth turned up in an

uncomfortable grin. "I'm sixty-two. After my initial cancer diagnosis, I only hoped to live long enough to see my son Michael graduate from college."

Valerie went on to describe her plight as a single mother. Despite lots of help from friends and neighbors, the road was tough. She praised the parents who took her son places when he needed a ride, but she was working. She marveled at how often people cooked for them or lent a hand in other ways after she got sick. Now Michael was gainfully employed as an actuary, living in Chicago with his girlfriend. He and Valerie talked often.

A warmth spread through Caroline's insides as she listened to proud Val speak about her son. "I hope I can share a similarly happy story about Kyle one day," she said. "I've always dreamed of him living in a big city with a fascinating career. My interpretation of life after baseball." She longed for him to reach that point—without a prison sentence derailing him.

"It's crazy how quickly things can change," Valerie said. "One minute, I thought I was a goner, and the next thing you know, I'm feeling optimistic and anticipating the future. I'll be much better off financially if I continue working until I'm sixty-five. I'm just struggling to find the strength. How did you do it?"

Still zigzagging in and out of her daydream about Kyle's future, Caroline was confused by Valerie's question. "Do what?"

"Remain balanced," Valerie said. "I've read your book and listened to your talks on YouTube. How did you manage to fight cancer while still keeping up with your other obligations?"

That was a delicate question—and a bit misplaced. Caroline's circumstances differed greatly from Valerie's because Jordan was there to pick up much of the slack. She'd also never describe herself as balanced. Her hyper-focus on recovery had come at the exclusion of almost everything else. For years, she'd chosen to concentrate exclusively on her physical well-being, ignoring her feelings and toughing it out alone while the rest of her life played on. She had compromised her role as a mother, tipping the scales in her own favor while often leaving her husband and kids to fend for themselves. None of that sounded balanced. And while she'd achieved her goal of being declared "in remission," she'd swallowed a fair share of anger and isolation along the way.

Maybe *she* should be the one seeking advice—from Valerie Saks. Val shared her emotions freely and had no problem leaning on others. Look at all the support *she'd* been offered and accepted. Caroline could count on one hand the times someone made her family a meal while she was undergoing treatment. Even the person who occasionally left flowers on her doorstep remained anonymous, as if revealing their identity would have crossed a line.

Was that the message she sent out to the universe? No wonder she felt so alone when allowing herself to dwell on it. Caroline might never understand why she'd kept things from Jordan and the kids, like excluding them from the ceremonial bell ringing to mark her last treatment. Valerie would be shocked if she knew about that.

More importantly, did Caroline have the capacity to change if she wanted to?

"I think you've got me all wrong," Caroline said. "I'm about as imbalanced as they come. I'm just good at

105

hiding it. Smoke and mirrors, I always say."

As the impromptu confession spilled from Caroline's mouth, she was struck by how complicated life could be—and filled with contradiction. In one moment, Valerie impressed her as a skilled and competent attorney. In the next, she smacked of someone who'd taken on more than she could handle. Despite Valerie's assurances, Caroline continued wondering whether they were being naïve in trusting her with Kyle's future. They couldn't afford to blow any chances at keeping him out of prison.

Valerie edged her chair closer once again. This time, Caroline allowed their legs to settle against one another until they stood to leave. Before exiting the room, they caught eyes, giving Caroline a close-up of that familiar look—the one that had stared down the C-word while enduring an arduous journey and now drilled into her soul searching for hope.

Caroline couldn't explain the unexpected connection she felt with Val, who, unlike herself, preferred getting up close and personal over keeping a distance. The hint of friendship was comforting and unsettling in the same breath. A clash of emotions left her frustrated and confused. But regardless of Caroline's misgivings about Val's capacity, having faith in the attorney they'd hired was in everyone's best interests.

If they wanted to clear Kyle's name, there were bigger battles to fight.

****

The sky turned dark earlier these days, and Ethan spent a lot of time in his room, playing video games and going to sleep early most nights. After dinner, cheese sandwiches and canned soup for the second night in a row, Ethan cleaned the kitchen and started heading upstairs. When George stopped him to ask whether they could hit the grocery store together, Ethan said, "Sorry. I'm tired. And I've got schoolwork to do before bed."

"Come on," George pleaded. "I still don't know my way around this town."

"It's a straight shot up the main road. It'll only take a few minutes."

"Let me put it another way then. Your dad asked me to get you out of the house. He thinks you spend too much time gaming. I think he's worried about you."

Ethan sneered. Funny how Dad made George do his dirty work. His father barely said a word at the dinner table and excused himself as soon as he finished eating. "Dad's not worried about me. He thinks I'm lazy. And I don't care."

Looking at his backpack, Ethan dreaded the makeup assignments stuffed inside. Earlier in the week, he finally returned to school, which should have pleased his father, although he'd yet to acknowledge it. Ethan mostly liked being back in the classroom. It gave him something to think about besides missing Mom.

The shock of her death had subsided for most of his classmates. Only a few still gave him awkward looks or tried too hard to say the right thing. Brad Sullivan and the rest of Kyle's baseball buddies hadn't given him any more trouble, and Ethan's teachers moved forward with business as usual. He even had to take a pop quiz on his first day back, which was completely unfair.

If Ethan had been an athlete like Kyle, he could have skipped all the schoolwork he wanted. Kyle hadn't attended a single class since the accident, and Ethan assumed that no one was sending his assignments home

107

or expecting him back anytime soon. That kid could write an entire paper in Pig Latin and still get passing grades. All anyone cared about was how Kyle would make the town of Shawnee Springs proud one day by playing Major League Baseball. Big fuckin 'deal.

Ethan could feel his temper rising, and the sound of Dad flipping through TV channels in the family room made matters worse. A quick trip to the store with George might give him the attitude adjustment he needed before tackling his physics worksheet. "Fine. I'll go with you. But let's go to the store in the next town over. It's not too far out of the way."

George gave him an odd look. "That's weird. Why? We're just grabbing food for tonight's game. Buffalo plays New York. Your dad invited all three of your uncles over."

"Of course, he did." Ethan rolled his eyes. He'd forgotten about Thursday night football on network TV. So much for getting to bed early. "I don't feel like running into anyone I know, that's all."

But that was only part of it. Ethan's mom enjoyed dragging him to the local grocery store, regardless of whether she was doing her "big shop" or just running in for a few items. He rarely minded unless he was in a hurry. Mom never got in and out of the store without seeing tons of people she knew. Never in a rush, she would stand and talk forever, or at least until Ethan nudged her along. It became their inside joke to count the number of times he'd have to interrupt his mom's chitchat in the aisles before they made it to the checkout line. Their record was six. It took them almost two hours to complete their shopping trip that day, and he remembered how annoyed he'd been.

Now, he'd surrender every video game he owned to patiently wait while she socialized, and he wasn't ready to shop the familiar aisles without her.

As soon as they entered the alternate store, George said, "Let's split up. You grab the snacks while I head to the cooler for drinks."

"Sounds like a plan." Ethan grabbed a grocery basket and scanned the overhead signs in search of some munchies. Just as he turned down the "Chips and Crackers" aisle, he stopped dead in his tracks. Only a few yards in front of him, Mrs. Beasley casually steered a full cart of groceries past the potato chips and pretzels as she strolled straight toward him. What was she doing in this neck of the woods? Probably the same thing he was—trying to avoid crossing paths with anyone she knew.

Ethan wanted to turn around and sprint from the store, but his feet wouldn't cooperate. He stood trapped in place as if concrete filled his sneakers. If he didn't hurry out of the way, she'd walk right into him. Quickly, he bent down and pretended to tie his shoe, hoping she'd pass without noticing him.

Nope. No such luck. They locked eyes before Ethan could look away.

"Ethan, what are you doing here?" Her eyebrows arched upward.

"Um, um, same as you, Mrs. Beasley. Grocery shopping."

"Oh, I mean. Why here and not the store in Shawnee Springs?"

Ethan glanced around awkwardly, staring at the contents of her grocery cart and trying to look anywhere but her face.

"I get it," she said. "Sometimes it's easier to be

incognito."

"Right." He mumbled.

"I'm glad we ran into each other. I've meant to call and apologize to you and your dad."

"For what?" Ethan played dumb, knowing exactly what she was sorry for but eager to watch her sweat.

"For showing up at your mom's service. I hope you realize my intentions were good. I'm an only child, just like you, and when I was in high school, I lost my dad. I remember how terrible that was. I just wanted to express my condolences. In retrospect, I made a poor decision. I didn't mean to upset you or your father."

Ethan half-listened and continued avoiding eye contact. Mrs. Beasley's nonchalance irritated him. Part of him wanted to pile on and say more about how inappropriate she'd been, but he felt so alone and couldn't find the courage. Once again, George was nowhere to be found when he needed him.

Without pausing, Mrs. Beasley continued. "I meant what I said at the funeral home. About always being there for you."

Oh, brother. She should have quit while she was remotely ahead. Her words angered Ethan like they had at his mom's wake. Something was seriously wrong with her. She seemed oblivious to the fact that Ethan could never forget her son was responsible for his mom's accident. And he hadn't shown the decency to stop and help when she was lying in the street—*dying*. Here was Ethan's golden opportunity to tell Mrs. Beasley what a piece of shit Kyle was and how he'd never need a thing from anyone in their whole goddamned family.

But George didn't give him the chance. He must have been lurking around the corner, listening to the whole conversation, because he suddenly appeared and bumped Mrs. Beasley's cart into the cracker shelves—not hard, but enough to make his point.

"Are you bothering my brother?" he said.

"What? Who?" she said. "Ethan, I didn't know you had a brother."

"Come on, lady," George squawked. "Leave us alone. Get the hell out of here. And tell your son we'll never forgive him for the pain he's caused our family."

The only other shopper in their aisle, an older woman wearing a khaki trench coat and an angry pout on her face, wheeled her cart past them and abruptly turned the corner.

Ethan backed away from the commotion and once again fixed his gaze on the contents of Mrs. Beasley's grocery cart. A bundle of bright red and pink flowers sat propped upright near the front basket. Poppies. He guessed Mrs. Beasley didn't know his mom was the one who occasionally left flowers on her doorstep when she was sick. Ethan was in middle school, and sometimes Mom would let him sneak onto the Beasleys' front porch with the anonymous bouquet. Pretending to be a ninja, he'd drop the flowers and run back to the car as fast as possible.

Mom had wanted to do more for the Beasleys back then. She contemplated offering to make them meals, help with their laundry, or accompany Mrs. Beasley to her chemo appointments to help pass the time. But Mrs. Beasley was intimidating, so his mom kept her distance most days. He should do the same now.

Ethan suddenly wondered whether Grace could be waiting outside in the car again. There might be enough time to hurry to the parking lot while Mrs. Beasley paid for her groceries. He didn't like how their last conversation had ended, and he hoped for another chance to talk with her. He hadn't stopped thinking about her since the football game and couldn't care less about Kyle's earlier warning to stay away from his sister. Fuck that! Kyle had no right telling him anything anymore.

His conscience stopped him from searching for her. The Beasleys were the enemy now. Talking with Grace was a terrible idea.

Too bad he didn't entirely believe that.

Considering how she'd looked at him from across the bleachers, she might be the only person who could understand what he was going through. But how could she? No one could.

In an unexpected fit of anger and confusion, Ethan stormed out of the store, leaving George to finish with Mrs. Beasley alone.

Chapter Eight

The grand jury was expected to decide on Kyle's case that afternoon. The secrecy of the closed proceeding troubled Caroline, and the waiting threw her into a serious funk. She hadn't made any public appearances since Kyle's arrest, which her agent Toby Stoll failed to understand, and Jordan rescheduled the few patients remaining on the day's calendar after the rest mysteriously canceled. Caroline craved anywhere else to go so she and Jordan could stop getting on each other's nerves at home.

Almost crashing into the refrigerator door as Jordan threw it open with unreasonable force, Caroline stopped abruptly and crossed her arms over her chest. "What's the big deal if Kyle's without a phone for a while longer?"

"It's inconvenient," he said without looking away from inside the fridge. "The police aren't hurrying to return the one they confiscated. Wouldn't you like to be able to reach him when you need to?"

"Reach him? How hard is that? He rarely leaves his room."

Caroline worried about Kyle's self-imposed isolation and wished he'd confide in her about his feelings. His refusal to unburden his heart arose straight from a chapter in the Caroline Beasley playbook, and she didn't like it.

With a yogurt cup in his hand, Jordan closed the refrigerator door, gently this time. "Can't we agree to disagree on this for now?"

Of course, Caroline thought, reflecting on how often they'd achieved a similar stalemate throughout their twenty-year marriage. Living in a state of truce had become customary, but she was tired of bickering and ready to escape the stress building inside the house. "Let's get out of here and grab some lunch."

Surprisingly, Jordan said, "Great idea."

A short time later, they arrived at their favorite lunch spot. Joe Magee, the owner of Joe's Diner and a longtime patient of Jordan's, greeted them at the employee entrance. Jordan had called ahead to make sure Joe was working, knowing he'd understand their predicament. Going out in public was a hassle lately, especially in the middle of town. The strange looks and rude comments didn't surprise them anymore, but they graciously accepted Joe's offer to sneak in the back and through the kitchen. Instead of their usual table—the one closest to the window with a breathtaking view of the waterfall— he seated them at a dark corner booth and personally took their orders.

"Thanks, my friend," Jordan said before Joe disappeared to deliver their orders to the cook.

"Did you detect a trace of the cold shoulder?" Caroline said.

"From Joe? No way."

"I don't know. He seemed less friendly than usual."

"For God's sake, Caroline. The man just offered us a discreet entrance and an inconspicuous table. Stop being so paranoid."

"Fine." She dropped it. But something about Joe's

demeanor struck her as different from his normal congeniality. Perhaps he was siding with the Shawvers. Maybe their families were friends.

As time passed, Shawnee Springs separated into two camps. The Beasleys and the Shawvers—kind of like the Hatfields and the McCoys. Long-standing friendships crumbled, and neighbors who once shared backyard barbecues kept their distance. Even if harmony could be restored after Kyle's case was resolved, it might take years for the community to fully recover from such a significant rift.

A young waiter promptly delivered their drinks. A beer for Jordan. Unsweetened iced tea for her. As soon as he walked away, Caroline said, "That kid barely looks older than Kyle. Should he be serving alcohol?"

Jordan sneered. "Oh, geez, Caroline. Stop picking at every little thing. I'm sure he is, or Joe wouldn't have him doing it."

Caroline cleared her throat and took a deep breath, determined to keep the tension from mounting. "You're never going to believe who I ran into yesterday at the grocery store."

"Who?" Jordan peeled the label from his beer bottle and guzzled his drink as if stranded in a desert.

"Ethan Shawver and his brother."

"His brother?"

"Yeah. Half-brother. Who knew he had one? He's older than Ethan and was a real prick to me."

"What?" Jordan looked at her skeptically. "What did he do?"

"I was trying to talk with Ethan, telling him how sorry I was for showing up at his mom's service, and his brother told me to get the hell away from them. He was rude. Very rude."

Jordan cocked his head to the side. "Wait a second. You went to Amy's service?"

"Yes, Jordan. I told you that."

"No, you didn't. I would have remembered." He closed his eyes and shook his head as if shaking water from his ears.

Even if Caroline hadn't mentioned it to Jordan, she was surprised Grace never did. She was such a Daddy's Girl and usually told him everything. "Ugh. I don't want to argue. I only wanted to tell you about our encounter. I offered to be there for Ethan and his dad if they needed anything, but if they're going to treat me like the enemy, I'm done. Done trying to be nice."

"Ha! Since when are *you* worried about being nice?" Jordan's booming voice turned a few heads in their direction. The hostess, a middle-aged woman who'd worked there for as long as Caroline could remember, lowered her gaze and whispered something unintelligible as she passed their booth.

Caroline furrowed her eyebrows. "That's a shitty thing to say," she said. "What do you think I am? Some sort of monster?" Jordan's words stung. She hated feeling like that's how he saw her. Her years of helping others fight cancer should count as *nice*. Sure, she'd been nasty to a few doctors and nurses over the years. Frustration came with the territory. Sometimes, it takes more than a wink and smile to get what you want, need, or deserve. But different rules applied to her family. She loved them more than anything in this world, and she didn't deserve such an ugly accusation from her husband. Would Kyle and Grace have agreed?

Once their food arrived, they ate in silence while

Jordan sucked down another two beers. She stopped herself more than once from telling him to slow down.

After clearing his plate, Jordan looked at his watch for the umpteenth time. "When do you think we're going to hear something?"

"It depends on how long the grand jurors deliberate. They need twelve affirmative votes to indict him." Caroline stared down at her lunch and slid her plate aside. She'd barely tasted her chicken sandwich, and the fries sat untouched.

"Aren't you gonna eat those?" Jordan grabbed her plate as he waved a hand at the waiter walking by. "Can you grab me another beer?"

Caroline rolled her eyes at how snippy Jordan got when he drank too much.

After much debate, Valerie had persuaded the Beasleys not to have Kyle testify before the grand jury, whose only function was to establish whether there was enough evidence to take his case to trial. It was unlikely anything their son could say would make a difference. Either the prosecutor's office had the evidence, or they didn't.

Even though Valerie predicted a negative outcome, Caroline hoped for a miracle. The same way she'd foolishly prayed for the charges to die on the vine during Kyle's arraignment. If the jurors only knew Kyle like she did—understood what a good kid he was, with such a bright future—they'd come around to see there was no point in taking this case any further. She needed to remain positive and believe anything was possible.

For a brief time, Caroline wondered whether keeping Kyle off the witness stand was a mistake. If the grand jury got to hear his side, in his own words and from his own mouth, this nightmare could end quickly.

But deep down, Caroline knew better. While she'd never practiced criminal law, she possessed a general understanding of how these things worked. With or without Kyle's testimony, the facts stacked up against him. Several witnesses would testify they'd seen a dark gray Jeep Liberty with a license plate beginning with KEA strike Amy Shawver while she was riding her bike. The driver failed to stop after she landed in the street. The elements of the crimes Judge McCaffrey charged him with were easily met. Plain and simple.

Their best chance of exonerating Kyle would be to prove he didn't actually cause Amy's death and provide a solid defense of why he left the scene. Both hurdles presented serious challenges, but Caroline needed to trust Valerie, who believed a trial judge would be easier to convince than a group of grand jurors. Valerie even alluded to the possibility of a favorable plea deal. "So let them indict," she'd told Caroline. "We'll have plenty of evidence to present to the judge suggesting Kyle doesn't belong in prison."

When Jordan's phone finally rang with the news, the outcome didn't come as a surprise. The grand jury had handed down an indictment on charges of criminally negligent homicide and leaving the scene of a fatal accident. Despite the friction between her and Jordan over lunch, Caroline leaned across the table to get closer to her husband, not wanting to put the phone on speaker in case someone could overhear Valerie rattling off a few more details. Their attorney promised to call again after she returned to her office, and Jordan hit the "End Call" button. Caroline slumped back into her seat and sighed slightly, relieved that the prosecutor hadn't tacked on a manslaughter charge.

"This is such bullshit." Jordan's words tumbled from his mouth with a slur.

An emptiness ached in Caroline's gut. She took her plate back from Jordan and devoured the remaining fries. "It's what we expected."

"Whaaat? You agreeee with it?"

"Of course not. But it's no shock."

Jordan looked around the restaurant. "Where's the server? I need another drink."

Caroline lowered her eyebrows and gave Jordan a long stare. "I think you've had enough. Besides, we need to get home to tell Kyle." She hated to admit being unable to call their son on his cell phone was inconvenient. Maybe Jordan was right about getting him a new phone.

When the server returned, Caroline spoke loudly over Jordan's plea for another beer. "We're ready for our check, please."

After settling their tab, she led Jordan through the kitchen the way they'd entered. He insisted he was okay to drive, but she had discreetly lifted the keys from the table and refused to turn them over. Nearing the car, Caroline clicked the remote to unlock the doors and noticed a few strange splotches on the driver's side. Moving closer, she recognized the smear of yellow and white dribbling down the side of Jordan's black BMW.

She wasn't being paranoid now.

Someone visiting their favorite lunch spot had egged their car.

****

Among the swarm of students clamoring outside after last period, Ethan stood alone on the sidewalk in front of the high school, waiting for George to pick him up. He had a monster headache and couldn't wait to get home. It was Friday, but he wasn't interested in going out. He'd stayed up too late the night before watching Buffalo pulverize New York while sneaking beers from his dad and uncles. No one besides George seemed to notice how drunk he got. His brother practically carried him up the stairs once the game ended. Dad never said a word, as if Ethan were invisible, not just last night, but ever since Mom had died. His father didn't care about much anymore. Moving out would be easier if things stayed that way.

He stared down the bus lane and spied Theo and Cole talking to a cluster of girls. Freshmen, he assumed, as he only recognized one of them—Grace Beasley. He still hadn't spoken with her since the funeral home, and she looked cute waiting for the bus in her soccer warmups. He guessed by how she hung her head that she was having a hard time. If her post-crash life was anything like his, she was trying to appear normal while her insides were doing somersaults.

Cole noticed him gawking and called out, "Hey, Ethan! You headed to the away game?" He and Theo left the girls and maneuvered down the crowded sidewalk toward him. As soon as they were in earshot, Ethan said, "Not tonight."

"Come on!" Theo caught up to him and smacked him on the back. "The Boosters sponsored a bus so everyone can ride together. After we pre-game at Cole's first, of course."

"Not today. I drank too much during last night's football game. I have a hangover and need to go home to sleep it off. Do you two need a ride? George is picking me up."

"No thanks," Cole said. "But back up a sec. Where did you watch the game? At your house?"

"Yeah. I watched with George, my dad, and my uncles."

"And they let you drink?" Theo said.

"Not really. I kept refilling my water bottle with what they thought was soda. Nobody pays attention to what I do anyway. I could have been doing shooters right there on the couch."

"I doubt that," Cole said. "And by the way, why weren't you at lunch today?"

"I was in the guidance office. The principal is worried about my mental health and wants me to meet with the school counselor regularly."

"That's cool, isn't it?" Theo said.

"I guess. So far, the counselor does most of the talking. I'm not sure what she expects me to say. My mom's dead. That sucks. It's not like I'm going to off myself or anything." Ethan adjusted his backpack on his shoulders. It was getting heavy—kinda like everything else in his life. "I saw you guys talking to Grace Beasley. What's up with her?"

Theo and Cole glanced at each other, smiling as if they shared a secret.

"Not much," Cole said. "She's quiet. Nothing like Kyle."

"But she's hot," Theo said. "Think she'd go to the homecoming dance with me?"

Ethan jerked his head back in surprise. "No offense. But that's not a great idea."

"Why not?" Theo said.

"Are you dense? It'd be awkward having her in our

group." He swallowed the pang of jealousy that snuck up on him. "I might not go this year anyway. Just not feelin' it. But it would still be strange if you took the sister of the kid who—you know."

Ethan could feel what he now knew was officially called a "wave of grief" churning inside his chest. The counselor had warned him that anything could trigger them, and they came out of nowhere.

His knees trembled, and he immediately removed his backpack to stay steady on his feet. His brother turned into the school driveway in Mom's minivan as if perfectly timed. With the windows rolled down, music blared from the radio. Ethan looked at Theo and Cole, picked up his backpack again, and hurried toward his ride. "Catch you two later!"

Chucking his backpack into the backseat, he hopped in the passenger's side. "Hey, George. What's up?"

"Not much. I stopped working early to enjoy the fall colors. We don't get this in my part of California, so I figured I should enjoy it while I'm here."

"Mom loved this time of year. Autumn was her favorite season."

"I know," George said with a faraway smile. "You hungry?"

"Not really. But I could always eat."

"Good, cuz I'm starving. Let's grab some tacos."

George stepped on the gas, and the tires squealed as they peeled out of the parking lot.

"Slow down!" Ethan screamed as his pulse rate skyrocketed. "This is still a school zone."

"Relax. I got this," George said in a voice that could have soothed a screaming baby.

But Ethan couldn't relax. Sometimes, even riding in

a car made him anxious, and his fear of driving was getting worse. He pictured himself veering off the side of the road and plowing down a pack of cyclists like a bowling ball striking a set of pins. Thankfully, George didn't appear to mind chauffeuring him around whenever possible.

"Seriously. Slow down. I feel sick."

George obliged, continuing at a slower speed until braking abruptly to turn into a fast-food drive-thru, where they joined a long line of cars waiting to order food. "Looks like everyone and their grandmother is hungry." He chuckled. "Since we're gonna be here awhile, I've got something to tell you."

"What?" Ethan glanced over at the side of George's head.

"I'm going home," he said, still facing out the front windshield and avoiding eye contact with Ethan. "My flight leaves late Sunday."

A lump the size of a golf ball lodged itself in Ethan's throat. "How come?"

"I can't stay here forever. I've got to get back to work."

"I know, but it's only been a few weeks. And I thought you worked remotely?"

"I do, for the most part. But I still have an office to go to occasionally. Besides, I have a life in California. Friends. Obligations. A gym membership. Even an on-again, off-again girlfriend who allegedly misses me."

"But what am I going to do without you?" In other words, Ethan feared being left alone with his dad.

"You'll be fine. It's been great getting to spend this much time together. And you can come stay with me whenever you like."

"Careful what you say. I might take you up on that offer sooner than you think."

Moving through the drive-thru line and finally coming to the menu board, they recited their orders into the microphone and then inched their way toward the payment window. "My treat," George said. "Mind grabbing me some cash from my wallet? I think it fell on the floor there in front of you."

Ethan leaned over and found George's wallet underneath the seat. When he opened it, a small bronze coin dropped into his hand. He'd seen something similar before but couldn't remember where. "What's this?"

Quickly, George said, "My one-year sobriety chip. Never leave home without it."

"Sobriety chip? You're an alcoholic?" No wonder he'd *really* been drinking soda during the football game.

"Yup. Been sober for more than two years now. That's why I was late to Mom's wake—so I could catch an AA meeting."

Suddenly, Ethan remembered where he'd seen a chip like that before. In his mom's dresser drawer, when he snooped through her room the day after she died.

"Wait a second! Mom had a bunch of these chips. Was she an alcoholic, too?" Ethan could barely believe he'd asked that question. Nothing could have been further from his imagination, and his mind leapfrogged to his conversation with George when he'd picked him up at the airport. Something told him he'd just stumbled upon a secret from Mom's past.

"You didn't know that? Wow! Yes, she's the one who encouraged me to join AA. She worried about me having a genetic predisposition to alcoholism because of her own struggles. She could tell I'd hit rock bottom even from across the country. Who knows where I'd be now if it weren't for her."

George's casual tone made his disclosure sound more like a routine news report than the devastating bombshell he had just dropped. "That's why you need to be careful. I know it's part of growing up, but you and your friends drink a lot. I was concerned about how drunk you got at home last night. No lectures, just be aware. Alcohol tolerance differs for everyone, but it could be dangerous if you're anything like Mom and me."

Ethan couldn't process George's curveball, especially with a killer headache that instantly pounded harder. He could barely believe there was such a significant other side to Mom that he knew nothing about. "I had no idea. I never saw Mom with a drink in her hand. Ever. Not even a seltzer or a glass of wine."

"Of course, you didn't. She'd been sober since I was a teenager, I think. That's why she lost custody of me as a kid. She was a real mess and couldn't care for me back then. She started working the program after she met your dad. Regardless of what you think about him, he saved her life by insisting she stop drinking before they got married."

George leaned out the van window to grab their food from the cashier. Ethan gagged at the smell of refried beans, and his appetite disappeared.

"Do you think it's weird she never told me?"

"Hard to say. Maybe she was waiting for the right moment. Mom never said anything about keeping it confidential, and I'm sure she worried about you the same way she did about me."

Ethan remembered the talks Mom had given him

about underage drinking, realizing now that her perspective was entirely different than she'd ever let on. He searched his brain for the words she had used when he got busted trying tequila at Cole's house in tenth grade. She was so mad, pretty much lost her mind. At the time, he thought her reaction was normal. Any mom would go ballistic if she discovered her kid drinking. Considering what George had said about alcoholism being hereditary, Mom's crazy reaction made even more sense now.

It hurt that Mom hadn't trusted him with her past. Knowing her history wouldn't have changed how much he loved her. He'd never know if she would have eventually opened up to him if not for the accident, making him question how well he ever knew his mom.

Chapter Nine

Caroline woke Saturday morning to the sound of heavy rain and a note stuck to the bathroom window.

"Ran out to buy vinegar to salvage my car's paint job. Be back soon, Jordan."

Still fuming about whoever egged Jordan's car, she hypothesized about what the vandal was thinking. Or vandals. Rumors circulated in town that she and Jordan initially planned on covering up Kyle's crime, that he'd never intended to turn himself in, and they tried disposing of the car before anyone could see it. She'd even heard a story that when the police arrived at their house, they all ran out the back door, ready to flee Shawnee Springs as fugitives. Although the thought had crossed her mind, she'd never seriously considered it. People could be so heartless, as if they had nothing better to do than spread false gossip about a family going through hell.

Caroline couldn't let rumors spoil her day. She needed to light a fire under Kyle and rescue him from the dark cloud of his legal troubles so he could feel productive again, even temporarily. While she had battled cancer, there were many days when staying in bed for hours and feeling sorry for herself seemed easier. Eventually, she had learned to distract herself from the heavy stuff to keep moving. She preached about maintaining some sense of purpose in every speech she ever delivered.

Maybe she should give Kyle a similar pep talk. Letting go of guilt is never easy, but coaxing him out of his room and back into reality could be the first step in helping him forgive himself. Besides, she wasn't ready to accept that giving up was the only option.

Caroline flashed to her conversation with Kira, the young woman she'd met in Las Vegas who thought her ridiculous publicity poster was "badass." Resurrecting the persona from that poster might show Kyle how to keep his chin up, provided she softened her approach. Jordan's accusation during dinner at Joe's Diner lingered in her mind, reminding her how easily good intentions can be misunderstood.

Relieved to find Kyle's door unlocked for a change, Caroline quietly entered his bedroom. Kicking aside the dirty clothes littering her path to his bed, she sat beside his face-down body and whispered in his ear. "Wake up, Kyle. I'm taking you to get a new phone this morning. We need to hurry so I can catch Grace's game."

He rolled over on his back and hugged a pillow to his chest. With his eyes barely open, he said, "Seriously?"

Aha! She'd guessed right at the way to evoke a response.

"Seriously. Now get dressed, and let's get going."

Minutes later, Caroline found Grace downstairs, pouting at the kitchen table in her soccer uniform. "Game's canceled," she said. "The radar's showing thunder and lightning all afternoon."

"Wanna come to the mall? We're headed there to get Kyle a new phone."

"Sure, why not? I'll go get changed."

Caroline smiled at the opportunity to hang out with both kids outside the house and without Jordan. She hadn't had much chance to do that in a long time. If something good were to come out of this tragedy, maybe the crash could draw them closer.

When they arrived at the cell phone store, Caroline signed in at the kiosk and groaned at discovering six customers ahead of them. While they waited, Kyle and Grace sat next to each other on a small bench as Caroline examined the selection of overpriced accessories. Kyle would need a new phone case, too, so she might as well narrow in on a few options for him to choose from.

After forty-five minutes, she'd grown impatient and looked for her own place to sit. Glancing at Kyle and Grace, she noticed how close they were to one another. Their thighs and shoulders touched as they huddled over the tablet computer wedged between them. They leaned into each other with obvious ease, revealing a connection that took Caroline by surprise.

Despite the hostility Grace demonstrated the morning after Kyle's night in jail, she clearly didn't hold a grudge. Whenever Caroline told stories about how much her kids fought, she'd chalk it up to typical sibling stuff, secretly embarrassed at how heated their arguments could get. But seeing them now, she sensed a bond she never thought existed, as if they'd become allies when Caroline wasn't looking.

Regret spread rapidly throughout her body, like a germ flowing through her bloodstream. She had been so self-absorbed that she neglected to notice her kids growing closer. What else had she overlooked while fighting for her life and sharing her story with the world?

Kyle stood up when their name was finally called,

with Grace quick at his heels. As Caroline walked to join them, she heard the employee behind the counter say, "I know you. You're Kyle Beasley. I saw your mugshot on Instagram."

Grace stepped in front of her brother. "What does that have to do with anything?"

Kyle touched her forearm. "Thanks, Grace. I can handle this kid on my own." He glanced over his shoulder at Caroline and pleaded with his eyes for her to come closer. "My mom here wants to buy a new phone. Can you help us without prying into our private lives, or do we need to speak to a manager?"

Holy shit. Both kids had bigger backbones than she gave them credit for. As proud as a peacock, she approached the counter and peered skeptically at the employee. He helped them purchase a new phone and accessory package without uttering another word about what he'd seen on social media.

As soon as they left the store, Kyle said, "Wanna grab something to eat? It feels good to get out of the house for a change."

Grace nodded in agreement, and Caroline followed her kids to the food court. Over lunch, things couldn't have seemed more normal. Kyle got stir-fry while she and Grace picked up pizza. They ordered milkshakes for dessert and exchanged ideas about what to get Jordan for his upcoming birthday, talking and laughing as if nothing had turned their lives completely upside down. As if a local mom hadn't lost her life and her son's negligence hadn't drastically altered his future.

"Kyle, what do you know about Theo Donaldson?" Grace chewed on her straw as she finished her milkshake.

Kyle coughed as ice cream sprayed from his nostrils. Wiping his nose, he said, "Not much. His dad's the athletic director, and he's friends with Ethan Shawver. I know that. Why?"

Caroline frowned at the mention of the athletic director, intrigued by whether Kyle would appear uncomfortable talking about someone who held his secret about the earlier texting and driving incident. But her attention shifted as soon as Grace cleared her throat to respond. Her daughter's cheeks flushed, and she nearly shredded the straw with her teeth. "Rumor has it Theo has a crush on me. That he might ask me to the homecoming dance."

"What?" Caroline interjected. "You're too young to go to a school dance with a boy."

"All my friends are going," Grace whined.

"With dates?" Caroline said. "Don't most freshmen go in a big group? Kyle, help me out."

"It depends." Kyle eyeballed Grace. "I took a girl my freshman year. Remember?"

Caroline searched her memory, trying to recall Kyle's freshman Homecoming. It was only a few years ago, but she couldn't picture it. She must have gone with him to pick out a suit, ordered a corsage for his date, and taken photographs at someone's house before the dance, but her mind drew a blank.

Then she remembered the text message she had received from Jordan that night, containing a photo of Kyle and a girl she'd never seen before. Caroline was away for a book signing, grateful someone had snapped and shared the picture. At the time, that seemed like enough. But for someone who lectured others about the importance of time, she sure wasted enough of it worrying about things outside her family. Was it too late to turn over a new leaf? She needed to check back into her kids 'lives—if they'd let her.

If today was any indicator, she was off to a good start.

Grace said, "I remember that girl. Crystal Baxter. She moved away, right?"

"Yeah. Her parents got divorced, and she moved to live with her mom in Michigan."

"I also remember the awful sequined dress she wore. She looked like a stripper!" Grace flicked her straw at her brother and splashed melted ice cream on his face.

Caroline laughed. "So back to this kid, Theo. Do you think it's smart to consider a date with one of Ethan's friends?"

"I don't like the idea," Kyle said. "I bet other guys are thinking about asking you, too. Why not wait for someone else? And don't forget that no matter who you go with, I'll keep an eye on him. A very close eye." He leaned across the table and thrust his face within inches of his sister's, plucking her straw from her fingers and putting it in his mouth.

"You're thinking of going to the dance, Kyle?" Caroline said. "You haven't even been back to school yet. Geez, you barely even leave your room."

"Funny," he said. "About that. I think I'm ready."

"Ready for what?" Caroline said.

"To head back to school. I can't hide out forever. It's been almost a month. Now that I've got a new phone, I'll text Coach Urbas about what I need to do to catch up."

The optimism in Kyle's voice both comforted and worried her. Caroline couldn't forget how untruthful he'd been. Hiding his Jeep in the garage. Lying about hitting a deer. Never providing a satisfactory explanation as to why he fled the scene of the accident. She could feel her mental energy plummet down the rabbit hole and hated knowing these things about her son.

A mother can forgive her child for just about anything, but Kyle needed more than that. She hoped he wasn't clinging to false hope. Even if the justice system took mercy on him, he may never be able to move forward after crashing into Amy and failing to do the right thing by stopping to check on her.

A guilty conscience could be far worse than a guilty verdict.

****

Dad insisted on taking George to a fancy restaurant on his last night in town to thank him for everything he'd done to help. While George waited in the kitchen for Dad to grab a sports coat, he hovered over Ethan, who was finishing his homework at the table. "Why won't you join us?"

His dad and brother had both begged Ethan to come along, but Dad knew when to quit. The extra eggshells they'd been walking on since their lives changed so dramatically remained underfoot. Without Mom in the picture, they needed to figure out how to coexist without getting in each other's way—at least until the end of the school year.

"I'm sorry," Ethan said. "I've got this party to go to. Please don't be mad."

"I'm not, bro. And please don't be mad at me for leaving."

Ethan bit his lip, afraid he might cry. He wasn't mad at George, just super bummed about his decision to

133

return to California. "I like having you here," he stammered.

"I know. It's been great. But there's something you need to understand. Mom's death has triggered some heavy thoughts for me. I've worked hard to stay sober, but lately, I've been craving a drink."

Thrown by the weight of George's confession, Ethan shifted nervously in his chair. "Oh, man. I had no idea. I hope watching me and my friends drink so much hasn't made that worse."

"Naw. It's more than that. I came dangerously close to cracking open a beer the other night. That's when I knew I needed to head home. Please don't think I'm abandoning you. I feel especially guilty for ducking out after I dropped that bomb about Mom and her history with alcohol."

"Don't feel guilty. I needed to know, and Dad may never have told me."

His father appeared in the room with his hand in a tight fist. "Told you what?"

Ethan and George stared at him but stayed silent.

"Never mind." Dad unclenched his hand and dropped a package of vape cartridges on the kitchen counter. "Look what I found in the bathroom hamper. Who do these belong to?" He shot Ethan a disapproving look.

"Oops! Those are mine!" George leaped toward the counter and swooped up the package. "Not sure how they ended up in the dirty laundry. Thanks."

Grateful to his brother for taking the bullet, Ethan could tell by Dad's expression he wasn't buying it. But for some reason, the subject got dropped. Good thing his father never found out about Mr. Leandry's note, which the principal never mentioned again. If he had, Dad would've lost his mind the same way Mom would have if she found those cartridges today, interrogating him until he confessed and punishing him by taking away his gaming privileges or not permitting him to use the car. The car was a moot point now. Ethan could care less about ever driving again. But his video games were a different story. Take those away, and you might as well chop off his arms and legs.

But Dad just watched George put the cartridges in his coat pocket and grabbed his car keys. "Let's get going." He walked toward the door. "I'm starved." Turning back to Ethan, he said, "You sure you don't wanna come?"

Ethan nodded and sat still until they left.

As soon as Dad and George disappeared down the driveway, Ethan flew into action. He threw on a pair of khaki shorts and a polo, stuffed a few beers from the fridge into his backpack, and walked next door to Cole's house, where Theo was already pre-gaming with shots of vodka. The three of them had ultimately decided not to go to the homecoming dance, so they were headed to a party—the kind Mom never would have let him attend without calling ahead to make sure a parent would be home. A classmate named Jason Crook, whose parents were home but let him do anything he wanted, was throwing a banger for kids who were either going to Homecoming or not, complete with a keg of nasty draft beer, gelatin shots, and random bottles of booze smuggled from liquor cabinets across Shawnee Springs. Ethan preferred BYOB, to ensure he knew exactly what he was drinking.

Cole's mom had promised to drive them to the party,

but she ran out for a quick errand and had yet to return. They finally gave up waiting and set out on foot. Jason didn't live far, but the party was in full swing when they arrived at his house.

"Hey, guys. Come on in." Jason opened the door. "Drinks are in the basement—gotta at least pretend we're hiding them from my folks."

Mrs. Crook called from the couch. "Hi, boys!" As soon as she recognized Ethan, she jumped to her feet. "Oh, Ethan. Good to see you out with your friends tonight. Again, I'm so sorry about your mom. Her service was beautiful."

"Thanks, Mrs. Crook." He nodded respectfully, then made a beeline for the basement door with Cole and Theo behind him.

The resounding base of an EDM song shook the stairs. The basement was dark, lit only by the flashing colors of a strobe light.

"Geez," Cole hollered over the music. "It's like a dance club down here!"

"I love it!" Theo yelled back. "Let's go find the girls!"

Easier said than done. Ethan and his friends stood like idiots at the bottom of the stairs, eventually moving toward the corner of the basement. They gawked at the different groups of boys and girls, whispering to each other about why so-and-so was talking with what's-her-face or who looked like they were hooking up with whom. Some kids wore semi-formal attire—those who'd gone to the dance—and others dressed down like Ethan and his buddies. Most partygoers looked familiar, but hardly anyone acknowledged them with more than a nod here or a fist bump there, clustering in cliques and drinking more than they should to fit in.

"Let's get this party started." Theo lugged a half-empty liter of vodka from the backpack he had placed at his feet.

"Pace yourself," Cole said. "Remember what happened last time you drank too much of that stuff?"

Ethan chuckled. "Oh, God. That's right. Why don't you stick to beer this time, Theo? We don't want to be cleaning up after you tonight."

"Relax, assholes." Theo twisted the cap off the bottle and took a swig.

"It's your funeral if you get busted again." Cole seized the bottle of vodka and took a swig for himself.

Ethan opened his backpack and held up a palm before grabbing his vape pen and a can of light beer. "Don't judge. I'm going easy tonight." He hadn't stopped thinking about what George said about the potential for alcoholism to run in the family, wishing he knew when his brother realized he had a problem and also wondering about his mom. How old was she when she figured it out?

Theo leaned sideways, thrusting the weight of his body onto Ethan's shoulder. "Check out the stairs!"

A pair of toned and tanned legs in bright red shorts appeared in the stairwell, followed by another similar set. Then another. The girls 'soccer team had arrived, at least the girls who hadn't gone to the dance, and Theo about to start acting like a buffoon. He ran both hands through his hair and swayed back and forth to the beat of a hip-hop song.

"Settle down," Ethan said. "If you're trying to look cool, you're not!"

Cole laughed as he punched Theo in the arm. "True

dat, you jackass. Stop trying so hard."

"Whatever," Theo said. "But do you guys see her? Is she with them?"

"Who?" Ethan said.

"You know who," said Cole.

"Um, no. I don't."

"Grace. Grace Beasley." Cole looked over at Theo, who appeared to be trying to stuff his hands in the pockets of his shorts when there were no pockets.

"You're that into her?" Ethan raised his eyebrows and sucked on his vape.

"I know. It's not a good idea. That's why I didn't ask her to the dance," Theo said. "But the heart wants what the heart wants."

"You're pathetic!" Cole said. "Too bad I don't see her. Maybe she went with someone else."

The trio of soccer girls whisked by them in a blur, not once even glancing in their direction. They made their way in synch through the basement, maneuvering among the mass of drunk and disorderly bodies, past the pool table and beyond the bar, finally stopping to knock on the bathroom door on the far side of the room.

With the strobe on pause and the rest of the basement cloaked in darkness, the door's opening allowed a bright ray of light to shine out like a beacon, but only for a second. The pack of girls rushed inside and shut the door quickly behind them, snuffing the light immediately. But Ethan had managed to glimpse inside the bathroom, catching sight of Grace Beasley cross-legged on the floor with her cheek resting on the toilet seat. Someone must have summoned her friends to help, maybe even Grace herself.

Ethan stared at the closed door for what felt like

hours as impatient teenagers formed a single-file line outside the bathroom. When someone banged on the door, Ethan edged his way closer.

"Hey," he said to the doorbanger, a kid from his Spanish class who went by Mateo. "Someone's in there."

"No shit, someone's in there," Mateo said. "What's taking them so long? I've gotta take a leak." He banged louder and kicked the bottom of the door.

Ethan elbowed him aside and tapped lightly on the door. "Hey, girls. It's Ethan Shawver. Is Grace okay in there? I can tell she's not feeling well. If you let me in, I think I can help."

The door cracked open, and one of the soccer girls peeked out. Ethan blocked the entrance so no one waiting could get through. "Hurry, let me in," he whispered into the crack.

A slim hand extended through the opening and grabbed Ethan's shirt, jerking him inside. "Ethan," the girl attached to the hand said. "I'm Stephanie. Thank you. We could definitely use some help." All three girls stood perfectly still, crammed hip to hip inside the stuffy bathroom, looking perplexed.

Ethan gagged at the foul smell inside as he wedged between the door and the toilet, trying to get closer to Grace, who was barely conscious. Her arms wrapped around the toilet seat like she was clutching a life preserver, and her head dangled into the bowl, almost touching the water. When she glanced up to see who was talking, she squinted as if looking directly into the sun. Streaks of mascara trailed down her face, and chunks of vomit clung to the ends of her long brown hair.

"Eeeethan!" Grace slurred. "Howw aarr youu?" She stretched her arms wide, attempting to hug Ethan and then trying to stand before surrendering to the linoleum floor.

Ethan texted Cole and Theo. —*I need your help. Try getting rid of those kids in front of the bathroom door. I'm inside lending someone a hand. I'll explain later.*—

Next, he texted George, asking for a ride home and sending Jason's address.

Minutes later, he could hear Cole riling up the crowd. Theo must have been too wasted by now to join in. "Come on!" Cole cried. "There's a bathroom upstairs, guys. This one's out of commission."

As soon as things quieted down, Ethan opened the bathroom door, letting the soccer girls exit first and following behind as he supported Grace. Her arms draped around his neck. He allowed her to rest her head on his shoulder and led her through the thinning crowd.

With each passing whisper, Ethan cringed.

"Get that bitch outta here," said some kid with a mohawk wearing a cheetah-patterned suit and black silk tie.

Another voice said, "Aw. What's the matter, Grace? Can't handle living with a killer?"

Mateo obstructed his path and got up in Ethan's face. "Drop her! Why are *you*—of all people—helping the Beasley girl?"

Ethan forced his way past, horrified at how cruel some of his classmates sounded. Dragging Grace's nearly dead weight up the basement stairs and out the front door of Jason's house, he sat her down on the concrete steps to wait for George. The temperature had dropped significantly since earlier in the day, and the cool breeze against his bare arms and legs gave him a chill. He put his arm around Grace to keep her warm, looking around to see where her soccer friends had gone. They disappeared. Some friends!

Leaning into his hold, Grace mumbled, "Nobody cares about me. Everything's about Kyle's trial. Before that, it was my mom's cancer, her book, her groupies. It's soooo annoying."

"I care about you, Grace. I care." He drew her closer, confused at how easily the words fell from his mouth.

When Mom's minivan turned onto the street, Ethan wrangled Grace to her feet and pinched her cheeks. "Grace, Grace," he said. "My brother's here. He'll drive you home, but you need to sober up a bit." He tapped her face a little harder with his palms. Her head bobbed side to side, but she couldn't hold it up.

His mom's van stopped in front of the house. Ethan opened the rear passenger side door and laid Grace gently across the seat before opening the front door and jumping inside.

"Hello." The familiar voice greeted him in a disappointed tone.

"Oh, God," Ethan said. "Dad, what are you doing here?"

Chapter Ten

After spending her day with the kids, Caroline
turned in for the night early, but she woke around
midnight with too much on her mind. Jordan's side of the
bed was empty. He must have fallen asleep on the couch.
She flicked on the television and surfed an excessive
number of streaming subscriptions, eventually stopping
to watch a show about women in the 1950s who had
nothing to worry about except what to cook for dinner
and how to play pinochle. At least, that's how the media
portrayed them. Caroline suspected there was lots more
to it, especially if those women had children.

The sound of a car door startled her around 1:00 a.m.
It couldn't be Kyle, because he'd been in his room all
night, glued to his new phone. If it were Grace, she
missed curfew. Caroline rose and peeked out the
window, but their bedroom didn't offer a good view of
the street. Hopefully, the sound had awakened Jordan,
and he would check it out. It was probably a neighbor,
anyway. But minutes later, Tanner barked at the front
door, and the hum of loud voices drew her downstairs to
find out what was happening.

The family room reeked of stale booze and vomit.
Jordan sat on the couch with his arms wrapped around
Grace as she sobbed into his chest. Caroline tiptoed
toward them, stunned at the scene, and quickly trying to
gather her thoughts.

"Let me handle this," Jordan said. "Go back upstairs—please."

Caroline took a stutter-step toward them but respectfully complied—probably like those women from the 50s would have done. Although she had plenty to say about her freshman daughter coming home after midnight smelling like a brewery and looking like she'd been in a bar fight, she wouldn't argue if Jordan wanted to deal with it. Time alone to process the situation could only help.

As she lay in bed and stared at the TV screen, she seriously questioned her parenting style. She had deferred to her husband's judgment for so long, allowing him to take the lead on most everything kids-related. Was that strange or out of the ordinary? It's not like Jordan was Mr. Mom. He maintained a busy career, just like she did, but somehow, he possessed the bandwidth to juggle both.

Maybe Caroline should have wrapped her arms around Grace, too. Her instincts usually directed her toward anger, making her more inclined to launch into a lecture about breaking curfew and the dangers of underage drinking. Comforting her child should come more automatically than playing it safe by stepping away. Did that make her a bad mother? Perhaps it required practice, like yoga—an indulgence Valerie Saks had encouraged her to try but that she hadn't found time for yet.

Caroline drifted in and out of consciousness for the rest of the night, mindful enough of what was happening down the hall. Jordan settled Grace safely in her room before coming to bed, slipping under the covers beside Caroline, where she pretended to be sound asleep. When the sun finally rose in the morning, she'd wasted enough time psychoanalyzing herself. She needed to do something productive. Her thoughts returned to Valerie, who had mentioned a Sunday morning yoga class. "I go every week. Join me sometime. You'll love it."

It may have seemed odd to be considering an invitation from her son's attorney to take a yoga class together, but something about Valerie put Caroline at ease. They shared a kinship beyond Kyle's case, a sisterhood only other cancer survivors could understand. On a whim, Caroline decided to go. She checked in on Grace and Kyle before leaving the house, careful not to wake the rest of her family.

Upon entering the lobby of the yoga studio, Caroline felt intimidated by the look of the crowd. Everyone wore designer athleisure wear and carried bright-colored yoga bags. Caroline stood out in her faded black leggings and a snug Martha's Vineyard t-shirt, revealing she was a newbie.

A girl with a tiny nose ring, a crude wrist tattoo of a bird, and a sweatshirt that said "NAMASTE" smiled at her from behind the front desk. "First time?"

"How could you tell?" Caroline smiled back. "Do you have a yoga mat I can use?"

"Of course, and welcome!" The sweet girl practically cooed as she spoke. She handed Caroline a mat and clipboard with a few "new yogi" forms to sign. "The first class is free," she said. "If you tell us who referred you, they'll get a free class, too."

"Valerie Saks."

The girl's face lit up. "Oh, Val! She's here already. You can find her in the far back corner of the studio. That's her regular spot."

Whew. Caroline felt better already, finishing the form and walking down the hall toward the studio with the borrowed mat under her arm.

The insides of her nostrils tingled as she stepped through the door and drew in the unfamiliar scent. She guessed citrus, sage, and lavender. How heavenly. She spotted Valerie right away, flat on her back in the corner, with her eyes closed and her arms stretched over her head. A collection of yoga accessories lay near her feet—two foam blocks, a long black strap, and a funky-looking cotton blanket like the ones sold in Mexico at street festivals. No doubt Valerie was a regular, complete with all the gear.

Val's outfit screamed professional yogi, too. She wore a high-waisted pair of tie-dyed yoga pants and a matching sports bra. Layers of beads adorned her wrists. Caroline couldn't help but stare at the odd yet enchanting attorney as she relaxed on the floor. Kudos to the sixty-two-year-old woman with metastatic breast cancer who looked like she didn't have a care in the world. Plus, she was ripped. Underneath the lawyer clothes that made her look inordinately thin, her arm muscles were almost as impressive as her six-pack abs. Damn! If that's what yoga could do for the body, sign me up.

She claimed a spot on the floor next to Valerie and unrolled her mat, tempted to say *hello* but not wanting to disrupt her obvious sense of Zen. Val may have opened one eye and winked, but Caroline couldn't be sure. The blinds in the room were drawn, and the room was dark. She leisurely stretched out on her back just in time for the class to begin. The adorable girl from the front desk doubled as the instructor, and Caroline tried hard to follow her directions by focusing on her own breath. No use. Her mind strayed like a meandering stream.

First, Grace. Last night was a shitshow. Who had she been with, and how much had she had to drink?

"Let me hear you inhale, then exhale." The instructor spoke with a calm and peaceful voice. "Draw your knees into your chest. Give yourself a squeeze."

Caroline tried it. It felt good. But her mind wouldn't stay quiet for long.

Her thoughts leaped to Kyle. Looks like his revelation in the food court was only temporary. Since then, he had barely emerged from his room and was still apprehensive about returning to school. A request for an extended absence sat pending with the school board. She and Jordan had disagreed on whether to ask for more time; unfortunately, her husband's wishes prevailed. She predicted the board would allow Kyle to continue doing his coursework from home to keep any drama surrounding his case out of the school a bit longer. If that happened, she might have to beg Jordan to reconsider. Kyle needed to return to the classroom. Facing his classmates would be hard, but he needed some fragment of normalcy. Criminal trials could drag on. She desperately wished they could agree on a settlement that wouldn't include jail time.

Breathe, Caroline, breathe.

"Close your eyes and set an intention for your practice," the yoga instructor whispered. "Take your time, then meet me in a downward-facing dog."

Before moving, Caroline looked around to see what the silly canine reference meant and mimicked what everyone else was doing. The room got hot. The music grew louder. Sweat soaked her shameful workout clothes. The rest of the class flew by without another thought of her family. No time for that. She became too worried about passing out from the heat or falling flat on her face if she couldn't balance in some of those crazy poses.

When she returned to her mat for the final resting pose, Savasana, as they called it, Caroline was exhausted and fully relaxed. She melted onto the floor and completely surrendered to the moment.

But once again, the moment didn't last.

Her quiet calm succumbed to an unbearable angst. A memory from her post-mastectomy hospital stay surfaced with a vengeance and landed on her heart with the force of an anvil falling from the sky.

As Caroline remained in Savasana, unexpected tears slid down the sides of her face, mixing with the puddles of sweat already pooled on the hardwood floor. She recalled the loneliness she'd felt in the hospital that first night after her surgery when Jordan had gone home to the kids. Despite the heavy drugs meant to sedate her, the incessant noise from the nurses 'station outside her room prevented her from sleeping, intensifying her feelings of isolation and fear.

Long after her discharge, that same insufferable loneliness haunted her, accompanying her to every subsequent doctor's appointment, infusion, and trip to the radiation lab. It didn't matter whether she was alone or surrounded by people. A deep hole had burrowed its way inside her soul and claimed ownership like a squatter over a prime piece of real estate.

Over time, she'd learned how to manage her body's new tenant, primarily by pretending it didn't exist. If she kept active, moving, and preaching to herself and others about how to get well, the lonesomeness might vanish. If not, she'd try drowning it out with excess noise.

The other yogis shifted to a seated position and joined the instructor in the sound of "ohm." Caroline stayed glued to the ground until the class was finally over, then rolled up her mat and dashed toward the exit.

Valerie called out moments later. "Caroline, wait up!"

"Oh hey! I didn't want to bother you." Caroline wiped her eyes, knowing darn well her mascara had smeared. "You looked pretty peaceful in there."

"What'd you think? Did you like it?"

She hadn't decided. "I think so. I hope I can walk tomorrow. I'll definitely come again."

"Oh good." Valerie removed her sweaty headband from her forehead and let it hang around her neck. "I couldn't live without my yoga practice. Literally."

"It sure keeps you in shape. You look great."

"Thanks. But it's more than that. The physical benefits pale in comparison to what I gain mentally. It's a great outlet for any anger or pain you might have. That's why I suggested you try it."

"You think I'm angry?" Caroline's voice rose an octave, maybe two.

"Anger might not be the right word. I guess you're just—um—not as positive as you could be. You have so much to be grateful for, but I get the impression you don't always remember that."

"Wow! Tell me how you *really* feel."

"I'm sorry. I didn't mean to offend you."

"It's okay. I can take it."

But could she? Sometimes, nothing hurts worse than the truth.

Caroline didn't appreciate hearing she was a

negative person. Time to change the subject. "Have you made any progress finding a new doctor for a second opinion about your treatment?"

"Progress? Not really. I made a few phone calls and settled on someone but need to schedule an appointment. Thanks for the reminder."

"Of course. How about Kyle's case? Anything new there?"

Valerie hesitated, as if uninterested in talking shop outside the office. Too bad. She couldn't let Val get away without asking for a quick update.

"So?" Caroline said impatiently.

Valerie nodded. "Now that the grand jury has indicted Kyle, he'll be arraigned again, this time in Erie County Court, where his trial will take place. They'll read the formal charges in the indictment and have him repeat his plea of *not guilty*. Don't be surprised if the prosecutor requests a review of the bail conditions and tries to increase the amount. I doubt the judge would agree to that. Since we're not ready to talk plea-bargain, we'll adjourn for a future court date."

Although Valerie hadn't told her anything she didn't already know, Caroline listened intently and tried not to look insulted. Their attorney had seemingly forgotten she was a lawyer, too. Scowling, Caroline said, "Why aren't we ready to talk plea-bargain? I'd love to put this behind us if we can."

"Forgive me if I'm speaking too simply," Valerie said as if she'd read Caroline's thoughts. Or maybe Caroline's facial expression gave her away. She should really work on her poker face.

"We need to gather more evidence first," Valerie continued. "Remember, we're still waiting on the autopsy report."

"Yeah. But you said that was a long shot. Why not negotiate a deal right away?"

"We also need to collect witness statements—not only the ones the prosecution will use, but for our side, too."

"Like from who?"

"There's a list of people scheduled for deposition during the discovery phase in my office. I can't remember them all off the top of my head, but one on the prosecution's list concerns me a bit. Someone with the last name Donaldson who works at the school. Does that ring a bell?"

Caroline tilted her head. Valerie must be referring to the high school athletic director, the guy whose son wanted to ask Grace to the dance. Ethan's friend. "Yes. I know who he is."

"Allegedly, this Mr. Donaldson has information about a previous incident when Kyle was texting and driving and hit a parked car. The prosecution plans on deposing him to show a pattern of behavior. I'll argue it's irrelevant to our case and, therefore inadmissible at trial."

At least Jordan had come clean about the earlier incident. Otherwise, Caroline would have felt foolish right about now. It still stung no one told her when it happened. She hated feeling like a stranger in her own home. When would that stop?

Perhaps Valerie's tough love in calling her *angry* served a purpose, cracking through Caroline's protective armor and allowing her to be more *present*—just like she'd chanted along with the yoga instructor.

****

Ethan stared into his locker Monday morning, trying to figure out how to jam his lunch bag inside without smushing his peanut butter and jelly sandwich. No more homemade cookies. No more notes on his napkin. Just a boring old sandwich he'd made for himself and a sample-sized pack of crackers. Gripped by a sudden hollowness in his chest, he attempted a deep breath but choked on air. His lungs hardened as if someone had stuffed them with rocks, and he leaned into the locker to stop from collapsing to the floor.

Just in time, Theo appeared from around the corner with a noticeable chip on his shoulder that Ethan could only ignore in his current condition. "You okay, man?" Theo said. "You look like shit."

"All good." Ethan steadied himself and managed to separate from the locker. "Just needed to catch my breath for a minute. How's it going? Were you in bed all day yesterday?"

"Nope. My parents made me get up early and rake the yard. I swear they know when I've been drinking and love torturing me after."

"At least they didn't say anything. You were pretty wasted Saturday." Ethan laughed, but Theo didn't look amused.

"Not as wasted as Grace Beasley." Theo elbowed him in the ribcage a little too hard. "What happened with her, dude? One minute, I'm standing there with Cole; he disappears and returns to tell me you two left together. That sucks. You knew I liked her. You broke the bro ' code. And besides, aren't you the one who said hanging out with her would be awkward?"

Ethan's face blushed red, and he turned his back toward Theo. He grabbed his physics folder and

151

calculator from inside the locker and shoved them into his backpack, adjusting his lunch bag on the top shelf so it wouldn't fall. "I'm surprised you remember anything from the party, but I didn't really *leave* with her. Not in the way you think. So, relax. She was puking in the bathroom, and some assholes were giving her shit, making stupid comments because of her brother. I just got her out of there and made sure she got home safe."

"You walked her home?"

"No. My dad picked us up."

"Your dad? No way! How did that happen?"

Shifting sideways to face Theo again, he said, "I know, right? I texted George, but he narked on me. Sent my dad instead."

"No shit. Did you get in trouble?"

"Believe it or not, my dad was cool. He even helped me get Grace up her driveway."

"What? That doesn't sound like him. How come he didn't rip you a new one?"

"Who the hell knows? He hasn't said anything about that night since, but I'm still waiting for the fallout. Don't worry. It'll come."

Theo nodded in agreement and crossed his arms over his chest. "So, what happened at Grace's house?"

"It was definitely awkward. And I was so nervous about what might happen. Luckily, my dad was already back in the car when Mr. Beasley came to the door."

"Did Grace's dad freak out?"

"Surprisingly, no. He thanked me for getting her a ride home and closed the door as fast as he could. He looked awful, maybe even wasted himself. His eyes were bloodshot, and he looked like he hadn't showered in weeks."

"It's probably pretty rough in that house these days."
Ethan sighed. "I know how that feels."

"So, why'd your brother set you up like that?"

"I have no idea," Ethan said. "He left for California yesterday. Dad drove him to the airport, and I barely saw him before he took off." He left out the part about why George had to leave—because he'd been craving a drink. Ethan was still trying to wrap his brain around that.

"Maybe he wanted to force you and your dad together," Theo said. "Like he figured you guys better start getting along now that it's just the two of you."

"I dunno. But I liked having George here. I hate he left so soon."

"It wasn't soon, man. He was here for a few weeks. He probably has shit to do back there in sunny California. Why stay here in Buffalo, where it's about to get cold and gloomy?"

"You're right. I should have given him a nicer send-off than I did. I was still pissed at him for telling my dad about the party. And about Grace."

Theo looked down at the floor and kicked his sneakers together. "Speaking of the Beasleys, you're not gonna believe this."

Ethan slammed his locker shut and spun the wheel on the combination lock to make sure it caught. "What?"

"My dad got a letter in the mail over the weekend." Theo paused and kicked his shoes together again. "From the County prosecutor's office about Kyle's case."

"What? What does your dad have to do with the case?"

"Nothing. Really. Unless someone found out about the warning he gave Kyle for that accident in the parking lot."

"Do you think that's it?"

"I dunno. Maybe they want my old man to confirm Kyle was texting and driving, to suggest that's what he was doing when he hit your mom."

"Wouldn't that be inadmissible evidence?"

Theo snickered. "You watch too many crime shows."

"Not anymore. My mom loved a good detective series, and we used to watch them together." Another wave of grief threatened his balance, and Ethan leaned back against his locker. His tears were so close to the surface that they welled beneath his eyes. But he was saved by the bell—nope, by the soundtrack—as the theme song from one of his favorite action movies rang through the halls.

Ethan swiped at his eyes. "There's the two-minute warning. I'll catch up with you at lunch." He raced around the corner toward the stairwell leading to his homeroom, which was in the basement at the opposite end of the school. No way would he get there before the late signal, but he hoped his teacher would take pity on him and waive the detention. He hated playing the "dead mom" card, but it worked. He'd dodged a few tardy marks already without ever saying a word.

Taking two stairs at a time, Ethan rushed down the flight of steps and jumped the rest of the way once he got closer to the bottom. Dropping his backpack, he nearly smashed into Grace when he bent over to pick it up.

"Oh gosh." He grabbed hold of Grace's arm. "I'm so sorry. I was trying not to be late."

Grace turned her head from side to side, scanning the nearly empty basement hallway. "Looks like we already are."

A thin elastic headband kept Grace's long, shiny hair from falling into her face. She looked at Ethan with her big brown eyes, dark as chocolate and just as sweet. Gripping his backpack, his palms grew clammy, and his heart rate broke out into a gallop. He studied the clock hanging on the wall behind her to conceal how nervous she made him. The second hand ticked like a disapproving tongue.

"I guess so." Geez. He could have said something less lame.

"I'm glad I ran into you." Grace batted her thick, upturned eyelashes.

"You are?" Ethan could barely speak.

"Thanks for the other night. I appreciate you rescuing me before I died of embarrassment." The freckles on her nose lit up as the rest of her face turned red.

"It was no big deal. Did you get in trouble?"

"Not really," she mumbled. "But my dad felt weird seeing you."

"Guess I should have thought about that."

"Don't worry. He'll forget about it. I'm pretty much invisible at home these days. My parents have other things on their minds, as I'm sure you know."

The clock's ticking grew louder as if scolding him for lingering too long in the hallway. Or perhaps because he was talking with Grace. He should get going, but he didn't want to leave. "I understand," he said. "My dad's pretty preoccupied right now, too."

"I'm sorry," she said, as if apologizing for much more than Saturday night.

An awkward tension filled the space between them. Of all the girls at Shawnee Springs High School, she was the last one he should be talking to.

But as he met Grace's gaze to say goodbye, Ethan couldn't help but feel sorry for her. She had nothing to do with his mom's accident, and too many people in town judged her for her brother's actions. In one way, her situation was analogous to his. They'd both suffered life-altering consequences that fateful Saturday afternoon.

When he took one last look at those big brown eyes before finally scurrying off to homeroom, he recognized the expression that had been staring back at him in the mirror since this whole nightmare began.

Beyond the shock and the pain, there was loneliness.

And Ethan could tell that Grace felt it, too.

Chapter Eleven

Caroline favored October over all the other months. No matter where her speaking engagements took her, a warm welcome home to fall hues and Indian summer weather always reminded her why she loved living in the Northeast. Since she hadn't traveled in almost six weeks, she witnessed the gradual shift from a bright green landscape to tones of red, orange, and yellow without interruption—a magnificent transition as the leaves turned color before her eyes.

She took advantage of being the first one up that morning and left the house before anyone could stop her, including Tanner, who would've begged for a walk if he hadn't been sound asleep in Grace's room. Caroline drove to the lake and parked her car behind the gazebo where Kyle had his senior pictures taken. She then claimed a seat on a park bench overlooking the beach.

The other benches sat empty, and she smiled at being truly alone with her memories from one of the last occasions she and her son spent one-on-one time together. The weather had been perfect that afternoon, and they took their time while the photographer followed them through the sand, convincing Kyle to hold cheesy poses and making them both laugh. They'd even posed for a few shots together. Those were her favorites. She could picture them vividly and closed her eyes to capture the images as long as possible. The faint sound of cars traveling east and west along Lakeshore Road behind her hummed in the distance like a lullaby, quieting her thoughts. Maybe she didn't need yoga after all.

Taking an extended break from work had its downside, and Caroline could feel herself growing restless as the walls closed in. Claustrophobia threatened her mental well-being, giving her more occasion to think and worry. She had grown accustomed to her hectic schedule—living out of a suitcase and checking in and out of her family's daily routine, sometimes like a visitor or a distant relative. She hadn't realized how segregated she'd become from Jordan and the kids until they were thrust into spending so much continuous time together. Somehow, they'd figured out how to proceed through life regardless of whether she was around, which was exactly what she'd always hoped for.

Whenever she allowed herself to worry about her mortality, her biggest fears centered around what would happen after she was gone. She found peace in knowing that if her cancer ever returned, her family would be fine. But staying home for this long gave her something far better—connection. She hadn't felt this close to her family in years, making her heart melt like a stick of butter left on the counter on a hot summer day.

The loud and obnoxious honk of a car horn interrupted her solitude. She turned in her seat just in time to watch the owner of the honking vehicle swerve to avoid hitting a group of bicyclists out for a morning ride. Their bright-colored cycling jerseys blurred in the distance like a traveling rainbow. The angry driver sped past them and shouted something indistinguishable out his window.

An image of Amy Shawver seared through

Caroline's mind like a raging wildfire. Had Kyle tried to warn her he was coming her way, or had he barreled forward and plowed her down without checking the bike lane? His story was difficult to follow. Split-second accidents could be hard to recall, but it seemed impossible that he couldn't remember more details. Perhaps he did, and he was too ashamed to explain.

She wished for a better understanding of the sequence of events. The zealous defense of her son would be easier if she knew the complete story. Maybe his radio *was* so loud that he didn't hear the siren, or the ambulance had neglected to turn it on early enough for Kyle to veer over sooner. Then there was the sun. Kyle claimed it was so bright that he hadn't seen Amy on her bike. Hopefully, that was true and not just a poor excuse. She wished someone could corroborate his story, like members of the landscaping crew or the nurse riding his bike. The nurse should be able to explain the extent of Amy's injuries when he stopped to help, shedding some light on whether she could have been saved or if she was killed on impact.

Caroline peppered herself with questions she couldn't answer on her own, stopping to massage her temples to prevent an emerging headache from worsening. Startled by the jingle of her ringtone, she struggled to free her cell phone to grab the call before voicemail kicked in. "Hello," she said in the nick of time.

"Caroline, it's Toby. Remember me? Your agent. Are you avoiding me?"

"What are you talking about? I don't recall you leaving any messages?"

"Didn't think I had to—thought I'd give you some space. But aren't you ready to get back out there by now?"

Toby didn't have children and had no idea how radically her life had changed overnight. She wanted to scold him for thinking that having a son charged with murder would only require a quick fix, but she lacked the fire to fight this morning. Besides, he'd never understand. "Not yet. I appreciate you handling my postponements for a while longer."

"I will. But we have a golden opportunity—the kind you've been waiting for—and I wanted to run it by you before it disappears."

"I'm intrigued," she said cautiously.

"Great!" His voice rang through the phone with a little too much enthusiasm. "As you know, The American Society of Clinical Oncology holds its annual meeting the first week of December. They're trying something new this year by featuring patient testimonials in the different cancer spaces—leukemia, pancreatic cancer, colon cancer, and, you guessed it, breast cancer. Someone threw your name out there as a potential speaker."

"Wow." Her voice was flat. "That's quite an opportunity."

"I know," Toby said. Caroline could picture him fluttering his hands like the wings of a moth, the tell-tale sign he was getting excited. "And it's in Chicago—an easy commute."

"Maybe next year," Caroline said, surprised at how effortlessly she declined the offer without a moment of deliberation.

"What? Who are you? What have you done with my favorite client, Caroline Beasley? The woman who always said her dream gig was to speak directly to medical professionals about the effects a cancer diagnosis can have on patients 'emotional well-being. There's no better opportunity than this, my dear. ASCO is the Mack Daddy of oncology conferences. You'd get to tell your story to hundreds of people with the power to improve cancer care. Imagine the impact you could have by sharing your experiences with *that* audience."

"It's tempting, but not the right time. I'm not interested in traveling anywhere before the end of the year. My family needs me here. Even if Kyle's case settled tomorrow, I need to focus my energy at home without distraction."

Most of what she'd said was true, although she still questioned whether anyone in her family truly needed her the way she hoped.

"Are you saying what it sounds like? Are you putting an end to your speaking career?"

"Not forever. Consider it a sabbatical." She laughed, knowing Toby wouldn't find any humor in her decision. She waited for a response until realizing they'd lost their connection. Toby wouldn't have hung up on her. But maybe he did.

Before she had a chance to call him back—to make sure he didn't think she'd hung up on him—an incoming call beeped through. Looks like he beat her to it. But when she clicked to answer, the voice on the other end of the connection was not Toby's.

"Mom," Kyle said. "Where are you?"

"Oh, good morning, honey." The warm fuzzies she felt whenever Kyle or Grace called spread rapidly throughout her insides. "I drove to the lake this morning to gather my thoughts. What's up?"

"Come home. Fast! I just got a call from Ms. Saks.

I mean, Valerie."

Caroline pictured Kyle sitting in his room, perched on the edge of his bed, chewing his fingernails as his knees bobbed nervously up and down. The urgency in his voice signaled something was wrong. What could Valerie have said to him? When Caroline talked with their attorney after yoga class, it sounded as if things were progressing slowly, and talks of a plea bargain weren't even in the works. Despite Caroline's eagerness to further things along, Valerie had subtly encouraged her to be patient while they worked through some evidentiary issues. Something must have changed since then.

"What is it, Kyle? Are you okay?" She rose from the bench and hurried toward the parking lot, almost dropping her phone as she steadied it against her ear.

"Yes, I'm fine. I'm actually great! We got some good news today. The autopsy report came back. Looks like I didn't cause Mrs. Shawver's death after all."

Approaching her car, Caroline froze. Her legs simply stopped working. "What?"

"She died of an aneurysm, whatever that means. It's what made her swerve into the road at the same time I let the ambulance pass. She might have been dead before she hit my windshield. Crazy, right?"

It took a moment for the news to register. When it did, Caroline dropped to the pavement. The cool of the blacktop seeped through her jeans, and she practically morphed into a puddle in the parking lot. Pressing a palm to her heart, she closed her eyes. If she'd heard him right, Kyle stood an excellent chance of being declared *not guilty*.

She remained motionless, afraid to budge, until a

van turned into the parking lot, and she needed to get out of the way.

"I'll be right home," she said. Relief mixed with uncertainty stormed her thoughts as she drove along Lakeshore, adhering to the speed limit and resisting the urge to step on the gas. The narrow bike path followed alongside her, ever-present in her peripheral vision. It served as a haunting reminder of what had happened to Amy Shawver. Even if it were a strange coincidence that she'd suffered an aneurysm and hit Kyle's windshield while he moved to avoid the ambulance, her son fled the scene. That was a difficult decision to defend, still leaving them with a significant issue to overcome.

Slow down. Baby steps. Don't get ahead of yourself.

Kyle had called to share big news. He asked her to come back quickly. As she traveled steadily toward home, Caroline's earlier doubts about whether he needed her lifted. Her mind filled with thoughts about how to help her son—not by lashing out against the truth, but simply by being present.

****

Standing at the kitchen counter, Ethan opened an oversized bag of mixed candy and emptied it into the plastic witch's cauldron they used every Halloween. He paused to gobble down a peanut butter cup. Dad walked in and slapped him on the shoulder.

"Are you sure you want to stay home tonight to pass out candy? I could drop you at your classmate's party on my way to Uncle Dave's. That bucket would be fine sitting on the front step."

Suspicious of Dad's *Mr. Nice Guy* routine, Ethan had zero patience for his father tonight. Or any night, for that matter. "Nope. I'm good." His words were sharp, and he didn't care.

When the doorbell rang, followed by a group of high-pitched voices shouting "trick-or-treat," Dad grabbed a piece of taffy from the cauldron and slunk out of the way. With a hurt look, he said, "You better get moving. You've got a few early birds out there."

Dad left the house after the first group of trick-or-treaters chose their favorite bite-sized candy bars and raced next door. Ethan placed the cauldron on the coffee table in the family room and sat on the couch, waiting for the bell to ring again. He didn't have to wait long, and when he answered the door this time, he was excited to see Grace standing on the porch.

After hearing Dad's plans to play poker on Halloween night, Ethan invited Grace over to pass out the candy, nervous about whether she'd come. He never considered mentioning it to his father, afraid Dad might change his mind about the card game and stay home. Dad still hadn't said anything about driving Grace home drunk after Jason's party, which Ethan found strange. He steered clear of any conversation that might spark the subject. As far as Dad knew, that was the first and last time Ethan had anything to do with Grace.

But Ethan and Grace had been texting regularly since running into each other in the school hallway. Grace always ended her messages with playful emojis— a smiley face, googly eyes, confetti, and sometimes even a heart. They'd oddly moved past their initial anger toward one another. He liked having someone to talk with who understood him, and he and Grace had more in common than Ethan had first imagined. They shared the same taste in movies, agreed binge-watching reruns of '80s sitcoms offered the perfect excuse to stay up late on a school night, and both dreamed about getting out of Shawnee Springs someday. He couldn't hate her just because she was a Beasley, and he hoped she wasn't only being nice out of pity.

He could tell Grace things he didn't feel comfortable sharing with his friends. Considering the circumstances, he hadn't told anyone they were talking, and she agreed it was best not to flaunt their budding friendship. That's why Grace showing up tonight still surprised him.

Ethan opened the door with a smile. "Hey! Come on in. Looks like it's raining."

Grace walked inside and unzipped her coat. "Just drizzling. I hope it holds off. I always hated trick-or-treating in the rain."

"Me too." Ethan extended his arms and helped Grace remove her coat. "Want something to drink?"

"I'm fine." She waited for him to hang her coat in the front closet and followed him awkwardly into the family room.

"Have a seat." Ethan pointed to the couch. He swallowed a lump and wiped his hands on his pant legs. Oh boy, maybe this was a mistake. Texting was one thing, but carrying on a conversation without the threat of being late to homeroom hanging over their heads might be a struggle.

Perched on the very edge of the couch, Grace said, "Thanks for inviting me over. I love passing out Halloween candy, but my parents are keeping the porch light off this year. They're afraid of getting more tricks than treats. You have no idea what people have said and done to us since the accident." She paused and folded her hands in her lap. "I'm sorry. I shouldn't have said that. It's nothing compared to what you and your dad are going through."

"That doesn't make it any less terrible for you. It's okay if you want to talk about it."

The singsong sound of "trick-or-treat" interrupted them, and Grace popped up from her seat. "Let me get it!" She grabbed the cauldron and raced to the door. He watched as she joyfully held out the candy and allowed each kid to pick a couple of pieces.

"Aren't you an adorable little princess?" Grace said to the blonde-haired, blue-eyed toddler from across the street.

"And you're a pretty scary-looking clown," she told the princess's older brother.

"Oh, what do we have here?" She leaned over and tapped a pirate on the top of the head. "I love all your costumes. Happy Halloween!"

Grace practically skipped back into the family room with the cauldron, beaming from ear to ear. Sitting again on the couch, she leaned back and brought a knee to her chest. "That was fun. I didn't mean to hog them all. I'll let you do the next bunch."

"We can take turns." Ethan smiled. "I guess you're not worried about anyone seeing you at my house."

"Are you?" She tilted her head to the side and wrinkled her nose. "I'm sure my parents wouldn't like it, but it's my life, right?"

"If you're okay with it, I am too."

"Cool!" She gave him a saucy wink.

The doorbell rang regularly for the next hour and a half, giving them little time to chat in between. The cauldron neared empty with another fifteen minutes of trick-or-treating left to go.

"What if we run out of candy?" Grace said.

"I dunno." Ethan was enjoying himself and didn't want the evening to end. "The bigger kids usually show up now. Let's make sure we only give them one piece." He wondered why Mom never ran out of candy. She probably planned better than he did, having a back-up bag stashed somewhere just in case.

"We can always turn off the light if we have to," Grace added. "But I like your plan better. Let's see what happens."

The doorbell never rang again, and as soon as it turned eight o'clock, they shut off the porchlight and sat together on the couch with the cauldron between them.

"At least the candy's not all gone," Ethan said.

"Oh good! I've been eyeing those caramels all night. They're my favorite."

"Help yourself. Are there any suckers left?"

"Just one." Grace handed it over. Her fingers brushed against his skin like a feather, sending goosebumps up his arms. "So, why didn't you go to that big costume party tonight? Don't like to dress up?"

"Not really. My mom used to dress up to pass out the candy. I always thought it was a little weird."

"She did? That's hilarious. Did she dress up scary or cute?"

"Never scary. Last year, she dressed up like a wizard, and she was a punk rocker the year before that."

"How fun!"

"What about your mom? Does she like Halloween?"

"She used to. When Kyle and I were little, she even made us coordinating costumes a few times. I remember going as a bumblebee and a flower one year, and then ketchup and mustard another. She stopped doing that stuff when she got sick."

"Understandable," Ethan said.

"I guess." The sides of Grace's mouth curved down, and her gaze turned sad. Ethan worried she might cry.

"It's funny how life can change overnight, ya know?" he said.

"I do." She scooched closer to him on the couch and tilted her head to rest on his shoulder, making Ethan's heart flutter.

The turbulence of his life spun him like a bobbin. He turned his body sideways without thinking, forcing Grace to adjust her head upright again. "I need to tell you something." Grabbing her hands, he said, "I like you—a lot. I've tried to convince myself I only see you as a friend, but it's not working. And I know I'm a few years older than you, but—"

Grace placed a finger to his lips. "Stop. I've never had a boyfriend before. I mean other than friends who are boys. And I like you too—lots more than them."

She closed her eyes and tipped her chin to the sky as if she knew exactly what he was planning. Imagining how it would feel to join his mouth with hers, he couldn't deny the attraction any longer. He leaned in and kissed her. Softly. Gently. Like he'd never kissed anyone before.

Grace responded with exactly the warmth and enthusiasm he had hoped for, and he savored the taste of her lips until they both needed to come up for air. When she finally backed away, Ethan opened his eyes and found her gaze already fixed on his face.

With an unnerving sadness, she whispered, "I wish spending time together like this wasn't so complicated."

"Me too." He rested his forehead on hers and breathed deeply. His next thought blew up in his mind like a firecracker, but he kept it to himself.

If only your brother hadn't hit my mom with his car.
Or at least had the decency to stop and help her.

Chapter Twelve

Caroline waited in the hallway outside the courtroom in the Erie County Courthouse, anxious for the pretrial conference to begin but filled with dread that the other shoe could drop. The wave of relief following the news of Amy Shawver's aneurysm disappeared as soon as Valerie reiterated Kyle's Jeep still struck Amy's body and that the prosecutor had also filed a hit-and-run charge. A conviction for this offense carried stiff penalties in New York State.

Learning Amy died from something other than colliding with Kyle's Jeep raised additional questions, including why the pathologist had taken so long to uncover the truth and why the police didn't wait until all the facts were in before arresting Kyle. In her heart, Caroline knew they were doing their jobs and following the law. But that didn't stop her from wanting to scream from the rooftops that her son was innocent. The medical personnel who tried to save Amy should have known better based on her injuries, and the cops jumped the gun trying to provide the public with a quick resolution.

Shame on them. All of them. She expected an apology for the shoddy investigation. If only Kyle had stopped to help. It always circled back to that. No one could erase that critical mistake. If they could, news of an aneurysm would have cleared his name.

Caroline sat on a worn upholstered bench and

scrolled through the comments on the Shawnee Springs Online Parent Page. Kyle had become Public Enemy Number One, depicted as a total juvenile delinquent, a sociopath with no sense of right and wrong. She'd never heard such garbage, such complete trash. People she'd known for decades posted about what a terrible kid he'd turned out to be, neglected from an early age with no moral compass. They had no clue what they were talking about. A short time ago, Kyle earned the title of *hometown hero*, the talented young athlete ready to make his mark on America's favorite pastime—the game of baseball. First up, Niagara University, and then maybe the minor or major leagues.

Loyalty seemed scarce these days as too many of their *supposed* friends turned on Kyle quickly. Cowards hid behind social media profiles, taking their shots at the rest of them, too. Someone accused Jordan of being "a spineless wimp who only cared about sports and never disciplined his son." If her husband was that awful, half of Shawnee Springs wouldn't trust him as their family dentist, and he wouldn't have earned last year's Outstanding Citizen Award.

As for what they said about her, the criticism hurt. More than she wanted to admit. One comment described Caroline as "distant and aloof, with an air of superiority that intimidated others." Ouch.

At times, Caroline wished she could be more like many of the other women in Shawnee Springs, putting herself out there and wearing her emotions on her sleeve. When the kids were little, she became part of the community's inner circle and enjoyed making friends with other moms and dads. She fondly remembered playing Bunco with the neighbors, spending summer days at the public pool, and going out for "wine time" with her tennis friends. Hell, she was elected president of the preschool PTA when Kyle was four years old.

But cancer changed her. Or perhaps the diagnosis sent her running back to her shell. "Like mother, like daughter," Caroline's father used to say before he passed away. As an introvert, Caroline preferred privacy over companionship in her personal life and stretched beyond her comfort zone for her profession. Sharing her experiences with other cancer patients—most of whom she barely knew—proved easier than opening up to her closest peers. Somehow, that seemed safer, less threatening, as if she hid behind *her* version of a social platform. As odd as her apprehension may have appeared, that's how she protected her heart and survived. She shouldn't feel ashamed of living life on her own terms or compelled to apologize for keeping her distance when she needed to.

Regret methodically crept down her spine like a spider leaving a silk trail in its wake. Immediately after her diagnosis, enough people had offered to help. But she'd shut them out like she assumed her mom would have done. Now, they were turning against her for loving her son and not wanting to see his life ruined.

Anyone's kid could have hit Amy Shawver. No one could be sure that their eighteen-year-old wouldn't have reacted the same way Kyle did—panicking and fleeing home in search of safety.

Incensed by the hypocrisy, Caroline's heart pounded inside her chest as her temper flared. Scrolling further on the page, she surpassed her tipping point after seeing how one of Grace's classmates called her daughter a "cold bitch." Enough already! The universe had sufficiently poked Mama Bear. She rose to her feet and paced the hallway.

"Where is Valerie? She's almost an hour late, and we can't enter the courtroom without her." Annoyed, Caroline's stomach churned rocks. Her feet fought through quicksand, and her mind filled with so much worry her brain was ready to explode.

Jordan leaned against the marble pillar in the center of the hall. His skin looked paler than usual, and dark brown circles sagged below his eyes. The stubble covering the bottom half of his face appeared longer than the thinning hair sprouting unevenly from his head. Kyle stood beside his father, so close their bodies seemed glued together from top to bottom.

The Beasley men bore a striking resemblance to one another. No one would honestly believe she'd had a fling with a delivery truck driver. Kyle and Jordan's profiles were identical. Strong jawlines, broad but not prominent foreheads, and perfectly sculpted cheekbones. After Kyle tilted his head toward Jordan and rested it on his father's shoulder, they both stared intently at the phone in Kyle's hand, whispering like teenage girls. Hopefully, they weren't reading the same social media page she'd been scrolling.

When the door to the courtroom finally opened, a baby-faced bailiff popped his head into the hallway and looked around until his gaze landed on Kyle, whom he presumably recognized from all the media coverage. "Judge Gallagher is ready. You can follow me to the judge's chambers if your counsel is present. You'll be meeting there today."

Valerie hurried toward them in a black suit-dress. The sound of her heels echoed through the corridor. She wore tortoise-shell glasses hanging from a long cord around her neck and had done something different with her hair. The gray color appeared brighter, less like steel wool, and loose waves fell past her shoulders. She extended her arm and gently squeezed Caroline's hand as if they shared a secret.

"Hello, everyone." Valerie pulled her glasses to her face and untangled the chain from her hair. "Ready to get this show on the road?"

Caroline nodded, then looked over at Jordan and Kyle, who were still captivated by Kyle's phone. "Come on, you two. Put the phone away."

The bailiff led them down a long hallway into a large corner office with several floor-to-ceiling bookcases. Volumes of legal textbooks and legislation filled the shelves. Kyle sat beside Valerie in a leather chair facing the judge's intricately carved walnut desk while Caroline and Jordan settled into a pair of simple wooden chairs off to the right. Seconds later, Caroline stood back up and stepped toward Kyle to pick at the nape of his neck, tucking the tag from his shirt back where it belonged and adjusting his collar. "It'll be okay," she whispered into his ear. "We love you."

Kyle strained his neck sideways in her direction and mouthed, "Love you, too." A tear slipped from the corner of his eye and slid down his cheek. He looked nervous and scared, like when he was a little boy and she'd taken him to the pediatrician's office for shots. Back then, Caroline could hold his hand and let him bury his face in her chest while a nurse plunged a syringe into his arm. Now, she sat helpless, obliged to remain still and watch as someone infused a new kind of pain upon her firstborn.

She bowed her head to avoid breaking down, noticing the Assistant District Attorney who had entered the room through a different door and sat in the chair to Valerie's left. His name was Dwight Wingassett, and he looked like a cross between an NBA player and a circus clown. He must have been at least six foot five, and his red hair and freckles clashed with the hot pink of his tie. Caroline had never met him, but she'd heard he was reasonable—as far as prosecutors go.

The bailiff left the room momentarily. When he returned, Judge Gallagher, a short and stocky woman who looked years younger than Judge McCaffrey, filed in behind him. She tripped slightly on the hem of her black robe before climbing into her chair. "Be seated," the judge said in a gravelly voice. They all stood until Judge Gallagher settled behind the desk.

"Ms. Saks. Mr. Wingassett. Please approach."

The attorneys stepped forward and leaned close to the judge, peering at the documents she held in her stubby hands. After some indistinguishable whispering, Judge Gallagher waved them away and toward their seats.

Enunciating her words slowly with a husky tone, the judge said, "Considering the autopsy report results presented today, I suggest both parties consider a plea agreement. The goal of these pre-trial proceedings is to see whether we can avoid taking this to trial. Among other things, compromise saves the taxpayer a great deal of money. So, please, Ms. Saks, discuss this with your client and get together with Mr. Wingassett to see if you can reach a mutually beneficial resolution."

Judge Gallagher overextended her neck to eyeball Valerie and then Dwight. "My clerk will schedule our

175

next meeting. Until then, case adjourned." She banged her palms on her desk, sprang from her chair, and toddled out through the door she had entered. Dwight trailed behind her, and a long silence followed until Jordan spoke up.

"How do they know Amy didn't get hit first and then have an aneurysm?" he said.

"I leave the science up to the experts, but the conclusiveness of the autopsy report is huge," Valerie said. "We couldn't have asked for a better alternative set of facts."

"What exactly does this mean for Kyle's case?" Jordan gulped.

Valerie's glasses had slipped down her nose, and she shoved them back in place. "It means now that we can show reasonable doubt, the prosecutor is likely to drop the negligent homicide charge."

Caroline's neck and shoulder muscles relaxed, only for an instant. She wanted to feel triumphant, but the road ahead remained long. It might appear they were one step closer to clearing Kyle's name, but this was no time to let their guard down. The nightmare would never end if she stopped fighting now.

****

Ethan sniffed his hot lunch and guessed at what the mystery meat could be until he gave up and pushed his tray aside. He wasn't hungry anyway. His appetite had all but disappeared since kissing Grace—a telltale sign he was falling for her. Hard. When they'd said goodbye on Halloween night, they agreed to take things slow, knowing their situation was messy. He thought they were on the same page until Grace ghosted him the following day. She had ignored his texts and declined his calls until he eventually stopped trying to reach her. If she needed space, fine. He just hoped she hadn't changed her mind about him. Despite their unfortunate circumstances, all Ethan could think about was getting to see Grace again.

When she finally responded a few days later, Ethan was relieved. And nervous. She asked if he could meet her after school. She'd be at the soccer field next to the waterfall in the center of town. Hopefully, she didn't plan on telling him to get lost, to leave her alone and pretend they'd never shared a kiss. The most amazing kiss of all time! He braced himself for the worst and hoped he was overreacting.

When he arrived at the field, he spotted Grace right away, shooting a soccer ball at the goal, over and over. Ethan knew little about soccer, but he could tell she was good. Impressed by the determination on her face each time she kicked the ball, he almost felt bad interrupting her focus.

"Hey, Grace!" He approached slowly.

After one last kick, she turned and smiled, reminding him of Kyle for a brief instant.

"Hi, Ethan!" She picked up her ball and jogged toward him. "Thanks for coming."

"Thanks for asking. I thought maybe you were mad at me after the other night."

"Sorry about that. My dad tells me I'm moody. I guess it's true."

"It's okay." Thankful things seemed normal, he considered kissing her again but knew it was too soon. Instead, he grabbed the soccer ball from Grace's hands and playfully kicked it down the field.

"Hey," she giggled. "Race you to the ball!"

They took off running, almost neck and neck, until

Ethan sprinted ahead and got to the ball first.

"Holy shit! You're fast!" He panted.

"So are you. I almost beat you. Did you ever play sports?"

"Only baseball when I was younger."

"I remember. You played with Kyle, right?"

"Yeah, we were on the same team for a while. I don't think my dad ever forgave me for quitting."

"Why did you?"

"I dunno. Sports just weren't my thing. Once I got my first 3D video game, that's all I wanted to play. My dad hates it. He says I'm addicted to what he calls my *nerd games* with my *nerd friends*."

"Are you? Addicted, I mean. I know you're not a nerd."

"I admit to being a little obsessed, sometimes playing way too late on a school night. But I can usually control myself. My dad would disagree, and he's constantly criticizing me for it."

"That's terrible." Grace picked up the ball and bobbled it in her hands.

"I don't let his insults bother me anymore. Besides, I'll show him. Just wait until I start designing my own games and apps. I'm gonna make lots of money doing that someday."

"Is that what you want to do after you graduate?"

"I think so. I applied to the University of Utah. They're one of the best schools in the country for video game design. But now that my mom's gone, I'm not sure what to do. I had hoped to get as far away from here as possible, but I feel kinda bad leaving my dad alone."

"Did you apply anywhere else?"

"University of California Santa Cruz. They have a

pretty good gaming degree program. I also applied to the University of Buffalo for a local option. They only offer a gaming certificate, but I could always start there and transfer somewhere else down the road."

"Sounds like you have a solid plan."

"Ha! For what it's worth. Even the best plans can go down in flames. Losing my mom taught me that. Planning anything in life seems pointless now."

"I know how you feel."

He hated when people said that, especially when talking about his mom's death.

"Really? How's that?" He spoke softly to hide his irritation.

Grace grabbed his hand gently. She must have picked up on his mood change. "Let's walk toward the waterfall." Leading the way, she said, "I didn't mean to upset you. But hear me out. Of course, I can't understand what you're going through. What happened to your mom is every kid's worst nightmare, and I'm so sorry you have to live through it."

Her sincerity soothed him, making it impossible to stay annoyed. She still gripped his hand, so he adjusted his fingers to interlace hers. Silently, they continued toward the waterfall, reaching a narrow dirt path hidden by a patch of tall trees and thick bushes and following it to the end. Ducking underneath the low-hanging branches of a willow tree, they sat on the grass outside a chain-link fence intended to keep people from getting too close to the edge. The sound of water rushing over the cliff and breaking on the rocks in the river below was captivating, almost magical.

"How did you find this place?" Ethan said.

"Isn't it beautiful?" Her eyes widened. "I come here

to clear my head. I thought maybe you could find some peace here, too."

Ethan stared into Grace's big brown eyes; conscious their hands had separated as soon as they sat down. "You sure seem older than a freshman."

"My dad says I'm an old soul."

"That's funny. People say that about me, too."

The glow on Grace's face suddenly faded. After a long pause, she said, "I don't know what your excuse is, but for me, I think it's because my mom got cancer when I was so young. I used to spend full days worrying about how long she'd be around."

"That must have been scary." Ethan drove a pop-up image of his mom lying in her casket from his mind.

"It was. The worst was seeing my mom in the hospital after she had surgery. I'll never forget the nurse wheeling her into the recovery room where we were waiting. Her face looked so weird—oily and pale. She wore this light blue cap on her head, like a shower cap made of see-through paper. I wanted to yank it off to brush her hair like she used to brush mine when I was little. She went bald later that year. I hated that, too."

Hypnotized by the water, Ethan remained silent and stared off into space. Heights frightened him, and even though he and Grace were behind the fence, sitting close to the edge made him nervous. A sudden urge to hurl himself over the cliff and into the water overwhelmed him—an irrational thought bringing genuine fear. Although some part of his brain that he should probably remember from science class would stop him before doing anything impulsive, he shifted farther from the fence to be safe.

"Are you okay?" Grace brushed her hand up and

down his arm.

"As good as can be expected. But back to your mom. *That's* what you meant by saying you know how I feel, right?"

"Exactly. For a long time, I couldn't stop thinking about the possibility of my mom dying. I was obsessed. I'd come here every day after school and kick the soccer ball as hard as I could, unleashing all my anger on the field."

"That's probably why you're so good," Ethan said. "And listening to you right now, I don't know which would be worse: anticipating someone's death or being blindsided by it."

"They both suck," Grace said. "Just in different ways. For so long, I'd lay in bed at night and promise God I'd never take my family for granted again."

"And do you?"

"It's complicated. You'd think almost losing my mom would make me more forgiving of how self-centered she can seem. But it's difficult living with her. She cares way more about other cancer patients than she does for her own family, especially me."

"I don't believe that. Maybe it's just hard for her to tell you how she feels."

"To describe how she feels, she'd have to pay attention to me first. I still have no idea what I can do to get noticed. It's like I'm invisible, living in the shadow of the golden child. I try not to hold that against Kyle. It is what it is. But he's the superstar, and I'll always be the runner-up."

"Even after what just happened?" Ethan heard the judgment in his question and hoped he hadn't crossed a line.

"More so," she said with conviction. "Kyle can do no wrong. Even when he does, my parents see him as a victim, and anyone who thinks otherwise is the enemy."

Grace's comment struck a nerve. Mistaking Kyle as a victim sounded absurd. Maybe Mr. and Mrs. Beasley were just as unreasonable as his dad said they were.

"What was your mom like?" Grace continued. The look of anticipation on her face made Ethan feel like he was the most important person on the planet.

"She was the best." His voice cracked.

"You don't have to talk about her if you don't want to." Grace placed her hand over his.

"No, it's okay. I like talking about her. It helps me remember. I'm so afraid I'll forget all the things that made her special." He paused, contemplating whether to share the information George had trusted him with. "If I tell you something—something I've never told anyone else—do you promise never to repeat it?"

Her eyebrows flashed, and she shook her head nervously.

Ethan swallowed hard and took a deep breath. "When my brother was here, he told me something I didn't know about my mom. It upset me, and I'm not handling the surprise well."

"Go on," she said.

He cleared his throat and stuttered. "Apparently, my mom was an alcoholic. She'd been sober since marrying my dad, but she still went to AA meetings."

There, he'd said it. He felt lighter already.

"Wow. I expected you to say something different."

"Like what? Don't you think that's terrible?"

"That she was a drinker? Not really."

"No, not that part. Just that I had no clue."

"I guess. But I'm sure she had a good reason to keep it from you, especially since it never really affected your life."

"But it does. Alcoholism can run in the family, and it often affects people with addictive personalities. That means *me* if you believe my dad about my uncontrollable gaming obsession. Besides, I can't help thinking I never really knew my mom. That she hid this whole other side of herself from me."

"Isn't that how parents are? I mean, they had their own lives before they had kids. Hell, they were kids themselves once upon a time. I don't know much about my parents and what they did before Kyle and I entered the picture. Sure, they've told me stories, but I admit sometimes I tune them out."

"There you go again."

"What?"

"Being wise beyond your years."

She fidgeted with her fingers and smiled uncomfortably. "If it bothers you so much, why not ask your dad? Maybe he can explain why she kept it a secret."

"My dad and I don't have that type of relationship."

"What type of relationship is that?"

"One that involves talking about anything other than my mistakes and why I'm nothing but a disappointment."

Anxious to stop discussing his dad, Ethan decided it was finally time for their second kiss. His heart pounded harder and faster than the rush of the waterfall, urging him to bow toward Grace and bring his lips near hers. Taking in her breath, Ethan closed his eyes and paused before moving closer.

Unfortunately, he hesitated seconds too long. Grace jumped to her feet and leaned against the fence to stare down at the waterfall. "Do you mind me asking what you hear about Kyle's case lately? I only get bits and pieces of the story from my parents, which makes me crazy."

"I don't get much either." He lied instinctively while still processing the rejection of his attempted kiss. Ethan had discovered he could follow the court docket online in real time, so he neurotically checked the website every morning. And unlike Grace's parents, Ethan's dad gave detailed updates whenever new information became available. Talking about the case was all they had in common anymore. Recently, Dad hired a lawyer to explore whether they should pursue a wrongful death claim against the Beasleys. They'd been advised not to mention the possibility to anyone. He hated keeping that secret from Grace and hoped nothing ever became of it.

"What do you know about the prosecution interviewing Theo's dad?" Grace said. "My mom says he might testify about an accident Kyle was in last year, supposedly because he was texting and driving."

Lying again and feeling terrible about it, Ethan stood to lean on the fence next to Grace. "That's news to me."

"Oh well. I guess we'll find out soon enough." Grace turned toward the soccer field. "I better get going."

Ethan wasn't ready to say goodbye. "Can I walk you home?"

"No thanks. I'm going to stick around and kick some more balls. I'll see you at school tomorrow." Grace raced ahead and never looked back, sending out a strange vibe and leaving Ethan confused about why she ran away so quickly and avoided his kiss this time. Grace was moody, like most girls, but he sensed something more was swirling around in that mysterious mind of hers. Something beyond the obvious predicament they'd fallen into together.

Chapter Thirteen

Caroline stood in front of the bathroom mirror wearing a silk nightgown, surprised to find that she still had some of her old lingerie. She hadn't worn anything remotely sexy in years, especially in the bedroom. But tonight, she tossed aside her ratty old t-shirt and boxer shorts and hoped liked hell Jordan would notice. She and her husband hadn't made love in a long time. She missed the connection they once shared and yearned to reignite the spark that used to burn hot between them. After today's news about Kyle's case, she felt like letting herself go, celebrating the small victory, even if only for a moment.

The gown's lace neckline looked peculiar, bunching unevenly over her lopsided breast implants. When she was in her twenties, a boob job sounded appealing. She had always been flat-chested and longed to easily wear those cute dresses or halter tops that she admired in the catalogs—especially the backless kind that never looked quite right without complicated undergarments. As a bonus to making her whole again, her post-cancer reconstructive surgery could have eliminated the need for a bra wrapping around her waist and fastening at her neck. Too bad things hadn't gone as planned.

Thanks to the hack plastic surgeon who lost his license shortly after he operated on her, Caroline felt like a failed science experiment. Instead of a one-and-done procedure resulting in a nice perky set of tits, she endured months of uncomfortable tissue expanders and three separate operations. She walked away with pockets of flesh, fat, and scar tissue molded together like clumps of clay and set too high on her breastbone to resemble anything natural. An entire chapter in her book addressed the importance of vetting physicians to best understand the risks of any procedure—a lesson she'd learned the hard way. If Caroline had been more thorough in her search for a surgeon, perhaps she wouldn't hate seeing herself naked now.

Fortunately, Jordan had already turned off the bedroom lights. She listened to him rambling about something from the bed before slowly opening the bathroom door and moving toward his voice.

"Geez," he said. "You took long enough in there. Did you hear what I said?"

"Not a word."

Her eyes hadn't adjusted to the dark, but she could hear him performing his nightly routine, smacking his pillow and fluffing it into shape.

"What do you think about Kyle's conversation with Coach Urbas?" he said.

On the way home from the pre-trial conference, Kyle told them about a phone call with the coach. Their son was in jeopardy of being cut from the baseball team, not because of his arrest, supposedly, or all the bad publicity that followed. Remote schoolwork didn't agree with Kyle, and he was failing most of his classes. He wouldn't meet the eligibility requirements of the State's athletic association.

"He still has time to get his grades up. He's only been back in class a few days." Caroline said. "You would hope they'd grant him some leeway based on what he's going through. Maybe the ramifications of Kyle's extended leave should have been considered earlier."

Jordan ignored her shot at why allowing Kyle to take his time returning to school was a bad idea. "Threatening to cut him after all his hard work and what he's done for the Shawnee Springs program sucks. One misstep, and they turn their backs on him," he said. "I'm tempted to call Coach and give him a piece of my mind."

Caroline sat on the bed and slipped under the sheets. "We both need to be careful about calling what Kyle did a misstep. Even though Amy died from something else, he still broke the law."

"We break the law every time we drive over the speed limit, Caroline. It's a stroke of luck Amy Shawver didn't die from a head injury, or anything related to Kyle hitting her with his Jeep. That should be enough to justify dropping all the charges."

"Let's hope so," she said. "Today was a slight win, but we're not out of the woods if they apply the law literally and prosecute him for the hit-and-run."

"All I'm saying is that if the prosecutor can't proceed with the homicide charge, the school should give him a chance to get his grades up and play this season. If they don't, Kyle will lose his scholarship at Niagara. Then what?"

Caroline was growing tired of the conversation. This wasn't the foreplay she had envisioned, and Jordan needed something to improve his mood. Otherwise, her sexy nightie would go to waste. Sliding over until their skin touched, she kissed his neck. His body stiffened at first, but he eventually turned sideways and kissed her on the lips.

"What's this?" His voice was full of surprise. "Wait a minute. What are you wearing?" He slid his hand up and down her torso, petting the silk and moving the smooth fabric over her thighs.

"It's been too long." She whispered into his ear, stopping to nibble on his ear lobe before trailing down his neck. Gently, she guided him upright and helped him tug his t-shirt off over his head. He seemed just as nervous as she was, but at least he hadn't frowned at the proposition.

Rolling on top of her and pinning her on her back, he returned her kisses with the same passion she remembered from their younger days. He plunged his tongue into her mouth and groaned, stopping for an instant to gaze into her eyes, then returning to explore the parts of her body only he knew existed.

His breath burned hot on her skin, and his lips traveled across the top of her chest from shoulder to shoulder. She winced when he got close to her breasts but grabbed hold of his hair and gently steered him away from the wreckage, down toward her stomach. He kissed her belly button and ran his tongue from hip to hip before moving back to her mouth. She seized the opportunity to thrust a hand beneath the covers to grab hold of his penis, expecting him to be rock hard by now and ready to go.

She was shocked to find he wasn't aroused, kneading his lifelessness in the palm of her hand like the dough of a breadstick before putting it in the oven.

"I'm sorry." Jordan let out a giant sigh, rolling off her and onto his back.

"What's the matter?" She suppressed the desperation in her voice. "Is something wrong with you?"

"With me?" He sprang to a seated position and rested against the headboard. "There's nothing wrong with *me*, Caroline."

"Then what? What is it? Don't you find me attractive anymore?"

"Of course I do. You're beautiful." He leaned sideways and kissed her on the cheek. "But in case you haven't noticed, we haven't done this in a very long time. And despite what they say, it's not like riding a bike."

"I don't understand."

"Seriously?" He turned to face her and scowled. "You sure are a mystery. For such an intelligent woman, you don't see what's happening here? You can't turn me on and off like a faucet. You've rejected me for years, pushed me away, and closed yourself off like a tomb. And now what? Just because we got some good news today, you want to pretend there's no baggage left between us? That we can pick up where we left off before the cancer?"

"Is that what this is about? The cancer? I thought it was about finally seeing a glimmer of hope that this nightmare we've been living might end. I'm sorry for wanting to feel close to you, to be intimate again. I know it's been a long time, but I'm ready to feel like your wife again—in every way."

"Well, now that *you're* ready, it's settled. Back to business as usual. The infamous Caroline Beasley has finally decided to share herself with her husband again. Who cares what he thinks!"

Sometimes, the truth hurts.

Other times, honesty grabs you by the neck, drags you down the stairs, and repeatedly kicks you in the gut before leaving you to suffer alone.

The contempt and resentment in Jordan's tone cut through her like a sharp knife. She hadn't realized how much she'd upset him over the years. Maybe she'd been too militant, too stubborn, about her independence. She'd only had good intentions, wanting to spare him some of the angst she endured by keeping her worries to herself. But now she could see the harm she'd caused by not trusting him when he offered support. How could she make things right and show her husband how much he meant to her?

Jordan's back faced her now. She slid onto her side and nestled against his body, wrapping her arms around his waist and burying her face between his shoulder blades.

Before she could say another word, Jordan launched himself from her grasp, grabbing his pillow and exiting the bed in a huff. "I'll sleep on the couch."

Caroline was left alone with her thoughts, plagued by the familiar loneliness that she'd lived with long enough.

****

Sitting at the kitchen table in front of his open laptop, Ethan waited for Dad to take him to school. After George returned to California, Ethan attempted driving again, but only if absolutely necessary. He still hated using Mom's minivan, and Dad never complained about dropping him off on the way to work each morning. If Ethan was lucky, they barely spoke during their rides, but Dad often filled the silence with updates on Kyle's case. Occasionally, Dad took advantage of having Ethan captive in the seat beside him to nag about his homework, college applications, and the future in general. That's when Ethan tuned him out—a skill he'd perfected over the last several weeks.

Ethan couldn't stop thinking about Grace. She was so pretty and easy to be around—nothing like any of the other girls he'd *talked* to, which only amounted to a casual few. His attempt at a second kiss with Grace was an epic fail, but he hoped for another chance soon. He'd never felt so comfortable with a girl before, and it didn't seem right to ignore their connection because of her brother's actions. Or inactions.

Would it be so wrong if he and Grace supported each other while trying to get through this awful time? Dad would disapprove. And based on the way his brother treated Mrs. Beasley at the grocery store, George would, too.

Listening to the hurried sounds of his dad getting ready upstairs, Ethan scanned the online court docket. Nothing new there. But, when he checked his email, a notification popped up that the ACT scores had finally been posted. Oh shit! The bagel he'd eaten for breakfast grumbled in his gut.

Dad entered the kitchen, straightening his tie. "Whatcha looking at?" He examined the computer screen before Ethan could snap the laptop shut. It wouldn't have mattered anyway. Ethan had to share his score with Dad sooner or later. Time to get it over with.

"ACT scores are up." His heartbeat thumped inside his chest. "Let's see how I did."

Dad sat across from him, and a fresh blend of toothpaste and aftershave wafted up Ethan's nose. Soon after the email link opened, Ethan slunk into his chair, bracing himself for his dad's reaction. "A twenty-eight," Ethan murmured. "Same as last time."

"Damn," Dad said flatly. "I guess that seals the

deal." Emotionless, his father stood and walked over to the coffeemaker, fiddling with the filter. "Do you know how to work this thing?"

Ordinarily, Ethan would have been quick to help. Making coffee was one of the many things Dad never had to do for himself. Mom always had a cup ready for him in the morning. But Dad's stupid comment about the test score enraged Ethan, especially because of his deadpan expression when he said it. His father didn't appear to give a damn about him anymore.

Ethan slowly rose from his chair and drew back his shoulders, ready to stand his ground. "What the fuck do you mean? What deal has been sealed?"

"Don't use that language with me, son. It's disrespectful."

"You don't respect me. Why should I respect you? I'm sorry I didn't do better, that I'm not smarter. I'm sorry you don't think I'm living up to my potential and that I'm not like you!" His voice grew louder and louder, and Ethan could feel himself teetering on the edge of losing control.

"Settle down." His dad walked toward him, but Ethan backed away. "Let's not get into this today."

"Get into this?" He shrieked as an uncontainable anger poured from somewhere inside him. "Get into what? My life? Your disappointment? How we're never going to be able to live in this house together without Mom? And speaking of Mom, why didn't anyone tell me about her drinking problem? Didn't you two think I was old enough to understand? Were you ever planning on telling me now that she's dead?"

"Ethan, stop. There's no point in getting hysterical. George told me that he let the cat out of the bag about your mother's alcoholism, which wasn't his place. I planned on telling you but was waiting for the right time."

"Oh, for fuck's sake! The right time? I think the right time would have been a long time ago. You guys lied to me. Each and every time she left this house for an AA meeting, you lied about where she was going. How could you do that to me? Why couldn't you trust me?"

Heat burned beneath his cheeks. The tears he'd been trying so hard to quash finally declared victory. Ethan covered his face with his hands and slumped forward, resting his elbows on the kitchen counter. Every emotion imprisoned inside him broke free, spilling from his heart and draining his spirit. A primal cry escaped his mouth as the intense pain and anguish frightened him to his core. He wept and blubbered until his body felt like an empty cavity.

Hollow and depleted, Ethan straightened up and looked pleadingly toward his dad, taking a small step away from the counter to test the water before going deeper. Mom would have known what to do at this moment. But she wasn't there. He needed a hug, and some reassurance they could get through this. Ethan took a second step forward, ready to wave the white flag and see whether Dad could fill the void.

"You need help, son," his dad interjected. "We'll get you therapy. From a licensed professional, not through the school guidance office."

Therapy. *That* was his answer? Ethan was beyond insulted that Dad suggested he talk with a stranger instead of his remaining parent. Suddenly, he felt stupid. Disappointed in himself for believing his father could offer any comfort.

"I'll drive myself to school today." He grabbed a tissue, wiped his eyes, and blew his nose. "There's no reason to leave Mom's van unused in the driveway anymore."

Ethan grabbed his backpack and walked toward the garage, turning to glare at his father one last time before leaving. "I'm not going to therapy. How's that for sealing the deal?"

****

Caroline woke up earlier than usual the morning after her disastrous efforts to revive her sex life. She had hoped to clear the air with Jordan, but he'd already left for work. His pillow lay back on the bed where it belonged, and he'd tossed his pajama bottoms into the hamper. Somehow, she'd slept through him taking a shower and getting dressed for the day.

After swapping the silk nightie out for a comfy pair of sweats and a long-sleeved t-shirt, she settled at the kitchen table with a cup of black coffee. A girl could get used to a leisurely morning like this. No outfits to fuss over. No planes to catch. No talking points to rehearse on the way to a speaking engagement. Nothing but peaceful reflection, even when regret was part of the package.

A newspaper would have been nice, but they canceled their subscriptions long ago, choosing to read all their news online. Caroline powered up her laptop, and like an addict looking for a fix, she logged onto social media first. Let's see how much mud people were slinging at her family today.

According to the Shawnee Springs Online Parent Page, the ACT scores came out overnight. Proud parents couldn't help themselves from bragging about their genius children.

"My son got a thirty-four," one mother proclaimed. "Harvard, here he comes!"

Another mom boasted, "My Simon does it again, raises his score another three points!"

Post after post of "my kid's better than your kid" made Caroline sick. No wonder today's high school students are so anxious and stressed. The pressure they face to outperform the rest of the world is ludicrous and unrealistic. No one talks about the well-rounded student anymore—the average kid who studies hard but enjoys a balanced life filled with friends and widespread extracurricular activities.

She'd even admit to that in her own home. Kyle and Grace had forfeited other interests, like scouting or playing musical instruments, to excel in their chosen sports. Kyle enrolled in travel baseball at age twelve, and Grace tried out for club soccer before finishing elementary school.

Looking back, Caroline didn't believe she and Jordan had pushed them too hard. Their kids 'primary motivation came from within. But the competitive culture of today's youth sports made it difficult to participate at any level other than overdrive.

Luckily, their choices turned out to be fruitful. If Kyle or Grace had failed to make their high school teams after putting all their eggs in one basket from an early age, their teenage years would have looked entirely different. She'd seen that happen to all kinds of kids in Shawnee Springs. Kids like Ethan Shawver who seemed a bit lost, at least according to the gossip Jordan picked up from his patients.

Now that Ethan's mom was gone, Caroline

wondered what would happen to him.

Without warning, she sensed Kyle's hands on her shoulders. "Morning, Mom." He leaned over and kissed her on the cheek.

"Well, good morning, honey. I didn't hear you come downstairs."

"Too wrapped up in online gossip, I see."

"Yes. Thanks for rescuing me. I don't know why I continue to look at social media. People are so full of themselves."

"True dat." Kyle opened a cupboard door and grabbed a package of chocolate toaster pastries.

"Want me to make you something else?" she said.

"Nope. I'm good." He ripped off the wrapper and dropped the pastries into the toaster. "Why did Dad sleep on the couch last night?"

"How'd you know that?"

"I couldn't sleep, so I came down for a snack around midnight. I heard him snoring like a power saw in the family room."

"He couldn't sleep either. I guess he dozed off watching TV."

Kyle eyed her suspiciously as he leaned over the toaster.

"What was on *your* mind in the middle of the night?" she said.

"Nothing in particular, just everything, I guess. Do you think the homicide charge will get dropped?"

"Sounds that way. I'll call Val this morning to hear what she thinks."

"That's good then, right?"

"Very good." She smiled. "I'm more optimistic about the potential outcome than ever."

"I wish I could say that." The toaster popped up, and Kyle immediately grabbed one of the pastries, burning his fingers. "Shit! That's hot."

"Let me help." Caroline rose from the table and walked in front of Kyle, grabbing a small pair of wooden tongs from the drawer and using them to place his breakfast on a plate. He remained standing and shoved the food in his mouth. "Geez, Kyle. You'll burn your tongue. What's the hurry?"

Chewing with his mouth open, he said, "I'm finally meeting with Coach Urbas this morning before homeroom. I want to get there early."

"What's the meeting about?" She leaned back against the countertop and folded her arms across her chest.

"My status on the team. What if I'm not allowed to play this year?"

It would be devastating, but she couldn't say that. Until recently, Kyle's whole identity centered around baseball. It's who he was and what he did. If the school wouldn't let him play, and even worse, if Niagara University reconsidered their offer, he'd go crazy. So would Jordan.

Suddenly struck by the absurdity of her train of thought, Caroline refused to let herself think about the worst-case scenario. Baseball wouldn't mean a thing if Kyle ended up behind bars. "Don't worry," she said softly. "We'll cross that bridge if we come to it."

Kyle slapped his forehead with his palm and rolled his eyes. "How many times have you told me that, Mother?"

"I know. I know. I'm a broken record. Wait until you're my age. You'll repeat the same stories and phrases to your kids. It's inevitable."

"Mom, I love you," Kyle said with surprising seriousness.

"I love you too." She paused to watch him finish the pastry and check the contents of his backpack. "Hey, before you go, did you see the ACT scores are up?"

"Yeah, I know." He zipped his backpack and slung it over his shoulder.

"Well—how'd you do?"

"I didn't check. I don't want to jinx myself."

"Jinx yourself, how?"

"It's not going to matter what I got on the damn test if I can't go to college next year. I can only handle one thing at a time, and right now, it's time for me to talk with Coach Urbas."

Caroline struggled to understand Kyle's logic, but the tension on his face was clear—he felt uneasy about meeting with the coach. She knew she couldn't press him any further; there was too much at stake.

Playing baseball this year might not be an option. He could lose his scholarship, and the risk of not overcoming the charges against him was real. He might even go to prison.

No matter what happened, Caroline was determined to keep their family from falling apart.

****

Happy to be in school and away from Dad, Ethan couldn't wait to see Grace. As soon as he'd found out she loved science fiction movies as much as he did, he bought tickets to the premiere of a new alien invasion thriller at the local theater. He waited at her locker before lunch and invited her to join him.

"That sounds like a date." She sounded hopeful.

Excited. He must have imagined the awkwardness when she left him at the waterfall earlier that week.

"Pick you up at six?"

She nodded and skipped a few steps down the hallway. Ethan shook his head and snickered at how unpredictable she could be.

Ethan drove to Grace's house later that evening and slowed in front. She hurried toward the street before the minivan stopped and grabbed for the door handle while the van was still moving. Ethan paused to look at the Beasleys 'crowded driveway, where three vehicles sat parked. Seeing Kyle's Jeep kicked him in the teeth even though the damage from where his mom hit the windshield had been repaired.

"Hi there," Grace sang as she rushed into the passenger seat. "Hurry up and drive. I don't want anyone seeing your van."

"You didn't tell them where you were going?"

"To the movies, yes. Just not with you."

"I get it. I didn't tell my dad either. But we're not exactly going somewhere private. We're going to a movie theater."

"I know. If my parents find out—oh well. I just didn't want them to stop me from coming."

Ethan shrugged. Sneaking around felt wrong but exhilarating at the same time.

"I'm psyched to see this movie," she said.

"Me too."

When they arrived at the theater, they bought an extra-large bucket of buttered popcorn to share and a supersized fountain drink. After settling into the seats Ethan had purchased and pre-selected online, a slight whisper drew his attention a few rows back. He peeked over his shoulder and recognized the couple catty-corner behind them as two kids from their high school, juniors Beth Barnes and Scott Weaver. They'd both been at Jason's party on homecoming night.

"I told you they were hooking up," Scott murmured.

"I can't believe it," Beth said. "Of all people."

Their whispers grew softer, indistinguishable. They must have realized Ethan noticed them. Oh well. He couldn't worry about what people thought of him anymore. Or what they thought about him talking to Grace. He tipped the bucket of popcorn in Grace's direction. "Help yourself."

She grabbed a tiny handful, slowly and daintily putting one piece in her mouth at a time. They extended their recliners as the house lights dimmed, and the previews began. Once the popcorn bucket was empty, Ethan wiped his hands aggressively on his pants before grabbing hold of Grace's hand and interlacing his fingers with hers. Neither attempted to break loose until the movie was over.

"What'd you think?" Ethan said.

"It was awesome!"

"Agreed." Spontaneously, he leaned over and spoke into her ear. "Let's stick around until everyone clears out."

"I'm in no hurry." She giggled.

If he were lucky, the theater would remain dark long enough to steal another kiss. But something occurred to him while they waited for the rest of the movie-goers to leave. He needed to get something off his chest. Since Dad had mentioned moving forward with his plan to file a civil suit against the Beasleys, Ethan debated when and how to break the news to Grace. She needed to hear it from him before everyone in town knew, but he feared it would hurt their relationship. He couldn't stand the possibility of losing her as they grew closer. He appreciated her comments about his mom and how it didn't seem like a big deal that no one told him about her alcoholism. He needed someone other than George to talk sense into him more often.

Skooching sideways, he whispered. "Can I tell you something while we're waiting?"

"Sure."

He adjusted himself in the recliner to face her, so close he could smell the buttered popcorn lingering on her breath.

"What is it?" she said.

Ethan's feet involuntarily shook as they dangled over the edge of the footrest. If honesty was the best policy, why wasn't he more confident in what he was about to reveal?

"I learned something the other day, and you won't like it. I feel bad keeping it to myself, but you'll find out sooner or later. Please don't hate me for what I'm about to say."

"I could never hate you." She brushed his arm, calming his nerves and easing the tension in the air.

"We'll see. So, it sounds like my dad is going to sue Kyle." There, he'd said it. Ethan swallowed hard.

"Sue him? For what?" Grace stuck her hand inside the side of the recliner and pressed the control button until her chair was upright again. Ethan did the same, staring at the movie credits still rolling on the screen and trying to think of how to explain.

"Wrongful death."

"Wrongful death? What does that mean?"

"I guess it means my dad's going to try and get money out of your brother for causing my mom's death."

"Wait, haven't you heard? He didn't actually cause her death. The autopsy report came in, and she died from an aneurysm. I wasn't supposed to say anything until after the prosecutor drops the charges, but he's going to. It's only a matter of time."

"I know. And I don't know much about how the law works, but apparently, it's easier to hold someone responsible for killing another person when they're being sued for money instead of being locked up in jail. That's how my dad explained it anyway. He wants to go after Kyle by saying my mom wouldn't have died if he had stopped to help, even with the aneurysm."

"That sounds stupid," Grace said. "But even if it were true, Kyle has no money. He's a high school kid."

"I thought the same thing. My dad has this crazy idea that the court can hold your parents responsible for your brother's actions. Kinda like when Mr. Leandry would threaten us about having parties and warn us our parents could get arrested. Remember those posters hung at school? *Those That Host Lose the Most*. Honestly, I think my dad's nuts, especially since Kyle's already eighteen."

"Even if he's right, why would your dad do such a thing? Does he want to ruin my family? It's not like you guys need the money."

"I know. I'm not sure where the idea came from, and I definitely disagree with him. My dad's all over the place right now—sad one minute, angry the next. I just wanted you to know where I stand in case he goes through with it."

"I appreciate you telling me, but this changes

everything."

Once again, Grace's demeanor shifted. Ethan was frustrated trying to keep up with her drastic mood changes, but this time, her feelings were no mystery. She was pissed.

Grace sprang from the recliner and marched up the aisle. "Don't follow me. I'll text my brother for a ride."

Chapter Fourteen

By now, everyone in Shawnee Springs had heard that the prosecutor's office dropped the negligent homicide charge against Kyle. Caroline hoped the people who'd been so quick to throw stones regretted it. Karma would catch up with them later. Some people seemed upset about the news, probably those who only paid attention to soundbites and talking points. The evidence clearly showed Amy Shawver died of a brain aneurysm before getting hit by the Jeep. But that didn't mean Kyle was off the hook.

ADA Wingassett appeared determined to pursue the hit-and-run charge to ensure Kyle paid for his actions. As quoted on the evening news, he said, "New York State imposes a legal duty on its citizens to provide their contact and insurance information to all parties involved in an accident if they believe someone sustained injuries at the scene. Failure to share that information and report the incident to the police can result in felony charges, significant fines, and up to seven years in prison. We need to set an example for all drivers, especially young ones. Leaving the scene of an accident will not be tolerated."

Caroline had been sitting on the couch in the family room and talking on the phone with Toby when the story first aired. Unable to interrupt her agent's barrage of ass-kissing as he tried to convince her to return to work, she muted the TV and set it to record the newscast so she could watch it later.

"Think of all the women out there who need you, who are missing out on your words of wisdom," Toby said.

"I see what you're doing," she said. "Stop trying to butter me up."

"I'm worried you'll lose momentum if you don't book one or two speaking engagements soon. It's important to keep your name out there. I still think the ASCO meeting is the golden opportunity you've been waiting for, but hey, what do I know? I'm just the agent who landed you a book deal with an advance most authors only dream about, and I've kept you busy ever since." Toby finally took a breath and gave Caroline another chance to speak.

"I need more time. I promise to think about it, but no commitments until the spring."

"Why? When is the trial?"

"Late January. Even if we don't settle and the case goes to trial as scheduled, I'll still need to get Kyle ready to leave for college."

"Um…eh…um," Toby said.

An awkward silence followed until Caroline realized her mistake.

"Come on, Toby, give me a break. I know what you're thinking. I'm trying to stay positive. Of course, there's a chance Kyle won't be going to college, and yes, maybe he'll end up doing some jail time, but I can't think like that. You shouldn't either."

"I'm sorry. But any chance you're in denial about what your son's future could realistically look like?"

"Maybe you haven't heard the latest news." She

raised her voice to emphasize the point. "They've dropped the negligent homicide charge. The autopsy proved that the woman he hit died from an aneurysm, not from contact with his Jeep."

"That's wonderful! With that behind you, shouldn't things progress more quickly?"

"Not necessarily. There's still the matter of the hit-and-run. That one might be harder to escape, but I'm hopeful."

Toby exhaled loudly into the phone. "Do you feel conflicted about that in any way?"

Caroline wrinkled her nose, wishing Toby could see the look of confusion on her face. "What do you mean?"

"Well, you say you're hopeful. Hopeful your son gets away with breaking the law, I assume. In saying that, you're suggesting you think it's okay he fled the scene and left that poor woman dying in the street. I don't mean to sound harsh. Not being a parent myself, I'm no authority on these matters. But I wonder whether you're sending the wrong message supporting his actions. You should think about how that could affect your career. Consider coming out with a statement to preempt any bad publicity that might follow."

"No statements, Toby. This isn't about me. It's about my son. I'd do anything for him, absolutely anything. You could never understand. But chew on this one—he's a kid. Kids make mistakes. Did you ever do something stupid when you were younger? Something you grew to regret? If so, were you granted a second chance?"

"Of course." Toby paused. "But at the risk of pissing off one of my best clients, I can't be silent. Nothing I did ever resulted in the death of another human being."

"Go fuck yourself, Toby!" Caroline disconnected the call and tossed her phone across the couch. He must not have heard a word she said. No amount of sweet-talking would convince her to resume speaking engagements now. Maybe she should look for a new agent, someone with more empathy for what she was going through.

Caroline stretched out on the couch and closed her eyes. She must have drifted off because the next thing she knew, Jordan was whispering in her ear. "Wake up, sleepyhead."

Disoriented, she rubbed her eyes and tried bringing his face into focus. "Hey, honey. What time is it?"

"It's after six. How long have you been asleep?"

"Oh, my. Over an hour. Wow! That never happens."

"You must have needed it." He kissed her on the cheek. "The kids should be home from school soon. Kyle waited for Grace to finish practice. What should we do for dinner?"

Caroline appreciated that Jordan never assumed she should take charge of what could be considered stereotypical female responsibilities. She should tell him that more often. Even now that she was home indefinitely, he still shared in caring for the kids and the house. And ever since her failed attempt at intimacy, he'd been overly affectionate and eager to make her happy, perhaps out of remorse for being so unkind.

Once again reflecting on the hot and cold of a long-term marriage, Caroline leaned into the moment and kissed Jordan back before sitting up and grabbing the remote control from the coffee table. "Let's watch the news before they get here. I missed the segment about Kyle's case, but I recorded it."

Jordan sat beside her and rested his hand on her knee. Together, they watched the video clip of Dwight Wingassett trying, in layman's terms, to explain the distinctions between negligent homicide and leaving the scene of an accident.

"Don't ya just love how these prosecutors perform for the cameras?" she said. "Trying to give the illusion they're speaking generally and pretending to be apolitical. It's such bullshit."

Once Dwight finished defending the dismissal of the first charge and grandstanding for the camera about how justice required applying the full arm of the law for the hit-and-run, the reporter interrupted with breaking news.

A young woman with big hair and a full face of heavy makeup reported, "This just in. While Kyle Beasley may have received a break in the State's case against him, his legal woes became more complicated as a lawsuit was filed in civil court today, alleging he and his family should be held responsible for the wrongful death of Amy Shawver. According to the summons and complaint filed in Erie County Court, Dan Shawver is seeking damages in the amount of one million dollars. Dismissal of the negligent homicide charge won't affect the civil suit since reasonable doubt of causation is not required in a tort action."

Jordan dug his fingers into her knee. "Did you know about this?"

"I had no idea. And how come we're hearing about this on the evening news instead of from our attorney?"

"I don't know, but let's not jump to conclusions. There could be a reasonable explanation for the media releasing this information before Valerie got it to us."

"Don't give me that. Let's get her on the phone and

find out what the hell is going on!"

But Valerie hadn't heard either. She'd been out of the office all day for an infusion and hadn't seen the news report. "Don't worry," she said after they filled her in. "Filing a civil action in matters like this isn't uncommon. I'm not worried. It seems more like a scare tactic than anything else, another way for Dan Shawver to prove his point and punish Kyle."

"So, what do we do?" Jordan said.

"Sit tight for now."

"Can't you at least get a copy of the complaint so we can see what basis they have?" Caroline said.

"I will. But it's after-hours Friday, and all the government offices are closed for the weekend. I'm sure the online portal only contains the basics of the allegation. It takes several days for the details to follow, but the damn news media loves to scoop the story before they have all the facts. I'll give the clerk of courts a call first thing Monday. Even then, we shouldn't be focusing on the tort action just yet. Let's take it one case at a time."

Caroline's patience faltered. One step forward, two steps back. She wasn't sure how much more they could take. At least she and Jordan weren't at odds with each other today. His presence beside her on the couch grounded her, made her feel safe and secure. She hoped he felt the same way about her.

Relying on loved ones to tackle tough times, which she often viewed as weakness, might actually signify strength. How long had she misunderstood that? Perhaps rekindling her relationship with Jordan could trigger a positive chain reaction, bringing their family closer and helping them meet the challenges yet to come.

****

Friday night ice skating had been a Shawnee Springs tradition since his dad was a high school freshman, the year the town built the indoor ice rink. Ethan rarely missed it. He was a decent skater but mostly loved to go because of the music. A legendary local DJ played up-tempo songs from all eras, giving Ethan the buzz he needed to circle the ice like a rockstar.

But Cole practically forced him to the rink tonight. The news story that ran earlier in the week brought a fresh set of problems. Although he'd grown accustomed to being the subject of town gossip, the increased media attention was a hassle. Everyone wanted to know how Ethan felt about Kyle getting out of the homicide charge and whether he believed the Beasleys would have to hand over a million dollars.

And that meant everyone, not just his friends and teachers.

The gas station clerk who sold Ethan his daily slushie interrogated him whenever he stopped in. The neighbor up the street, who'd never uttered a single word to him before, grilled him at the drugstore. And their mail lady suddenly delivered the mail precisely when Ethan came home from school, ready to cross-examine him as soon as he stepped foot in the driveway.

The renewed interest in Ethan's life made him want to disappear, especially since his chances of ever spending time with Grace again faded after the recent developments. She hadn't spoken to him since the movies, and his occasional messages went unanswered. Except one. After the latest news report, he texted to see how she was doing, which prompted a lengthy reply.

—*Stop texting me! My dad says I'm not allowed to talk with you anymore. Not like I was planning on it anyway. But you're not getting the message. Let me spell it out again. STAY AWAY FROM ME. I'M SORRY ABOUT YOUR MOM. TRUTH! BUT IF YOU AND YOUR DAD WANT TO SEEK REVENGE ON MY FAMILY, I WANT NOTHING TO DO WITH YOU.—*

This time, a string of not-so-playful emojis followed—the image of a stop sign, an upright palm, and a hand holding up the middle finger.

Okay, message received. He needed to quit hoping that Grace would ever forgive him, but that wasn't easy. He missed her terribly and could barely function without someone to talk to who understood him.

So, when Friday night rolled around, Ethan planned on staying home to watch a movie. But it was his dad's turn to host poker, and Ethan didn't feel like fetching beers all night for his uncles and Dad's random card buddies. When Cole came next door and grabbed Ethan's cell phone, threatening to hold the device hostage until he agreed to come skating, Ethan weighed the pros and cons of his options and eventually caved.

"But I'm not skating," Ethan said. "Just watching."

"Suit yourself." Cole clutched the phone and held it high over his head. "We're pre-gaming at my house first. Theo's already there."

After a round of shots, Ethan and his friends arrived at the ice rink halfway into the two-hour "open skate." Teenagers of all ages cruised counterclockwise around the rink with different degrees of skill, stumbling and laughing and trying to look cool. Theo and Cole rented skates while Ethan stopped to people-watch behind the tempered glass surrounding the ice. He recognized almost everyone there. One of the employees, a kid named Antonio from his homeroom, zipped past like an

Olympic speed skater. He wore a bright yellow jacket with the word "GUARD" in big black letters across the back and looked like a traveling billboard. A pack of young-looking girls, probably freshmen, huddled together and clung to the railing. As soon as one of them fell, they all collapsed and remained sprawled on their backs, laughing hysterically.

After several minutes, Theo sprung from behind and tapped Ethan on the shoulder. "You're honestly not skating?"

Cole followed, wobbling on his skates to stay balanced on the rubberized floor. He clung to Theo for support.

Ethan shook his head. "No. I'm gonna enjoy watching you two make fools of yourselves instead. Funny how your skating has barely improved after all these Friday nights."

"Screw you," Theo said before hopping onto the ice and towing Cole behind him.

Ethan's stomach growled as soon as his friends disappeared. He wandered over to the concession stand and groaned at the long line, claiming his place behind a boy and a girl he'd never seen before. They couldn't keep their hands off each other, and Ethan tried not to stare. The girl grabbed the boy's ass before he wrapped an arm around her shoulder and stuck his tongue in her ear. She threw her head back and giggled, then launched her face into his chest and pawed at his shirt. Ethan gagged. Get a damn room.

When it was finally Ethan's turn, he bought a soda and a double order of nachos with extra cheese and spicy hot peppers before settling at a corner table facing the ice. He spotted Theo and Cole right away, trying to catch up with a pair of sophomore girls who were much better skaters than they were. One of the girls looked so much like Grace that Ethan did a double-take to make sure it wasn't her. He had assumed she wouldn't be there tonight. Earlier, her Snapchat story showed her watching a movie in someone's basement with a few girls from her team. Maybe they'd get bored and show up at the rink. Wishful thinking but not entirely impossible.

Kyle probably wouldn't be there either. Thankfully, he was still keeping a low profile. The last time Ethan and Kyle crossed paths in person was in Mr. Leandry's office before the crash. Since then, Ethan had imagined their next face-to-face encounter, picturing endless reactions to seeing Kyle after Mom's death. What he'd do in the moment was entirely unpredictable. He could demand an explanation. Wait for an apology. Or take a shot and pray he didn't miss.

But when Kyle appeared out of nowhere near the concession stand, none of those possible scenarios registered. Ethan froze, holding his breath and hoping Kyle wouldn't notice him.

Too late. As soon as they locked eyes, Kyle charged in Ethan's direction. For as long as he'd anticipated this moment, Ethan completely blanked. He sat speechless, choking on his anxiety but never looking away.

Kyle kept coming—fast. He adjusted the visor of his baseball cap over his forehead before swiping his long arm across the entire length of Ethan's table and knocking the tray of nachos to the ground. "Dickhead!"

What the fuck? Stunned, Ethan squeezed the life from his cardboard cup and chewed on the straw like a rabbit nibbling on a carrot. If anyone deserved to be called *dickhead*, it was Kyle!

"Stay away from my sister. If I ever hear you're talking with her again, I'll kick your ass!"

Alarmed by his racing heartbeat, Ethan stared at the ground and chomped harder on his straw, hoping to avoid a scene.

Kyle leaped to Ethan's side of the table and got in his face. "You understand me?"

A rapidly growing crowd gathered inside the concession area. A few guys whooped and hollered, egging them on. "Fight! Fight!"

Ordinarily, Ethan would have walked away. Someone like *him* should never stand up to someone like Kyle. A challenge like that had disaster written all over it, and the odds of escaping without a broken bone or with his dignity intact were slim.

But a raw anger shot through Ethan like a lightning bolt. A searing heat burned a path through his body, setting his insides on fire. He pictured Kyle driving recklessly down Lakeshore Road, listening to the radio full blast while texting and scrolling social media. Ethan's mind sucked him further into the flames as bursts of agony blazed around him. He envisioned the front end of Kyle's dark gray Jeep crashing into his mom while she was doing what she loved. Her bike tires flew sideways as she smacked her head on the pavement and landed in the street. Her helmet cracked in two, and her heart stopped beating.

But Kyle barely glanced up from his phone. He kept driving, running his fingers through that thick head of hair the girls drooled over. Flashing those perfectly white teeth without stopping or caring about the wreckage he'd left behind.

Ethan knew this vision was a figment of his

imagination—most of it, anyway. But in that moment, his exaggerated version of how things played out couldn't have seemed more real. He rose from his chair, puffed out his chest, and leaned forward within a millimeter of Kyle's face.

In a steady, controlled tone, he said, "You've got some balls. After what you did to my mom, I should have taken care of you a long time ago."

Seconds later, Ethan hauled off and punched Kyle in the gut, catching him by surprise and causing his head to drop and his body to fall forward. Ethan struck again without giving Kyle a chance to recover, screaming like a crazed animal and decking him in the face as hard as he could. Blood sprayed from Kyle's nostrils. He fell back against the wall before crumpling to the floor.

Antonio arrived in his yellow "Guard" jacket, yelling at Ethan to stand back so he could tend to Kyle. Ethan didn't budge. He'd never actually hit anyone before, not even a slap. It surprised him how good it felt. Something inside him had just snapped, followed by a surge of aggression—like a grizzly bear pouncing on a buck.

He flexed his fingers to make sure they weren't broken and put a lid on his lingering adrenaline rush. His mom's voice cut in and echoed in his ears. "I'm disappointed in you, Ethan," she would have said before launching into a long-winded lecture.

Luckily, Mom never stayed mad long.

But Dad. Free from Mom's interference, he would have an entirely different reaction.

Unsure of the punishment awaiting him now, Ethan hurried from the ice rink and slowly headed home.

****

When Kyle walked through the back door holding a blood-covered towel over his face, Caroline couldn't fathom a guess at what had happened.

"Oh my gosh, Kyle!" She jumped from the couch where she'd been reading on her tablet. "Are you okay? Who did that to you?"

In a muffled voice, he spoke through the towel. "How do you know someone did this to me? Maybe I walked into a wall or fell down a flight of stairs."

"Okay, wise guy. Did you? Is your injury self-inflicted, or whose mother do I need to call?"

After entering the room from the basement, Jordan took one look at Kyle and winced. "I warned you not to go out tonight, especially to the ice rink. I'm surprised this is the first time someone's roughed you up."

Caroline leered at Jordan. "Wait a second! You let him go ice skating? Why didn't anyone tell me?"

Ignoring her question, Jordan walked closer to Kyle and looked under the towel. "Ouch! What did the other guy look like?"

"Very funny, Dad."

"Jordan, I thought we agreed Kyle should lay low for a few days," Caroline whined meekly. "To wait for the hysteria over that news report to die down."

"He's eighteen years old, Caroline. We can't control him." Jordan turned back toward Kyle. "Where's your sister? Did you give her a ride tonight?"

"No. She decided not to go. I thought she was home with you guys."

"She hasn't been here all night," Caroline said. "Oh, God, should we be worried about her, too?"

"Relax, Mom. I'm sure she's fine. She probably went out with girls from the soccer team. It's not even past curfew yet." Kyle removed the towel from his face and stared at the blood. "Sick!"

"Let me help," Caroline said. After neglecting to intervene when Grace came home drunk, she refused to make the same mistake twice. She hurried into the kitchen and returned with a handful of ice wrapped in a clean towel. She gave it to Kyle. "Here. Put this on your nose."

Kyle followed instructions but stood in the middle of the kitchen like a helpless toddler. Jordan guided him to the table and pressed him into a chair. "Now tell us what happened. You can trust us with anything. We're your parents. We love you."

Caroline blinked to keep from crying.

Kyle sighed. "It was nothing. And I only decided to go to the ice rink when I found out Ethan Shawver was there."

"Why would you want to see Ethan, of all people?" Jordan said.

"Let's stop pretending we didn't know Grace was seeing him," Kyle said. "The whole town was talking about them being at the movies together."

Caroline shot Jordan a questioning look, suspecting he knew about the movies, too. Even if he didn't, she assumed her husband had been clear in telling Grace to stay away from Ethan after he and his dad gave her a ride home from Jason Crook's party. Maybe that warning made a relationship with Ethan seem more enticing. Caroline had been young once, too, recalling how her teenage crush on the class "bad boy"—a kid named Paul Brown— grew more intense after her parents got wind of it and banned her from seeing him.

Her daughter's minor rebellion didn't concern

Caroline much for some reason. They were talking about Grace, after all. And Ethan. Both good kids with little to no experience in the dating department, as far as she could tell. Considering their extenuating circumstances, there couldn't be a more unlikely couple in the universe. They'd probably just latched onto each other for comfort, someone new to talk to during a difficult time. Their friendship, or whatever was emerging between them, would be a passing phase. Nothing to get fired up about, but she was still curious to know more.

"When you say *seeing him,* do you mean they were dating?" Caroline said.

"They don't actually call it dating these days, Mom. All I know is I picked her up at the theater after he told her about the civil suit, and she told him to fuck off."

Caroline smiled uncomfortably. "That's my girl. Although I like Ethan. I'm sure he had nothing to do with the lawsuit. But it's nice to know Grace is defending her family."

"How could you like Ethan now? After what he did to my nose?"

"So, tell us how that happened," Jordan said.

Kyle described the incident at the concession stand, but Caroline wondered if he was leaving anything out—again. "That doesn't sound like Ethan to me," she said. "He's always so kind and sweet."

"You should have seen the look in his eyes before he punched me in the stomach. It's like he was possessed, and then he just turned batshit crazy."

A familiar feeling washed over her. "That poor kid. He's probably been walking around like a zombie since his mom died, with all that rage bottled up inside."

"Poor kid?" Kyle said. "So, it's okay that he took it

out on me?"

"Well, Kyle, you are the most obvious choice of punching bags," Jordan said. "But it doesn't excuse what he did. He still assaulted you. We could press charges."

"Oh no! No more lawsuits. Enough is enough," Caroline said. "Besides, living with suppressed anger is unhealthy."

"You should know," Jordan said.

Ouch. Guess she'd been naïve, thinking their marriage only needed a minor repair. Years of damage couldn't be fixed after leaning into each other a few times. "What's that supposed to mean? I'm not overly angry, considering everything I've been through. Is that how you see me?" She already knew Valerie did.

Jordan stomped over to the bookshelf behind the couch, snatched a copy of her paperback from inside, and held the book in front of her face. "Does this look like a peaceful woman to you? You look like a professional wrestler before stepping into the ring. Clenching your fist. Gritting your teeth. And the tagline—*I'll Kill You First.* If that's not anger, I'm *People* magazine's next *Sexiest Man Alive.*

Caroline's body went numb. She should be offended, embarrassed, sad, or pissed off. But instead, she felt nothing, like she'd fallen into a bottomless black hole. Eventually, she dug a fingernail into her forearm to make sure she was still alive. The pain barely registered, and she waited for someone else to say something. Anything.

Jordan finally rescued her from the silence. "We need to get Kyle to the emergency room. If his nose is broken, it should be set sooner than later."

"I'd like to come, too," she said softly.

"Someone should be here when Grace gets home," Jordan said. "I'll take him, but I promise to keep you posted."

"Thanks." She waited until they were gone to let her guard down, curling up in the fetal position on the couch. Tears streamed down her cheeks as she wept, louder and louder until she gasped for air. Tanner lumbered toward her but hurried away when a guttural sound croaked from her mouth. Remembering the cute little instructor from her one and only yoga class, Caroline took a deep breath in through her nose, out through her mouth. If she couldn't control the crying, at least she could make sure she didn't suffocate.

As time passed, the sobbing subsided. Her insides warmed as if they'd been emptied, cleansed, and restocked with a new glow. When the door to the garage opened and Grace stepped inside, Caroline didn't attempt to move. She remained still on the couch and allowed her daughter to see her as she truly was—hurt, frightened, and in need of someone to comfort her.

"What's wrong, Momma? Are you crying?"

Without a word, Caroline stretched her arms out and invited a hug. Grace melted into her embrace as she'd done as a young child, huddled tight with no space between them. Caroline breathed in the familiar smell of Grace's hair and cried some more, gently this time, as if her fresh tears originated from an entirely different place. When Caroline sensed her daughter shudder against her chest, she placed a hand on her chin and slanted her head upward. A single teardrop pooled in the corner of Grace's eye and slipped down her cheek until Caroline brushed it away.

"We've been through a lot," Caroline whispered. "Let it out. There's no shame in crying."

Chapter Fifteen

Ethan slept late Saturday morning. The house was eerily quiet when he finally made his way downstairs. A note from Dad hung taped to the refrigerator door. "Headed into the office for a few hours. Clean your room and water the plants."

Water the plants? That was random. Looking around the house, he understood why. Only a few houseplants survived after Mom's death. The hoya in the living room she raved about whenever it bloomed. The rubber tree that craved the bright light of the sunroom. And some viny thing that belonged on the kitchen counter; he could never remember its name. The others had all died since neither he nor his dad cared for them. Mom would have been bummed, maybe even mad. She loved her plants, watered them religiously, and talked to them sometimes as if they were his siblings. He and Dad had neglected them. If someone didn't start tending to the survivors, they'd be gone, too. Just like her.

Dad must have come to the same realization, thus the note. Ethan filled a pitcher from the kitchen faucet and started watering, wondering if Dad had any other *aha* moments this morning. When Ethan arrived home last night from the ice rink, walking in from the garage and asking his father about the poker game, there was no mention of his fight with Kyle. Thank God.

The ice rink manager had warned that he would

notify Ethan's *parents*, somehow not realizing who Ethan was or that he only had one parent left. He must not have meant immediately, but Dad would eventually find out. Ethan had no intention of sharing the news himself.

By noon, he'd watered the plants and picked up his room. Now what? Weekend days were dull, and Ethan was restless. He didn't feel like gaming, and his homework could wait until tomorrow.

He texted Cole.

—*Whatcha doing?*—

Three dots immediately appeared on his phone screen. Cole was already typing.

—*Nothing. Wanna day drink?*—

George's cautionary words about how alcohol affected people differently gnawed at him, but Ethan shut them down.

—*Sure. Just you and me?*—

—*Yeah. Theo got grounded. I'm not sure why. Come on over.*—

Cole's house was a mess. Dirty dishes filled the sink. Piles of mail sat on the countertop. A basket of unfolded laundry blocked the steps to the upstairs.

"Your mom's not home?" Ethan said.

"No. She has a new boyfriend. I think she spent the night at his house." Cole walked over to the makeshift liquor cabinet—an old TV console that had been painted and repurposed. "Pick your poison," he said with a mischievous grin.

Ethan lacked much experience with the hard stuff. After the tequila incident in tenth grade, he mostly drank beer. But he was feeling adventurous after last night's scuffle with Kyle. "How about a vodka tonic?"

"One vodka tonic, coming up!" Cole said.

After a few sips, Ethan understood why he preferred beer. "How the hell does my dad drink these things? They're terrible."

"Yeah," Cole said. "Let's just do shots. That way, we really don't have to taste anything."

They sat at Cole's kitchen table, talking nonsense and getting drunk. Cole teased him about his fight with Kyle, and they roleplayed the incident until they ended up wrestling together on the floor, cracking up over how surprised Ethan had been by his own behavior.

At one point, when their conversation took a more serious turn, Ethan was tempted to open up about Grace and everything that happened between them, including their unforgettable kiss. But starting from scratch with Cole seemed like too much trouble. His friend wouldn't understand anyway, and Ethan didn't want to be a buzzkill by bringing up his girl problems.

By two o'clock, Ethan felt no pain. His lips tingled, just like they did when he had his wisdom teeth removed. When he took another shot, the vodka dribbled down his chin and onto his sweatshirt. The kitchen spun like an amusement park ride, and he couldn't get his hands to cooperate as he wiped his mouth. His gaze lagged when he looked over at Cole, who was face down on the tile floor pretending to swim.

"Look at mmeee!" Cole shrieked. "I'mmm racing a shharrrk!"

Ethan laughed so hard he could feel the muscles in his stomach ready to rip, then hurl. Oh no. He was about to get sick.

He stepped over Cole and stumbled to the bathroom, just in time to throw up in the toilet. A few small chunks of last night's nachos splattered on the floor. Ethan doubted Cole's mom would notice, so he left them there to avoid losing his balance. After splashing water on his face and rinsing his mouth, he decided to go home for a nap. He tiptoed over Cole, who had stopped swimming and passed out on the kitchen floor.

Three hours later, Ethan awoke in his own bed with a pounding headache and a mouth full of cotton. It was already dark outside, and he stumbled through the blackness to use the bathroom. In a few seconds, he was back under the covers. He pulled a pillow over his head, tossing and turning and trying desperately to fall asleep again. No use. His mind was racing in overdrive.

Muttering to himself, he shot out of bed and sat at his desk to fire up his laptop. He stared at the browser, wracking his brain at how to phrase the question that weighed heavily on his mind.

His fingers pecked at the keyboard, quickly at first, then hitting the backspace and trying again continually until he got it right. "What are the signs someone has a drinking problem?"

Dr. Google was no expert. Mom used to say that all the time. When Ethan was a sophomore, the school nurse sent him home after noticing a spot of ringworm on his arm. Afterward, he searched the internet for pictures of what he believed were creepy little worms slithering across his skin. When he couldn't find what he was looking for, Mom warned him to resist using the information highway as his resource. "Please come to me first with those questions," she'd said. "I could have saved you some worry."

But reading up on the symptoms of becoming an alcoholic before sounding alarm bells with anyone else made perfect sense. Some of the online answers comforted him. He never drank alone (if drinking with Theo and Cole didn't count), and he never missed school or neglected his appearance because of his drinking. He'd never blacked out, either. That was a relief.

But several of the responses troubled him, starting with how other addictions could be seen as red flags. He worried about his so-called gaming addiction and that he vaped more frequently than his friends. He also read alcoholism can be triggered in people under extreme pressure or experiencing emotional distress. He could check both of those boxes. And the ability to drink greater and greater amounts of alcohol before feeling its effects suggested an increased tolerance, an early warning sign, according to a few sources. Maybe he should be concerned that he'd recently tried vodka.

A tiny voice inside Ethan's head tried reassuring him that he was only being paranoid. But he couldn't unsee some of the alarming comments.

Alcoholism can run in families.

Having an alcoholic parent increases your chances of becoming an alcoholic.

Like fireworks on the Fourth of July, the warnings exploded in his mind. He shrank into his seat and braced himself for the heart-thumping finale, closing his eyes and covering his ears while beads of sweat dripped from his forehead. A sharp pain ripped through his chest, and he suddenly feared being alone. He needed to call someone to talk him down. But who?

He thought about Grace. He missed her. She was the first person he'd ever met who truly understood him, like his mom did in some ways, but different, too. He grabbed his phone and searched for her contact, admiring her picture when it popped up. But she was still ignoring him. If her last text message hadn't been clear enough, she sure as hell wouldn't want anything to do with him after his fight with Kyle. Contacting her was a bad idea. But he had to talk with someone.

George picked up on the first ring. "Hey there, buddy. What's up?"

Ethan released the breath he'd been holding, but his words barely eked out. "It's nice to hear your voice."

"Yours, too. But you sound weird. Is something wrong?"

The tightness in Ethan's chest intensified. He curbed the discomfort, hoping to sound normal. "I got my ACT scores back. Same as last time."

"That's okay. A twenty-eight is good. It'll get you in plenty of places."

"Oh, I know." His voice cracked. "I'm fine with it. Dad's the disappointed one."

"Give him time. He'll come around. But I can tell something else is bothering you. What's going on?"

Ethan's burning concerns spilled from his mouth. He admitted to wondering whether he had an addictive personality and how he was afraid he'd been drinking more than usual. Did it sound like he might be turning into an alcoholic like George and their mom? Fighting back tears, Ethan begged for advice. "Help me. I feel like I'm spiraling out of control."

"Don't worry, little brother. I'm here for you. The fact that you called me about this is huge. You're fine. You're a teenager in high school, experimenting the way teenagers do. And you just suffered a tragic loss. You're bound to be feeling unstable. From what I witnessed when we were together, you're not acting like someone with a drinking problem. But now that you know about our family history, you need to be careful. Awareness is half the battle, and you're miles ahead of where I was at your age."

"Really? Do you mean that?"

"Of course. But feel free to call me whenever you need to talk. I've got your back."

After a deep sigh of satisfaction, Ethan said, "If things get any worse here, you know, between me and my dad, can I come live with you? Just temporarily. Until I graduate high school and settle on a college."

"Of course. I told you that before I left. I'd love to have you. Any time."

An odd rustling sound startled Ethan. He turned to see Dad frowning at him from the doorway.

"Gotta go," Ethan whispered into his phone before hanging up on George. He wondered whether Dad had been standing there long enough to catch part of their conversation.

Dad raised his eyebrows. "Have you been drinking? Your room reeks of alcohol." His tone was neither angry nor sad, just flat. Without waiting for a response, he turned and walked down the hallway to his room.

Wait! That was it? No checking his breath to confirm he'd been drinking. No mention of Ethan's desire to leave home and live with George. Surely, his dad would have said something if he'd overheard Ethan's paranoia about becoming an alcoholic. He hadn't mentioned his fight at the ice rink, either. If Dad knew about that, he would have handed down some type of punishment by now.

Avoiding any of those conversations should have come as a relief. But the only thing worse than one of

Dad's lectures was his cold shoulder. Feeling the sudden drop in temperature, Ethan flung himself back in bed and buried his head beneath the covers.

****

Caroline and Jordan called a truce after their most recent spat. Jordan promised never to call her *angry* again, admitting she'd made progress and no longer resembled a professional wrestler. Caroline thanked Jordan for recognizing how far she'd come and pledged to keep working on her temper, which should be easier after recognizing her flaws—at least theoretically. Plus, she'd joined the yoga studio with Val and had high hopes that a regular practice would help her achieve better life balance. If only the effects could be immediate!

This morning, Caroline, Jordan, and Kyle sat apprehensively in a conference room outside the prosecutor's office. Caroline stared at the clock as intently as Jordan stared at his phone, and Kyle chewed on his fingernails as if they were covered in chocolate. The dark purple bruises beneath Kyle's eyes made him look like a raccoon, but at least the swelling had gone down, and his nose wasn't broken.

Kyle spit a fingernail. "How long is this going to take? I've missed enough school already. Too many more days like this, and I'll never catch up."

The way her son spoke made Caroline uncomfortable. His impatience and anger mounted daily. Had he learned to fall back on those emotions from her?

"Look at you, Kyle. Never in my wildest dreams would I have imagined you complaining about missing school," she said in an upbeat tempo.

"When I met with Coach Urbas, he agreed to give me a chance. If I work hard and get my grades up, he'll

230

do what he can to keep me on the starting roster."

"Good to know your baseball coach will go to bat for you." She chuckled at her lame attempt to make him laugh. "Get it? Go to BAT for you?"

Kyle flashed one of his famous Hollywood grins. "Funny, Mom. Good to see you haven't lost your ability to deliver corny jokes." A lightness brushed across her heart like a flower petal. Teasing one another again felt nice.

When the doorknob finally turned, tension reentered the room. Dwight Wingassett walked in with an armful of overstuffed files and loose paperwork, followed by a flustered-looking Valerie. A bright red pair of glasses sat high on her head, wedged deep into the bird's nest of today's hairstyle. Wrinkles overpowered her blouse, and her trousers hung too low beneath her waistline. Even her Mary Janes screamed that it had been a rough morning—with one navy, one black.

"Sorry, I'm late, Beasleys. I had an appointment with my new doctor today. It was the only time he could squeeze me in." She shot Caroline a quick look of thanks. "And yes, I know I'm wearing different-colored shoes. I'm just putting it out there before anyone can make a wisecrack." No one did. Val's effort to lighten the mood fell short.

Still standing and towering over Valerie's petite frame, Dwight cleared his throat and dropped his files on the conference table with a thump. "Shall we get started?"

"By all means." Valerie dug a legal pad from her briefcase and plunged further into the pockets before untangling a pen from the hair behind her ear. She paced the room like a caged tiger. Why couldn't the attorneys sit down like the rest of them?

After much lawyer talk, which Caroline didn't miss one bit, Dwight boiled things down to the nitty-gritty. "We offered to drop the negligent homicide charge, expecting Kyle to plead guilty to the hit-and-run."

Valerie snapped, "Nice try, Dwight. Too late to backpedal. Dropping the homicide charge was a no-brainer, considering the autopsy report. If that evidence had been available when the grand jury deliberated, they never would have indicted him on that charge."

Without hesitation, Dwight said, "Fine. So, let's focus on the hit-and-run. If your client pleads guilty to that, I'll recommend a light prison sentence. One to two years max."

Valerie vigorously shook her head. Her eyeglasses stayed put, snarled in place. "No prison time. He's a kid. With no criminal record. He made a mistake."

"He committed a felony. The victim is dead. Someone needs to pay the price." Dwight crossed his long and lanky arms in front of his chest.

"The death of the victim is irrelevant to this discussion. We should only be talking about what Kyle did after she went down."

"Think again, Ms. Saks. Consider the elements of the crime outlined in the statute. New York law allows for up to seven years in prison for fleeing the scene of an accident involving a fatality. The critical word there is 'fatal.' There's no getting around that one."

"I won't let you use my client to send a message to the masses."

"I suggest you talk things over with him and his family," Dwight said. "I would hate to see such a fine young man jeopardize a bright future to prove a point.

Agree to the guilty plea now, and there's a chance he can resume his baseball career after he gets out. Seven years is a game changer for an athlete, don't you think?"

Listening to their legal mumbo jumbo made Caroline sick. She couldn't bear her son going to prison, not for one second, and she couldn't sit there without reacting. Her make-believe options ranged from throwing herself at Dwight's freakishly big feet and begging forgiveness for Kyle's mistake to pouncing on his face and ripping every one of his freckles from his skin for threatening her boy's liberty. She bit her lip and chanted words of restraint in her head to prevent herself from doing either.

Valerie looked at Dwight. "Mind if I spend some time alone with the Beasleys? I need to explain a few things so perhaps we can carve out a resolution."

"Take all the time you need." Dwight gathered his untouched mound of paperwork and raised it to his chest. "My offer expires at the close of business tomorrow."

After Dwight left the room, Valerie sat at the conference table and set her legal pad in front of her. Not bothering to free the red eyeglasses from atop her head, she mined a pair of purple ones from her bag. "What are you all thinking? About the criminal case only. We're not talking about the civil filing today. One matter at a time." She held her pen over the pad, glaring down at her hand as if waiting for the signal to begin a timed exam.

Jordan spoke up first. "We don't want our son to go to prison."

"Not even for a day," Caroline said. At least they were on the same page.

"If his case goes to trial, what are the chances Kyle could be found *not guilty* of the hit-and-run?" Jordan

233

said.

"That's the million-dollar question now, isn't it?" Valerie said before further suggesting the prosecutor's office wanted to make an example out of Kyle. The number of hit-and-run cases had risen over the last several years and primarily involved drunk drivers. The New York legislature recently amended their vehicle and traffic laws to capture other types of reckless driving, like texting behind the wheel. The lack of any suggestion Kyle had been drinking made his case ripe for setting a strong precedent, allowing the State to take an otherwise "innocent" offender, someone distracted without being under the influence, and try holding him accountable for not stopping to offer help or contact the authorities. Putting forth that argument would be a bold move. The kind district attorneys loved to make, especially during an election year.

"So, what does that mean for us?" Jordan said.

"It means we need to be smart about our strategy and consider all angles before making big decisions," Valerie said.

"Okay," Caroline said. "What are the best defenses available if we go forward?"

Valerie put her pen down and leaned back in her chair. "An associate from my office did some research. I skimmed her memorandum this morning. The strongest argument I can put forth is claiming Kyle didn't realize he hit someone. He got confused by the lights and sirens signaling behind him at the last possible minute. He panicked, swerved aside to avoid being hit by the ambulance that appeared out of nowhere, and hit Amy Shawver on her bike without comprehending it." She looked at Kyle. "Does that sound about right?"

Kyle nodded his head reluctantly while chewing on his fingernails.

Caroline said, "What's the legal basis for that argument?"

"Mistake of fact," Valerie said. "It's our best chance. I can't argue Kyle never felt his car make contact with anything. There's no doubt something smashed into his windshield. But because he was so shaken up by almost getting hit by the ambulance, it's reasonable to suggest he believed it was something else, like a deer, as he initially said. If he had no idea he'd hit a person, that might explain why he never stopped."

Kyle slumped in his chair. His fingers remained in his mouth.

"But what about the witnesses?" Jordan said. "Weren't there people on the scene who saw what happened? Could anyone testify that Kyle *did* see Amy Shawver? That there's no way he could have mistaken her hitting the windshield as anything other than a person."

"Possibly," Valerie said. "But only Kyle knows what he truly saw in the moment. Witnesses can say whatever they want, and I'd argue to keep any damaging statements out of evidence. If that doesn't work, it'll come down to whose testimony is more credible."

"I'm feeling good about this," Caroline said.

"Me too," said Jordan. "It sounds like you think we have a good chance of beating this thing at trial."

"I do," Valerie said. "And right now, I'm leaning toward having Kyle testify as I think he can tell his story best. But I don't want to sugarcoat things. Dwight will come at Kyle hard. He'll portray him as an egocentric teenager driving recklessly down the road and not paying attention to anything other than the music on the radio or, most likely, his phone. That's a tough thing to prove, but not impossible."

Kyle squirmed in his seat and whimpered softly, but Jordan talked over him. "So, summarize our options for me."

"We could go with the mistake of fact defense, take our chances at trial, and hope the prosecutor doesn't have enough evidence to prove Kyle knew he hit a human being. If we succeed, he'll be acquitted, and you can all get on with your lives."

Kyle cleared his throat and said, "Or?"

"Or you can plead guilty to fleeing the scene and accept the prosecutor's offer to serve one to two years. You'd most likely get out after six months with good behavior."

"Nope. No way," Jordan said.

"I agree," Caroline said without looking at Kyle first. When she did, her heart crumbled. When this nightmare began, clearing his name altogether sounded like the only option, but maybe they needed to be more open-minded. "Are those our only alternatives?"

Valerie removed her glasses and wiped them on the sleeve of her blouse. "We could present a counterplea, agree to plead guilty to the felony if they recommend no jail time. Is that something you'd consider, Kyle?"

Kyle's gaze darted back and forth between Caroline and Jordan. He looked perplexed.

Confused herself but desperate to help her son process such a big decision, Caroline yanked Kyle's fingers from his mouth and held them in her hand. "Even if you could avoid serving time, a felony follows you forever. I don't think that's a great idea. I'd recommend we take the case to trial."

Kyle recovered his hand and resumed biting his nails. "But that sounds risky. What if I choke on the stand and can't convince the jury I never saw Mrs. Shawver as she flew over the windshield?"

"Valerie won't let that happen." Caroline turned sideways and looked at her husband. "What do you think, Jordan?"

Looking at Kyle, he said, "If you're uncomfortable testifying, you don't have to, but I tend to agree with your mom about the felony. You don't want that on your record." Turning to Valerie, Jordan said, "Any chance they'd reduce that to a misdemeanor in exchange for a guilty plea?"

"No. Dwight's already said the felony charge is here to stay."

"Then forget it," Jordan said. "It would create too many problems for our son's future. For starters, Niagara University would revoke his scholarship, and he can kiss his baseball career goodbye."

Oh, brother! Here we go again. Would Jordan ever see how insignificant baseball was at a time like this? The risks involved much more than losing a college scholarship. But she couldn't argue against avoiding a felony. "Looks like we've reached a consensus to see this thing through."

Kyle shifted in his seat again. "Wait a second. Isn't this my decision, Ms. Saks? I'm the one on trial here, so I should be the one with the final say."

"Yes, you are, Kyle. No matter what your parents want to do, the decision is all yours. So, what are you thinking?"

Droplets of sweat flooded Kyle's face. Once again,

he looked pale and ghostlike—the same way he appeared the afternoon of the accident. "I'll take Mr. Wingassett's plea offer—as is."

Caroline's jaw dropped. Despite her recent progress in maintaining a greater sense of peace and calm, her natural instincts took over. "What? Why? You could do jail time. No way. I won't allow it."

"Won't allow it? What am I five years old?" Kyle shouted.

"It doesn't matter how old you are. You'll always be my son. You've got to fight this—to the very end!"

Caroline stood up brusquely and accidentally knocked her chair to the floor. When Jordan leaned over to pick it up, she swatted his arm away. "Don't touch that! I don't need your help. I need you to talk some sense into our son."

Jordan backed away. "Relax, Caroline. There's no reason to get so worked up."

"Are you kidding me? There's every reason to get worked up here. Kyle just announced he's willing to bend over and take whatever's coming. We must stop him!" She waved her arms wildly and patrolled the room, unleashing her temper beyond the point of no return. *Bring it on Kyle*, she thought. *Give me everything you've got cuz I'm not backing down.*

In a cautious but deliberate tone, Jordan turned his back to Caroline and spoke directly to Kyle.

"Ignore what the prosecutor said about resuming your baseball career. If you take the plea, those days are over no matter what. I assume you have a good reason for making this decision."

"If I end up serving time, so be it. Ms. Saks said I'd probably get out before serving the whole sentence. It'll be okay if I can't play baseball or even go to college anymore. I just want to put this behind us."

"Kyle," Jordan said with an uptick of urgency. "I agree with your mother. You're making a mistake."

"I'm not, Dad. Trust me."

With unexpected panic, Caroline launched herself between her husband and son and planted her hands firmly on the conference table in front of Kyle. "No. You need to listen. Sometimes, parents know best, Kyle. Let's talk this through some more."

"Can you even do that, Mom? You stopped talking a long time ago. Calm down. Besides, I've made up my mind. I'm pleading guilty."

The pain in Kyle's eyes gave way to an expression Caroline couldn't identify. His face blanked and his shoulders drooped, reminding her of a ninety-year-old man.

He'd given up and abandoned the fight.

Moving forward, nothing she said or did could alter the outcome of his case. A guilty plea would mean he'd be at the court's mercy, and she'd no longer have the power to impact his future.

Perhaps she'd been foolish to believe that she ever could.

****

The silent treatment had grown worse over the last two days. No matter how hard Ethan tried to make conversation, his dad barely spoke to him anymore.

"How was your day?" Ethan said Monday after Dad returned home from work.

"Fine," he said without looking up from the newspaper in his hand.

"What do you feel like for dinner?"

"I'm not hungry. You go ahead and eat without me."

"Okay. So, by the way, who's hosting Thanksgiving this year?" Ethan randomly asked about the upcoming holiday to see if he could finally get his father to say something more significant, but also because the anticipation was killing him. Mom loved entertaining, so they always hosted Dad's family for Thanksgiving dinner. This year would be different, and Ethan needed to mentally prepare for what to expect.

Dad folded the newspaper and placed it on the kitchen counter. "We haven't decided yet. I have a headache. I'm going to catch a cat nap."

Under any other circumstances, Ethan would have assumed something else was bothering his father. He could be a prick, but he'd never been this cold and unengaging. Was he pissed Ethan had asked George if he could move in with him in California? Or maybe he was mad about his fight with Kyle Beasley. There's no way he hadn't heard about that by now. Everyone in Shawnee Springs was talking about it, and his dad was pretty tapped into local gossip. But Dad *still* hadn't mentioned the night at the skating rink, not one peep.

Ethan devoured a ham and cheese sandwich before sitting at the kitchen table to start his homework, flipping on the television for background noise. When he opened his backpack, he discovered that his laptop was missing. Shit! He must have left it in his school locker. He texted Cole to ask about coming next door to print their calculus assignment.

Cole answered immediately, as if he'd read the text in real time.

—*Sure, come on over.*—

Ethan threw on a heavy hoodie that had been

hanging in the front closet since last season. It was already pitch-black outside, and the temperature had dropped at least fifteen to twenty degrees since returning home from school. Winter was coming, and he didn't look forward to the upcoming months without his mom, especially if Dad kept shutting him out. Thank God he didn't live in China, where a three-hour per week limit was being imposed on video game time. That would totally suck.

When Ethan jammed his hands into the hoodie's front pocket, he found a wad of yellow paper the size of a ping-pong ball. Almost tossing the paper in the trash, he uncrumpled it first to find a short grocery list in his mom's handwriting.

"Milk, eggs, bagels, something chocolate—you know what I like."

Her signature smiley face inside the outline of a heart stared at him from the bottom of the paper. At one point, she must have given him the list and sent him to the store. He couldn't remember anything about the errand that day, but he probably complained about it at the time.

Oh, how he wished he could take so much back. Like when he griped about having to help Mom around the house. Or when he chose to stay in his room playing video games instead of keeping Mom company while Dad was gone. And when he ignored her at school events where she was volunteering because he feared his classmates would tease him for being seen with his mother.

Ethan would always be troubled by memories of backing away to avoid long hugs, believing he was too old for them. If he'd known their time together would be cut so short, he would have done things differently.

Mom's scribbles on the yellow paper left him breathless. His insides tightened as if being squeezed by a boa constrictor while he stared at the smiley heart. Instead of following his gut and heading directly to bed, he powered through the pain and ran upstairs to confront his dad. He'd had enough of the awkward silence. Mom would have been mortified to see how the two of them were behaving. It was time to have it out.

Expecting to find Dad sound asleep in his bed with the bedroom door shut tight, Ethan was surprised to see the door open a crack. A sliver of bright light shone into the hallway. He peeked inside and caught Dad pacing in front of the dresser with a look of distress on his face. "You need something, Ethan?" Dad barked, approaching the door and staring him down.

Ethan took a step back and considered his options. He'd come upstairs to clear the air. What a wuss he'd be if he chickened out now.

With his heart racing, he said, "Yes. We need to talk." He opened the bedroom door and marched toward his father, digging into the same courage he'd discovered when he punched Kyle at the ice rink.

"Agreed." Dad folded his arms and pursed his lips. "Me, first."

"Fine. Go."

"I know about your fight at the ice rink. Tell me what happened between you and Kyle Beasley. I need to hear it from you."

Ethan's first instinct was to look away, to remain silent and wait for whatever his dad intended to dish out. Both his parents had always frowned upon any type of violence. He could almost predict what Dad was about to say. *There was never an excuse to hit someone. He should be ashamed of his actions. Ethan had embarrassed their family and owed the Beasleys an apology.*

But fuck that! Regardless of the actual cause of his mother's death, Kyle Beasley had ruined their lives. He deserved more than a punch in the face for his arrogance and reckless disregard for human decency. Kyle earned everything the law would throw at him, even if he ended up in prison. Ethan wasn't about to defend his role in their altercation, especially to his dad.

"There's not much to say." He said with a defiance that seemingly astonished his father. "I was minding my own business at the snack bar when Kyle confronted me and called me a dickhead. All I did was stick up for myself."

Dad raised an eyebrow. "Why would he do that? If I were him, I'd stay as far away from you and me as possible."

"I guess he was pissed I've been hanging out with his sister. That's not news to you either, right?"

"Of course not. And I don't like it."

"Too bad. It's none of your business anyway."

"Anything involving the Beasleys is my business now. Don't you forget."

"Whatever!" Ethan threw up his hands and spun around to face the wall.

"Don't turn your back on me! Look at me when I'm talking to you."

Slowly, Ethan complied. Dad balled his hands up tightly, pressing them to his sides.

"Or, what? What are ya going to do to me, Dad? Ground me? Take my video games away? In less than a year, I'll be far away from here, and you won't have a say in anything I do anymore."

Dad's face turned purple. He clenched his teeth. "It's not that simple, son. How do you expect to pay for college? You couldn't survive without my help for too long, so watch what you say."

"Get over yourself. I don't need your money to go to college. I can figure that out on my own. I don't need a goddamned thing from you anymore. Once I'm outta here, I can finally be free of all your criticism!"

Without warning, Dad raised his fist over his head and swung at Ethan's face. He stopped short as if realizing the irony in the situation—condemning Ethan's attack on Kyle with a punch of his own.

His father had only raised a hand at him one other time. When Ethan was little, he ran out in the street after a baseball, almost getting hit by an oncoming car. Mom had intervened before Dad could spank him, but even then, everyone knew the attempted blow was an effort to protect him and teach him a lesson.

The punch he avoided there in the bedroom originated somewhere much darker. In the heat of the moment, his father had lashed out in anger. Anger for how Ethan talked back, behaved in public, and, in all truthfulness, failed to meet his father's expectations.

But his father wasn't the only one in the room with unmet expectations. Ethan's disappointment in how Dad continuously nagged him and found fault in everything he'd done in his life was overwhelming. He deserved more than a parent who wished he had greater talents and different dreams. But with Mom gone, that's all he had left. And it wasn't enough to keep him in Shawnee Springs.

"My turn." Ethan stood tall with an eye on Dad's clenched fist as he tucked it under his armpit. "I assume you heard me talking with George on the phone. He said I could stay with him whenever I wanted. I want to go now. There's no point in us trying to make this work anymore. I'll book the earliest flight and finish high school in California. Until then, I'll move in with Cole to get out of your way."

Dad stepped aside and allowed Ethan to pass through the bedroom door without a word or a glance. Pausing in the hallway to be sure neither of them wanted to take another jab, Ethan nearly collapsed. Despite the friends and family members remaining in his life, he'd never felt so alone. He'd hit rock bottom. Not in the same way Mom or George might have in realizing they needed to quit drinking to stop spinning out of control, but strangely similar.

Ethan needed to make a significant change and pursue a fresh start—a new beginning that didn't include his father.

Chapter Sixteen

Once Kyle announced his intent to plead guilty, Valerie packed her bag and turned to leave. "Sleep on it," she said before exiting the conference room. After disappearing into the hallway, her voice trailed off as she added, "You've still got time to discuss your options. I'll call Dwight in the morning with your final decision."

But Caroline knew her son had made up his mind. No one said a word during their ride home from the prosecutor's office. Jordan drove while Caroline quashed a mind full of bad ideas to get Kyle to reconsider. They planned on waiting for Grace to return home from soccer practice to fake their way through a "normal" family dinner, which consisted of mediocre Chinese takeout that smelled like ginger and too much soy sauce. When Grace texted to say she'd be late, they took their places at the kitchen table without her.

Caroline set the cardboard container of chicken and broccoli in front of Kyle, but he stuffed his hands underneath his thighs. She watched with concern as he rocked side to side in his chair like he'd done as a child when refusing to eat his vegetables, proving that certain personality traits were impossible to outgrow. She recognized the defiant look on his face and recalled how he could challenge her to a standoff that she would lose every time. No amount of bribery, trickery, or logic would sink in now. His decisiveness might be admirable if it weren't about to sabotage his future.

Caroline looked at Jordan, who wasn't eating either. She gathered the takeout containers and put them in the fridge, conceding that she was clueless to believe anyone would be hungry at a time like this. Her heart ached, and her head pounded. She couldn't wait to run to her bedroom and hide beneath the covers. Nothing appeared on her calendar for the next few days. Maybe she could sequester herself until she figured out how to stop feeling so useless.

Just as she was about to leave the room, Kyle moaned and tugged at his hair with both hands before bowing forward and resting his head face-down on the table. "I can't take this anymore," he shrieked. "You need to understand why I can't go to trial."

The affliction in Kyle's voice made her muscles stiffen. Cautiously, Caroline approached him and lightly rubbed her hand along his back. His broad shoulders confirmed that he was a man now—no longer her little boy. "If there's something more you need to say, please say it. We love you, Kyle. We're here to help."

His body trembled beneath her touch. She wanted to grab hold of him, wrap him in her arms, and rock him gently until the pain disappeared. The lullaby she sang to him as an infant played in her head. When he turned to face her, she leaned in close and kissed him softly on the cheek, glancing at Jordan, who sat motionless across the table. *Thank you,* she thought*, for giving me space to be here for our son*.

Keeping his ear to the kitchen table, Kyle whispered. "I remember, Mom. I remember."

She'd been so focused on reminiscing about Kyle's younger years that she had no idea what he was talking about. "Remember what, honey?"

"Mrs. Shawver." He sobbed. "She wore a blue helmet, and her face crashed into my windshield right before my eyes. I remembered running into her from the beginning and can't live with the lies anymore. It's killing me."

Oh, God! What was happening? If she'd heard Kyle correctly, he hadn't forgotten the crash at all. He had been lying from the get-go. Omissions, half-truths, and white lies were one thing. But she never expected *this* from her son. No wonder he wanted to take the deal.

Kyle had been carrying that horrific image of Amy Shawver around since the accident. All this time, they'd been worried about clearing his name, keeping him enrolled in college and playing baseball, and preventing him from going to prison when the gravest consequence was witnessing someone he knew and cared about die a tragic death in front of him. The guilt of knowing he had something to do with it must be eating him alive.

Kyle sat up slightly and wrapped his arms around Caroline's shoulders. Burying his face into her chest, he let loose and cried uncontrollably. A toxic blend of grief and shame splattered all over her, triggering a meltdown of her own.

Tears poured from Caroline's eyes as she struggled to see a way out. Predicting how long Kyle would spend in prison after receiving his sentence was a waste of energy. Even if a crystal ball miraculously fell into their laps, no one could foresee the long-term emotional impact on any of them.

Continuing to cry, Caroline clung to her son with the same desperation he bared. She flip-flopped between trying to stay strong on the outside and yielding to the weakness within. Her mind revisited the last public speech she'd delivered—the one in Vegas when an audience member embarrassed her by getting her to admit how seldom she relied on anyone else in the face of adversity.

"Getting through tough times is easier when you don't have to go it alone," he'd said, making it sound so simple.

She'd already grasped the benefits of allowing Jordan to get closer. Instead of trying to control Kyle's fate, perhaps all he needed from her was unconditional support. Was she capable of opening her heart and sharing his anguish without trying to fix things? Considering her history, it might be a stretch. But anything was worth a shot to save someone she loved.

****

When Ethan appeared at Cole's door looking for a place to escape his father, a warm welcome greeted him. But three days at his best friend's house already felt like three years. Good thing the arrangement was only temporary. He only planned on staying until he could get to California. So far, he'd shared the bare minimum with Cole about his plans to move in with George or his blowout with Dad. The details of their fight haunted Ethan, but he resisted talking about them after getting a first-hand glimpse of Cole's difficult family life.

For as long as he'd lived next door, Ethan never came close to knowing what it was like to walk in his best friend's shoes until now. Cole's mom kept a messy house and hardly spent much time there, coming and going constantly. She'd surfaced once since Ethan took over the guest bedroom, only to pop home for a quick change of clothes and a shower. She never said goodbye,

Susan Poole

and they hadn't seen her since.

Stretched out on the living room floor, drinking a beer and eating cookies, Ethan looked over at Cole beside him. "Is it always like this?"

"Like what?" Cole belched.

"Quiet. Carefree. With no rules to follow or chores to do."

"Pretty much."

"Don't you wish your mom was home more often?"

"Sometimes, but I manage."

Over the years, Cole had occasionally admitted to wishing his father was around. His comments took on new meaning now that Ethan understood how often Cole was left alone. No one nagged his friend about homework, ACT scores, or future plans. But it didn't appear that anyone cared for him, worried about him, or kept him company, either.

Ethan wondered what his own father was doing at this very moment. It must be even quieter next door. Did Dad like it that way, or did he wish Ethan would change his mind and come home?

That wouldn't happen. Ethan kept scouring the discount airline sites for cheap flights, wishing he had enough money in his savings account to pay for a one-way ticket to California immediately. When Ethan called George back to make sure it was okay he came to stay, his brother offered to cover the cost. But Ethan needed to start on the right foot, not wanting George to feel burdened by having his little brother living with him.

Ethan grabbed another beer from the six-pack on the coffee table before deciding not to crack it open. He slid the can over to Cole instead. "When should we start our homework?"

Cole snapped. "Why do you even care about your homework now? When do you leave?"

"After the holidays. Submitting my transcript and transferring my credits is a process. It'll be easier to finish the term here and start my new school in January."

"I still can't believe you're abandoning us, man. What the hell am I going to do without you?"

Ethan felt guilty leaving his friends behind, especially Cole. "I'm not abandoning you. I'm only leaving town six months earlier than I would have anyway."

"But what about our plans? Spring break. Senior prom. Graduation. None of those will be the same without you."

Cole was right, and the FOMO was real. Missing those things bothered Ethan, too. But not as much as spending the rest of the school year dealing with Dad. Even if Ethan stayed next door long-term, he couldn't avoid his father altogether. Not unless they lived far apart. "Hey, maybe you can visit me at George's during spring break."

"We'll see." Cole frowned and got up from the floor. "I'm tired and going to bed. I need to get to school early tomorrow to see my counselor. She's gonna help me fix something on one of my college apps."

"It's only nine o'clock."

"I know. Make yourself at home. Watch some television. Eat some more cookies. Fold some laundry if you're bored." Before running up to his room, Cole grabbed a t-shirt from the laundry basket sitting at the bottom of the steps—a place Ethan now realized was its permanent spot.

After locating his phone, Ethan clicked on the Erie

County website and checked the court docket for news on Kyle's case again. There hadn't been any updates lately, but he knew the lawyers met to discuss a plea agreement.

Before he and his father had stopped speaking, Dad explained how the percentage of cases advancing to trial was generally low, especially in criminal matters. They could consider it a *win* if the parties reached an agreement holding Kyle accountable for his actions without actually trying the case before a judge and jury. The same would be true of the civil case. Dad claimed to be less interested in collecting money from the Beasleys than suing them on principle, hoping to force Kyle to admit what he'd done was wrong. No amount of money would bring Mom back, but Dad believed an admission of guilt would somehow make them both feel better.

Ethan disagreed. After practically memorizing the alleged circumstances surrounding the crash, he hated to admit some part of him understood why Kyle fled the scene. It would have been scary and chaotic, and it wasn't too farfetched to think he might have done the same thing under a similar set of facts. He should have explained that to Grace. If only she would talk to him or answer his texts. He could tell her he didn't hate anyone in her family, not even Kyle. He didn't want his dad to ruin them. He wanted to be with her.

Cole's house suffered from a sketchy internet connection. When the case summary finally popped up with a string of acronyms next to today's date, Ethan jerked his head in surprise and got busy cracking the code: "PLD GLTY – N/C LIO-AMEN." His palms itched as he pounded on the keyboard and googled the cryptic message. If he understood correctly, Kyle pled guilty to an amended complaint, and once the prosecution dropped the homicide charge, Kyle admitted to the hit-and-run.

Holy shit! It looked like Kyle had agreed to go to prison for what he'd done. Ethan never saw that coming. He shouldn't get too excited; perhaps he'd misunderstood. By now, Dad must have heard about this, so Ethan shot up from the floor and rushed to the side window to see if the lights were still on next door.

Darkness cloaked his house, and the garage door sat closed. Maybe Dad was out for the evening. If so, where could he be?

Ethan padded out Cole's front door and returned home, entering through the unlocked glass slider off the back of the house. The kitchen was spotless as if Mom still lived there. Or maybe Dad shared her meticulous housekeeping habits. Funny how Ethan had always credited *her* as the neat one. Regardless, he loved not seeing dirty dishes in the sink and clutter across the countertops like at Cole's house. Ugh. He could feel himself turning into his parents already.

The hum of the dishwasher welcomed him back. Dad must be home, but it was awfully early for him to be in bed.

Ethan tiptoed up the stairs toward his parents 'room. "Dad?" He whispered, afraid to startle him but not wanting to wake him if he was already asleep.

The warm glow of the bedroom television illuminated the hallway, and Ethan smiled at the familiar theme music introducing an episode of his mom's favorite detective series. Some things never change.

Approaching the door, he stopped abruptly at the sound of something else. A low moan echoed from inside the room, where Ethan found his dad curled in a ball on the right side of the bed—Mom's side, not his own. Dad clutched a pillow and cried into the shadows. His suffering cut through Ethan's heart like a scalpel.

"Dad. It's me." He whispered a bit louder. "Are you okay?"

His dad sat up in bed. The stream of tears flowing from his eyes glistened in the dim light. His unrecognizable expression could pass as nothing other than sheer grief. Ethan didn't need a response. He felt it, too. Neither one of them was okay.

Dad muttered something under his breath Ethan couldn't understand. No matter. Without another thought, Ethan looked past the harsh words they'd exchanged earlier in the week and the physical altercation that almost occurred between them. He climbed into bed beside Dad, melting into his arms and leaning into their mutual pain. The fresh smell of fabric softener tricked him for a second, making him believe his mom was still present. And maybe she was.

"I miss her," Ethan cried.

"Me too, son. We were lucky to have her as long as we did." Dad squeezed him tight and wiped his tears on the sheets. "I miss you too, though."

Ethan rolled over on his back and folded his arms behind his head, staring at the ceiling. Tears ran down the sides of his face. "I'm sorry, Dad. I just—"

"It's okay. Please don't apologize. I'm the one who owes you an apology."

"For what?"

"For being a coward. I didn't know what to say after you got in that fight with Kyle. I thought if I waited, something would come to me. That I'd get some clarity.

Your mom was always better than me at handling tricky situations, and I got used to relying on her."

"I wondered why you waited so long to mention it." Ethan turned over to face Dad. "I'd been waiting for you to tell me how disappointed you were in my behavior."

"Seriously?" Dad sat up straighter, leaned against the headboard, and put his pillow in his lap. "Why would you think that? Did I seem mad when I asked you about it?"

Ethan's mind flashed to their recent argument. He couldn't recall anything but a few questions about the incident at the ice rink before they'd gone off on a tangent and lost their tempers. "I guess not. It was weird you didn't confront me right after it happened. I thought you were trying to torture me with the silent treatment."

"That wasn't my intention. I was just trying to avoid saying something stupid."

"Like what?"

"Like how proud I was of you for standing up to Kyle, for not taking any shit from him. At the same time, I didn't want to encourage you to strike out when you're angry. And boy, did you look mad—like you were avenging your mother's death."

"Wait. How do you know what I looked like?"

Dad tossed the pillow aside and put a hand on Ethan's knee. "I watched the fight on YouTube. Some kid with a camera captured the whole thing and posted a clip online. Uncle Dave saw it first and told me what a badass you were."

Ethan's cheeks grew hot. "Oh, God. Again, why didn't you call me out on it?"

"I couldn't ignore your mom's voice rattling around in my brain. She would have wanted me to say something other than *atta boy*."

Ethan laughed. "Yeah. She wouldn't have liked it. Probably would have made me apologize to the entire Beasley family."

"Or made you bake them a cake," Dad said with a lightness in his voice that had been missing for the last two months.

They laughed together through tears.

"She sure was something, wasn't she?" Dad said.

Ethan nodded. "The best."

"Just like you. You inherited some of her best qualities."

Ethan shuddered at what else he may have inherited from his mom but shoved his fears aside. "Too bad I didn't turn out more like you. Maybe we'd have more in common then."

Dad flinched. "Is that how I make you feel?"

"Sort of. I know how disappointed you were when I quit baseball, and you're not crazy about my future plans."

"Stop right there. I push you pretty hard sometimes when I shouldn't. You are your own person, and I admire how you dig in for what you believe. That's a sign of a strong man, and I couldn't be prouder of who you've become. I'm sorry if I don't tell you that enough. Like the other night. Wow! You sure have an impressive right hook. Let's hope your mother didn't see that from heaven."

"Somehow, I think she did." Ethan grinned. "But she'll forgive me. She always could."

"Will you forgive *me* and stick around?" His dad's tone sounded desperate, similar to how Ethan felt himself. He couldn't forget about everything that had happened between them or make any sweeping resolutions in the heat of the moment. He'd just gotten used to the idea of leaving Shawnee Springs to see whether a change of atmosphere would be good for him.

"I can't make any promises, and George is looking forward to having me come stay or a bit. How 'bout I return home from Cole's for now, and we see how things go?"

A flicker of what looked like hope appeared in Dad's eyes. "Works for me. And when you head next door to gather your things, please ask Cole if he'd like to join us on Sunday for the AFC Wild Card game. We've got an extra ticket. Assuming you'd like to come too?"

"That would be awesome." For the first time since his mother's death, Ethan felt cautiously optimistic that he and Dad could survive without her, regardless of whether he stayed in Shawnee Springs or moved to California.

Chapter Seventeen

The sentencing hearing, the only remaining piece to Kyle's case, loomed large over their lives. His decision to plead guilty came as a shock. Valerie may have suspected their son was holding something back, but Kyle's admission that he'd been lying about what he remembered blindsided Caroline and Jordan.

Tempering her anger hadn't been easy, but after serious reflection, Caroline was proud of her son for taking responsibility for his actions. Perhaps his plea felt easier to swallow because somewhere deep inside, she needed to see Amy Shawver's death adequately acknowledged. Kyle's mistake involved the death of someone's mother. Someone's wife. A beloved member of their community. Even if he hadn't caused her to fall into his path, he should have stopped to help. Plain and simple.

At the same time, Kyle's future had changed on a dime, and Caroline could do nothing about it. Helplessness typically inspired her to try fixing things. Once again, she pictured herself on her book jacket in that outlandish headscarf, rebelling against the institution and demanding a better alternative—anything other than waving the white flag.

But all she could do now was follow Kyle's lead.

A sense of peace washed over her as she pondered her little boy's journey into adulthood. Her son had shown remarkable strength, especially in the past few months. The prosecutor's office would recommend one to two years in prison, but the ultimate decision rested with Judge Gallagher. Even if she followed the recommendation, Kyle could handle it. They all could. They'd have to.

When a last-minute cancellation left an opening at the American Cancer Society's conference in Pittsburgh, Caroline cleared the date with Jordan before allowing Toby to reschedule the speaking engagement she'd postponed after the accident. Although Caroline threatened to fire her always-sweet-talking agent, he apologized for his insensitivity and buttered her up until she gave him another chance. She didn't have the time or energy to hire a new agent anyway. She needed to get back in the saddle, and the Pittsburgh conference presented the perfect opportunity. No one at home would skip a beat. It was only a two-hour drive, and Caroline was scheduled to speak for less than an hour at eleven o'clock. She could get there and back while Grace and Kyle were at school.

When Caroline arrived at the convention center, her stomach twisted in knots out of fear she couldn't do this anymore. Toby had warned her about other clients who had stepped away from the speaking circuit for personal reasons and didn't return—either in the same capacity or never at all. That's why he'd insisted she keep going, regardless of the turmoil at home, and how he convinced her to book this gig. After Toby announced he'd be joining her this time, she wondered whether he worried about his paycheck more than anything else. He hadn't accompanied her to an event since her book debuted. His appearance today suggested that he didn't trust her to show up and do a good job.

She spied Toby with a group of women near the coffee station. His bald head looked recently polished, and his chubby cheeks reminded her of a chipmunk with a mouthful of nuts. He held a Styrofoam cup in one hand while the other flitted wildly in the air, and his lips moved so fast Caroline presumed the ladies around him wanted to make a run for it.

Caroline approached the group but stood back, not to interrupt. When Toby noticed her, he placed his cup on the table beside him and moved in for a hug. "Oh, Caroline!" he screeched. "It's so good to see you. You look fabulous!"

The women he'd been standing with stared. "Hi, I'm Caroline Beasley." She held up her palm and wiggled her fingers, making eye contact with each of them. They talked over one another excitedly, introducing themselves and rattling off random questions.

"Please, ladies, please!" Toby interjected. "Let Ms. Beasley catch her breath. She's just arrived from Buffalo and needs to freshen up. Join us in Room 212. She'll have plenty of time to take your questions there."

Toby placed a hand on the small of her back and led her toward a quieter end of the hallway.

"Thank you," she said. "It's so good to see you."

"And it's better to see you, darling! Ready to do your thing?"

Caroline laughed at Toby's dramatic expression. Always the cheerleader. No wonder he was so easy to forgive.

"Is there somewhere private I can go to review my notes?"

"Sure, you've got a few minutes. There's a small

office across from Room 212. Gather your thoughts there, and someone will call you when it's time to begin. I'm going to grab another cup of coffee. Do you need anything?"

"No thanks. I'll see you in a bit." Caroline settled in the office to review a set of index cards stashed in her purse. Even though she'd long ago memorized her presentation, she kept the cards handy in case she needed a crutch. She flipped through them and felt her blood pressure rise. Something didn't seem right. Several of the bulleted points didn't resonate anymore, and she wished she had reread them at home. She glanced at her watch and concluded there wasn't enough time for a rewrite. She'd have to wing it—something she'd never tried, and going off script terrified her. But not as much as sounding like a phony.

Upon hearing her name announced across the hallway, Caroline tucked the cards in her purse before handing it to one of the conference staff for safekeeping. She walked toward the podium, shoulders back and spine straight, trying to appear confident despite dying inside. *Fake it, 'til you make it*, she reminded herself.

The audience members stood and applauded. For a brief instant, she believed their enthusiasm would summon the fire that typically burned fierce in her belly. Her fans could give her the strength she needed to carry on. But as she scanned the sea of attentive expressions, the air in the room thickened. She grew hot and breathless, choking on a lack of oxygen, as her inner voice preached that being fierce wasn't always the answer. Not everyone could fight the way she had. It wasn't always worth it. And sometimes, factors beyond our control ultimately prevail.

Caroline's vision turned cloudy—like someone put a high-powered magnifying glass before her face. When all she could see was a pinprick of light inside a fuzzy gray circle, she clutched the podium to remain steady, afraid she might turn blue and suffocate in front of the crowd. She closed her eyes and focused on the silence. Her fans were watching, waiting, and probably wondering what was happening. Somehow, she managed to squeak out a sound. "Hello, Pittsburgh!" She opened her eyes and blinked.

"Thanks for coming today." Her knees wobbled as she lifted one hand off the podium to adjust the microphone. What the hell was happening? Whatever it was, she didn't like it.

Deep breath in, deep breath out, she chanted to herself.

The applause returned, louder this time. Someone in the back of the room called, "Thank you for coming, Carol!"

Caroline fixed her gaze on Toby sitting in the back row, baring his teeth with apprehension on his face. He knew how much being called "Carol" bothered her. She held a flat hand over her eyes as if searching for the caller. "Who said that? Please stand up."

A woman wearing a soft pink sweatshirt with an embroidered breast cancer ribbon across the chest rose to her feet.

"What's your name?" Caroline said.

"Rachel," the woman said.

Caroline looked at Toby again, nodding and gesturing with her hand that she was okay. No doubt, he feared she'd bite poor Rachel's head off for abbreviating her name. How silly that seemed now, but she enjoyed seeing him sweat.

"Nice to meet you, Rachel. Tell me why you're here today." She anxiously veered off-script. Caroline had never opened with questions from the audience before and worried how it would go.

Rachel gave a lengthy explanation of her cancer diagnosis three years ago and how Caroline had inspired her. After reading *I'll Kill You First*, she fired her oncologist and interviewed two more before deciding on a new one. "Thanks to you, Carol, I had the confidence to advocate for myself. I never would have persisted without your book."

Caroline took a deep breath and held it in, slowly counting down from ten. "I'm flattered, Rachel. But you would have. My book tells of my *personal* approach to battling cancer. It was only intended to represent *one* woman's crusade, not to put forth a call to action or suggest every reader should follow my footsteps."

Caroline doubted whether her explanation accurately depicted her initial book goals, but it rang true today. The anger shared in her book may have sent the wrong message. Experts often know what they're doing, and minimizing their experience and training can be a mistake. Admitting that, even to herself, wasn't easy.

She thought of Valerie and how savvy she'd been representing Kyle. At first, Caroline judged her and doubted her ability. But her early instincts proved wrong. Val had gained Kyle's trust and helped him make an independent decision. Maybe it was time for Caroline to make a change and amend her own narrative—to rebrand herself as a facilitator instead of a warrior.

"Thanks for being so open." Caroline looked around to assess the crowd's reaction, surprised at how engaged they seemed in Rachel's story, especially the medical professionals in the room. Hearing Rachel's frustrations could be incredibly eye-opening to them, and Caroline had long dreamt of sparking that dialogue.

She continued. "Instead of standing here and regurgitating more of what most of you read in my book, let's try something different than what I had planned. Does anyone else feel like sharing?"

Caroline set a cell phone alert to ring in thirty minutes and instructed the audience to break into small groups. "Don't be shy," she said. "Get close with the strangers at your table. Exchange your deepest secrets and biggest fears. You might be surprised at how good it feels to get a few things off your chest to people who've walked in your shoes. We'll reconvene as a large group and report back what we've learned."

"What are you doing?" Toby mouthed the words at Caroline when she eyeballed him from the podium.

Improvising, she thought.

Relinquishing control.

Letting go to see where that could lead.

Lively conversation filled the room as a spirited energy took over. Caroline held her breath, giddy with anticipation and a sense that she was onto something powerful.

****

Ethan sat at the breakfast table eating a bowl of cereal before school, listening to the back-and-forth shuffle of footsteps overhead as Dad got ready for work. Things were far from "back to normal" after he moved home from Cole's. Maybe living with his father again was just more tolerable, knowing it was only temporary. He still planned on going to live with George in January.

Then off to college who-knows-where. But for now, instead of pretending every square inch of their lives didn't remind them of Mom, they paid tribute to her whenever the chance arose. He and Dad competed to see who could water the plants first whenever they looked dry, tried their best to replicate her favorite recipes, and printed some of the thousands of family photos living online to be framed and hung around the house.

Not everything revolved around keeping Mom's memory alive. The football game he and Cole attended with Dad and his uncles was awesome. Buffalo beat Cleveland, 28-7, and advanced to the next playoff game. During halftime, his father whispered in Ethan's ear. "I'm sorry we gave your ticket away this season. It's yours again next year, but only if you want it. And no pressure. Honest."

Ethan appreciated the peace offering, but any future plans depended on where he decided to attend college. Buffalo never played anywhere near the University of Utah.

They also arranged to attend group grief counseling, even though Ethan remained skeptical. He didn't need anyone telling him how to get over his mom's death. That was impossible. It could never happen. He gave in because he could see how important getting professional help meant to his dad. Besides, it was something they could do together until he left for California. Maybe they'd learn how to understand each other better or find a way to talk about Mom's alcoholism and how it might affect him.

So far, he liked the counselor—an older woman named Claudia, who matched his impression of a 1960s hippie. Long, kinky hair dyed bright orange. Loose, flowy outfits. And a raspy voice suggesting she smoked a pack a day. Somehow, her earthiness put him at ease, and she immediately got him to open up more than he had to anyone.

Anyone but Grace.

Ethan sure missed hanging out with Grace. She still wouldn't give him the time of day and avoided eye contact whenever they passed in the hallway. He texted her occasionally, but she never answered. He even went old-school by slipping a handwritten note into her locker, explaining how he hoped his dad would drop the lawsuit. She never acknowledged it.

Word broke that Kyle finally pled guilty to the hit-and-run charge, and Ethan stopped stalking the online court docket. What a relief to stop obsessing over that. Now, they only waited on two things: the sentencing hearing, scheduled for Thanksgiving week; and the tort action. Maybe Grace would speak to him again if Dad changed his mind about the civil case. So far, no luck. Dad wouldn't budge, insisting they proceed on principle.

His father entered the kitchen and placed a firm hand on Ethan's shoulder as he was drinking the milk from his cereal bowl. "What have you got going today?"

"Morning, Dad." A splash of milk dribbled down his chin, and he wiped it on his sleeve. "Nothing much. Same old, same old. What about you?"

"I'm in court most of the day today. Nothing big. A few traffic cases, a dissolution of marriage, and a minor drug charge. I hope to leave there by three o'clock, so you and I can head to the cemetery as soon as school lets out."

"Why are we going there?" Ethan hadn't been to the cemetery since Mom's funeral. He had zero interest in returning this soon.

"I thought I told you, but maybe I forgot. Your mom's headstone is ready. I want to be there when they place it in the ground, and I'd like you to join me."

Dad hadn't mentioned the stone was ready. Ethan would have remembered. But, as soon as the words "in the ground" escaped his mouth, Dad's face turned white as chalk, and his bottom lip quivered. Ethan hated to see his father so sad.

"Of course, I'll come. How long do you think it'll take? I just remembered there's a girls 'soccer game tonight. It's the first one in the playoffs, under the lights at the big stadium. I told Cole and Theo I'd go with them." He left out the part about his most recent text to Grace, telling her he'd be there, cheering for her from the stands.

Dad's expression grew even more grim. Uh oh. Ethan had said the wrong thing. Suddenly, he got hit with a vague recollection of his dad suggesting they make an event out of the installation by going to Mom's favorite Italian restaurant afterward.

Ethan continued. "Sorry. I almost forgot. You were hoping to grab a bite at Fortella's, too, right? Don't worry. I can skip the game—unless you think they could place the headstone on a different day." He crossed his fingers behind his back.

"No. The crew needs to install it before the weather gets bad, and it's supposed to snow by the end of the week. I don't think we should reschedule, but I assume they'd want to finish up before dark. Can we play it by ear? If there's time for dinner, great. If not, we'll go another time."

"Sounds like a plan." But another time wouldn't cut

it. Ethan could tell Dad was struggling. Considering how far they'd come in such a short time, he couldn't let his father down.

Grace hadn't answered his text anyway.

She wouldn't care whether he was at the game or not.

****

Caroline could almost feel the adrenaline pumping through her veins as she finished her Pittsburgh presentation. She hadn't been so moved in a long time and barely had to speak. The audience ran with the discussion while she moderated—asking a few questions and pointing to the people waving their hands, eager to tell their own stories. Thankfully, another workshop began in Room 212 at one o'clock. Otherwise, they'd still be there.

Caroline sped down the highway, hoping to make it to Grace's soccer game on time. The high school team had advanced to the playoffs, and Grace made the starting lineup. Caroline regretted allowing Toby to take her for coffee before she hit the road, but he'd insisted. Now, she was behind schedule. Toby had wanted to discuss additional booking opportunities, which was a waste of time since they all required overnight travel. Once again, he hadn't been listening. She wouldn't consider an out-of-town engagement, at least not through the end of the school year.

But her agent could be relentless. No wonder he was so good at his job.

Before Caroline cleared the Pittsburgh city limits, her phone rang. It was Toby. "One more thing. Why did you decide to change the format today?"

She sighed and stepped on the gas pedal. "I'm not

sure. When I looked at my notecards, my talking points seemed too hostile. I hadn't referred to them in a long time, and something didn't feel right anymore."

"That makes sense. You've been through a lot. You've changed. But your book's message hasn't. You've helped thousands of women stand up against mediocre healthcare and demand answers when they're not getting any."

"I know. But do you think my approach was too aggressive?"

"What do you mean by that?"

"I mean, at times, I encouraged women to defy their healthcare professionals when treatment wasn't working or a diagnosis didn't make sense. I got lucky after choosing to challenge the initial advice I received. That approach doesn't work for everyone. My anger and distrust could easily have backfired. How many women wasted precious time or suffered negative consequences by following my lead?"

Caroline paused for a breath before continuing. "Life isn't always fair. No matter how hard you look for answers, sometimes none exist. And there's not always someone worthy of blame, either. Maybe I should have been more sensitive to that before beating the drum and making it sound like anyone could overcome cancer if they screamed loud enough."

"Who are you? And where has Caroline Beasley gone? I can hardly believe my ears hearing you doubt yourself like this."

"Like you said, I've been through a lot. Trying to protect my son when my heart tells me he did something wrong has been humbling. I'll never look at the world the same way again. There are always two sides to the

Susan Poole

story, with real people on each side of every equation. It's hard watching Kyle struggle to rethink his future while waiting for the court's decision, but I also can't stop thinking about the Shawvers. Ethan lost his mother. Dan buried his wife. Their lives have been turned upside down more than ours have. Even if Kyle gets off with a light sentence, I'll never feel good about it."

"What does that have to do with your book?" Toby sounded annoyed.

"Everything." Caroline gripped the steering wheel and raised her voice. "I used to see the world as black and white. There's good and bad. Right and wrong. There's a solution, or there's not. Now, that sounds so naïve. I'm even embarrassed to be saying it out loud."

"Okay, I don't like what I'm hearing. It sounds like you're abandoning your mantra. You might want to think about that before killing your career."

"I'm not abandoning anything. I'm inspired to take my career to the next level by rebranding myself—maybe writing a new book about the downside of setting your expectations too high."

"Hmm. A new book? I love it! Now you're talking!"

But as soon as the words rolled off her tongue, Caroline's enthusiasm faded. Her plan lacked something. Something substantial. She liked the idea of writing a second book, but it needed more than an accounting of lessons learned like the last one. She wanted to dig deeper and connect more with her readers the way she had with today's attendees. She needed to figure out how she'd tapped into their emotions so easily. She'd done something different. Not them, but her.

Caroline glanced over at the navigation screen and yelped. "Oh shit! I turned the wrong way. I've been

270

driving in the opposite direction the whole time we've been talking. Gotta go, Toby. Time to pay attention and turn myself around."

She hung up and looked at the clock on her dashboard. She was really cutting it close now. Grace would never forgive her if she missed kickoff. Caroline got back on course and merged onto the highway toward Buffalo.

She couldn't disappoint her family today. They needed her, and nothing was more important.

Chapter Eighteen

The wind kicked up, and the temperature dropped below forty degrees, making their trip to the cemetery more miserable than Ethan had imagined. By the time he and Dad arrived for the installation, heavy rain fell alongside icy droplets shooting sideways from the sky.

After covering his head with the hood of his rain jacket, Ethan followed Dad from the car in search of someone from the cemetery staff. He chuckled at how his dad gripped a dorky bucket hat with both hands to keep it from flying away. The rain poured harder and harder, and the sky turned black, with only the dim glow of landscaping lights to lead the way.

As the only living people in the entire cemetery, they walked several yards and dodged gravesites until taking shelter under the maple tree chosen to watch over Mom's final resting place. After adjusting his hat, Dad retrieved his phone from his pocket to reach someone from the office. The call went straight to voicemail.

"Well, this is it, kiddo," Dad said. "You spend your whole life doing the things you love, taking care of others, and trying to be a good person, and this is where you end up—buried beneath a mound of dirt and destined to be surrounded by weeds and covered in bird shit once your loved ones are dead and gone. Seems meaningless, doesn't it?"

Unsure of what to say, Ethan kept quiet. Dad

sounded a bit too philosophical. Ethan didn't feel like debating the afterlife while standing in the cold and rain.

His father continued, "Somehow, I've got to do right by your mother. Avenge her death however I can, starting with the victim impact statement I'm giving at Kyle's sentencing hearing."

Ethan cringed at the sound of Kyle's name. If Dad wanted to talk about the upcoming trial, they could at least wait until they got to the restaurant.

After a long and wet twenty-minute wait, Dad announced, "It doesn't look like anyone's coming. Maybe I put the wrong date in my calendar. Or perhaps something came up on their end, and they called my office instead of my cell. Either way, today's a bust. Let's get the hell out of here and have some pasta. Your mom can wait."

"Yeah, it's not like she's going anywhere, right?"

"Right. And at least we haven't lost our sense of humor, which would make her happy."

Dad *was* right. Seeing the two of them together like this would have pleased Mom. She had wanted nothing more than "her men" to get along, to share in a *normal* father-son relationship, whatever that meant. It bothered her they'd grown apart. She would have hated the idea of Ethan leaving home to live in California—a topic he and Dad chose to ignore most days.

Less than half an hour later, they entered Fortella's, a mom-and-pop place in the center of Shawnee Springs with the best baked ziti outside Sicily (according to his parents). The powerful aroma of fresh garlic welcomed them as they greeted the maître d, a short and slight Italian man with a pencil mustache, wearing tight black pants, a white ruffled button-down, and a bright red dinner jacket. His name was Giuseppe, and he'd attended Mom's service in a similar get-up.

Giuseppe shook Dad's hand and patted Ethan on the head, even though Ethan was at least a foot taller than the tiny man. "Oh, Mr. Dan. Mr. Ethan. So good to see you. I'm still reeling over the loss of Miss Amy. We all loved her, and I pray for you both."

Ethan watched Dad nod in appreciation and followed his lead. Fielding condolences never got any easier. People meant well, but it was still awkward. A shooting pain pierced his heart, and his stomach growled. "I'm starving. Can we sit over there by the window?" Ethan pointed to a booth in the corner of the room, away from the other patrons.

"Sure." Giuseppe led them to their table. Ethan kept his gaze on the ground to avoid acknowledging anyone he might know, hoping Dad would do the same. They typically ran into at least one other person from the neighborhood or the school when they ate at Fortella's.

"What's the rush, son? You still hoping to make it to the soccer game?"

"Uh, no," he said, although unsure. Maybe the rain would delay or postpone the game. He wanted to be there to watch Grace, even if she never acknowledged his presence. But Dad needed him right now. Heck, they needed each other. They'd just spent the afternoon picking at scabs barely covering their wounds. If his dad's insides ached anywhere near as much as his, he shouldn't be left alone just yet.

After devouring the basket of warm homemade bread in the center of the table, they waited for their entrees. When Dad excused himself to use the restroom, Ethan seized the opportunity to check social media. The rain had stopped, and the soccer game was underway, tied at halftime with a score of 1-1. He texted Theo and Cole, asking them to tell Grace why he couldn't be there if they got the chance, even if she didn't give two shits.

Looking closer at his phone screen, he noticed an unopened text message. It was from Grace. How had he missed the notification? It must have come in when they were at the cemetery.

—*Thanks, Ethan. I'm glad you'll be at the game. Meet me in the stands afterward.*—

The absence of emojis after her words disappointed him, but at least she finally responded. She wanted to talk. Nothing could make him happier.

Quickly, he shot her a response even though she wouldn't see it until later.

—*I messed up my schedule. Long story, but I had to go with my dad to the cemetery. Now we're eating dinner. Can we meet somewhere after the game? Sorry, I had to miss it. I hope you played well.*—

Dad returned just as the server arrived at the table with their meals. Ethan set his phone next to his plate, screen-side down, so he wouldn't be tempted to check it during dinner.

"Can I get you two anything else?" the server said.

"We're fine." Dad turned to Ethan and raised his water glass. "Cheers!"

"Cheers!" He clinked his dad's glass with his own, daydreaming about Grace and how much he missed her. "Can I ask you something, Dad?"

"Of course."

"Promise not to get mad, okay?"

His dad swirled a gob of spaghetti around his spoon and stuffed it into his mouth. "I can't promise until I hear the question. But go ahead. Ask me anything."

A rush of courage propelled him forward. "Why are you suing the Beasleys? Can't you drop the lawsuit now that Kyle pled guilty?"

Dad rested his spoon on the table and sat back in his chair. With a serious look, he said, "I've considered that already. I have. I'm just not ready to back off."

"But why? It seems unnecessary. Do we need the money?"

"It's not that. I can't accept that Kyle didn't cause your mom's death. After they dropped the negligent homicide charge, I figured a civil suit would be the next best way to show he was responsible for what happened."

"But he wasn't. Mom died of an aneurysm."

"That doesn't mean her chances of survival wouldn't have been better if Kyle hadn't hit her with his Jeep. That's the part everyone seems to be missing. Okay, the prosecution didn't think they had enough evidence to prove he caused her death after the autopsy report. I get it. As a lawyer, of course, I do. But I'm not ready to drop that theory. Not yet anyway."

After swallowing a big piece of chicken parmesan, Ethan wiped his mouth with a napkin. "I still don't understand. You have no idea how much this upsets me. You never even asked for my opinion."

"I'm sorry. But adults don't always need to discuss grown-up matters with their kids."

The muscles in Ethan's neck tightened as his opportunity presented itself. Here was his chance to revisit the conversation about Mom's alcoholism. "Is that why Mom never talked with me about her past or her AA meetings? Was that a *grown-up matter* I couldn't be trusted with, too?" He suddenly lost interest in dinner and folded his hands on the table.

Dad's eyes glossed over with tears. "It's not that she didn't trust you, but parents aren't obligated to tell their children everything. Sometimes, we just know better, or at least think we do. In that case, we wanted to protect you for as long as possible."

"Protect me from what? The truth? Knowing who Mom really was?"

"Nothing you didn't know about your mom mattered. She loved you more than anything in this world. The woman she was in California didn't exist by the time you were born, and she wanted to put that behind her as much as she could. Alcoholism is a lifelong battle. Look at your brother George. He needed to leave because he feared falling off the wagon."

"I know, he told me. Don't you worry I could turn out the same way?"

His dad paused as if carefully considering his answer. "Your mother and I talked about that a lot. We never settled on how to approach the subject with you, so we muddled through the best we knew how, waiting for the right time as if we had all the time in the world."

Ethan scoffed. "You don't get how that makes me feel. Like you don't see me as mature enough to deal with adult issues. And ya know what's funny? Grace Beasley once encouraged me to ask you about it. Now she won't even look at me because of your damn lawsuit."

There, he'd said it. Now Dad knew the real reason he wanted the lawsuit dropped.

"Grace Beasley? Since when does what she thinks mean that much to you?

"Since none of your business." Ethan unfolded his napkin and placed it over his uneaten chicken parm. The ups and downs of this father-son relationship tortured him. "I'm not hungry anymore. Can we leave?"

"Not yet." Dad scowled and poked at his spaghetti with his fork. "If my silence after the night we drove her home didn't convey my disapproval, let me clarify things now. I shouldn't have to tell you this expressly, but I forbid you from having contact with anyone in that family."

"You can't tell me who I can and can't talk to. Grace is my friend. That's all there is to it."

"What will *your friend* say when she hears you give a victim impact statement during her brother's sentencing hearing?"

"What?" Ethan raised his voice.

"That's right. I'm not the only one expected to say a few words at the sentencing to explain how Kyle's actions have affected our family. And since George can't be here, it's up to you. I wanted to go over that with you tonight."

Ethan questioned the reason his brother gave when George called to say he wouldn't be making the trip. Something about a work conflict. It sounded more like an excuse, but Ethan figured George was struggling and couldn't handle coming back to Shawnee Springs right now. "Oh, no. I'm not doing that," Ethan snapped. "The Beasley family may still be intact, but they've suffered enough from this experience, too. What happened was an accident. A tragic one. Trying to ruin their lives won't bring Mom back, and if you ask me—which you rarely do—kicking them while they're down will only make things worse for everyone."

Dad gently placed his fork on his plate and slid his chair away from the table. "Let's go. I'm ready now."

But before Dad got to his feet, Ethan detected a slight shift in his demeanor. He didn't appear as angry or irritated as Ethan expected. His expression contained a hint of enlightenment, maybe even acceptance.

They silently filed out of the restaurant, and Ethan hoped something he'd said made sense to his dad. Maybe he'd earned some respect over dinner tonight so the pendulum could swing again. Things could look different moving forward—if only Dad could stop being stubborn and admit he was wrong.

****

Caroline's brain functioned like a minefield. With each fleeting thought, another explosive device detonated. Her creative juices flowed, and she couldn't wait to get home and start drafting her new book, rebranding her message, and rethinking her life.

But first things first. There was a soccer game to watch. Even after traveling in the wrong direction for several miles, she could still make it before the end of the game. Distracted by the nervous energy burning inside her, she made a few phone calls. Jordan first, then Kyle. Neither answered, and it was too late to call Grace. When she left the house this morning, her daughter seemed so anxious. Starting on the varsity squad as a freshman was a huge accomplishment, but the added pressure of making it to the playoffs might have been too much for her to handle. Had Caroline offered enough support and encouragement? Self-doubt snuck up on her like a shadow.

When Caroline was a teenager, she often wished for a mother more like the other women in the neighborhood—the ones who still helped with homework and insisted on eating dinner together every night. But that wasn't possible. Her mom returned to nursing after Dad died, working the night shift so she wasn't around much in the evenings. Caroline became very self-sufficient. She had no choice.

Caroline never wanted her kids to grow up the same way she had. She'd found comfort in Jordan always being around, clearing a path for her to step away to pursue a career. But could the presence of one parent truly replace the desire for the other? She and Jordan played different roles in their kids 'lives, fulfilling separate needs. They were fortunate the choice never had to be all or nothing. She should have realized that earlier. She should have known better, learned from her own childhood experiences, and paid closer attention to Grace during these critical years.

At least it wasn't too late. Lately, Caroline had been more tuned in, but sometimes, she still focused too much on Kyle at the expense of the rest of her family. From that point forward, she'd spread the wealth and balance her attention across everyone who loved her. Caroline stepped on the gas and dialed Valerie next.

"Valerie Saks." Her attorney answered on the first ring with her usual pleasant tone.

"Hi, Val. It's Caroline Beasley. Just checking to see if you've heard anything about Kyle's sentencing hearing."

"Hi, Caroline. I was going to call you this afternoon. Yes, it's scheduled for the Monday before Thanksgiving. It'll be nice to get some closure before the holiday."

"Depending on what closure looks like." Caroline shook the doom and gloom from her thoughts. "Is there anything we can do to prepare?"

"Yes. Kyle should be working on his allocution. I'll need to review his statement as far in advance as possible. I know he's remorseful, and I'm sure you'll coach him on what to say, but I can offer an objective eye to ensure he doesn't say something that might trip him up."

"Of course. We'll get right on that. Anything else?"

"Prepare him for the victim impact statements, too. Hearing Dan and Ethan talk about losing Amy won't be easy for any of you, but I'm particularly concerned about Kyle. Any guilt he feels now could worsen after listening to the Shawvers speak in court. I don't want him to be completely blindsided."

Caroline swallowed hard, trying to dislodge the bowling ball in her throat. "Thanks for the advice. I'll talk with him for sure."

"How are *you* doing, Caroline? Are you holding up okay through all this?"

Wow. When was the last time anyone had asked about *her* mental state? Val had a knack for always knowing the right thing to say, and her empathy did not go unnoticed.

"I'm fine," Caroline croaked.

"You don't sound fine."

A phantom sensation rested on Caroline's knee as if Val sat beside her in the car offering comfort.

Val continued, "When all this is behind us, let's you and I get together for coffee or a smoothie after another yoga class."

"I'd like that. A lot."

"I hate to go, but my next client is here."

The sound of Val's call breaking from the Bluetooth

echoed inside Caroline's car. She sure got lucky when Jim Doughman recommended her attorney-turned-potential-friend for Kyle's case. Valerie Saks was one-of-a-kind, and Caroline was grateful for their synergy.

She drove farther north on the highway, feeling calmer after speaking with Val. Caroline's post-workshop enthusiasm from earlier in the day hadn't disappeared, but the rapid-fire ideas became more manageable and less frantic. A rough mental outline for her next book took shape.

Before long, she was cruising down the road, listening to music, feeling energized and alive. Out of the blue, her car sputtered. The steering wheel stiffened and grew difficult to control. She glanced at the fuel gauge. Oh shit! She hadn't checked the gas since leaving Buffalo that morning, and it was already below empty. A power surge caused her to jerk in her seat. Moments ago, she passed a sign reading, "Next Rest Area 52 Miles." Oh, God. Don't panic.

Caroline slowly veered to the right shoulder and turned off the car. When she tried the automatic start button, it didn't make a sound. Her car was dead. Thank goodness she reached the side of the road in time.

Calmly, she called Roadside Assistance. They could be there soon. She tried Jordan and Kyle again to tell them she'd be late, but they still didn't answer, so she sent texts instead. The sun was starting to set, and it began to rain. She leaned her seat back and listened to the drops pummeling her windshield.

As she waited, the raindrops grew louder and the sky darker. Caroline eventually understood that her chances of getting home before the end of the game had vanished.

Then, something inside her snapped like a dam

breaking, releasing the full force of raging floodwaters. She fought against the powerful current until it turned pointless. The weight of emotion was too strong. Caroline cried openly, sobbing so hard her ears rang. She let it all out alone in her car with the windows closed. Years of fear and anxiety flushed through her body, washing away what remained of the guarded version of herself, leaving her open and vulnerable yet surprisingly unafraid.

By the time a Roadside Assistance technician arrived with a gas can, Caroline felt depleted. Her tears had dried, and she was left with an inexplicable void. After he filled her tank, she thanked him for the rescue and drove the rest of the way home. Halfway there, an added thought about overcoming tough times hit her from nowhere. All these years, she'd been directing her attention in the wrong spot—outward, not inward. Healing depended on allowing herself to truly feel the emptiness as she leaned into her loved ones for help.

"It takes a village," she said aloud. "Not just for the kids, but for the rest of us, too."

****

Dad went directly to bed as soon as they got home. Ethan wasn't tired, but he didn't feel like going anywhere. The soccer game was over, and according to Instagram and Snapchat, most of his friends were at a victory party across town. Since no one had texted him back, he figured he'd stay radio silent and spend his evening alone.

He turned on the television in search of something new to stream, but he'd seen almost everything, so he turned it off. Then he signed into his gaming console, but no one he knew was online, and he didn't feel like playing with a virtual stranger tonight. Now what?

His new counselor suggested that he start journaling. Whenever he felt like talking to his mom, he should write down what he wanted to say in the cloth-covered book Claudia gave him during their first session. Why not? He had nothing to lose. He searched the kitchen drawers for a pen and located the journal, opening it to the first page. Lines and lines of blankness begged for his input, but he couldn't think of one word to get started. Not one. Without his mom's presence and probing questions, Ethan's mind was impenetrably numb, stuck in place like he was standing in cement.

Grace. He could only think about Grace, and nothing was new there. He ruined their relationship by telling her about Dad's lawsuit. His willingness to forgive what Kyle had done—or not done—didn't matter. Grace made herself clear, drew a line in the sand, and refused to cross over it. But what about her last text? She had invited him to meet her after the game. Maybe she was ready to forgive him for something he had nothing to do with anyway.

He grabbed his phone and stared at her text again, trying to read between the lines.

—I'm glad you'll be at the game. Meet me in the stands afterward.—

The response he'd sent from the restaurant read "Delivered" but wasn't marked "Read." Damnit. He should have been there. She might not have seen his message. The stadium got sketchy cell service. Maybe she'd waited for him, and now she was mad.

Hopefully, Theo or Cole remembered to tell her why he couldn't make it. She'd have to understand. She wasn't that unreasonable, was she?

Quickly, he drafted another text, his version of a Hail Mary.

—Grace. I'm sorry. I don't think my last message went through. I had to spend time with my dad tonight. Long story. I can still meet up if you're out. If not, are you free another time this weekend? I'm wide open. Would love to hear what you wanted to tell me. Text me. And congrats on your big win!—

He read the message three times before pressing the "Send" button, then waited to see whether three dots would appear, hoping she was already crafting an answer. But instead of the dots, a crescent moon lit up next to her name. Her phone was set to "Do Not Disturb." Had she done that for his benefit? His gut feeling that she was still angry returned. Yup. He'd blown it for sure.

He looked down at the journal again. Its emptiness still called him. He swiftly thumbed through the pages like a cartoon flip book and wondered how long it would take to fill in the blanks. Months, if not years, especially at the rate he was going. If this is what writer's block felt like, he never wanted to be an author. Sorry, Mom. You'll have to settle for reading my mind.

A loud banging outside startled him. The sounds of Theo and Cole wrestling and laughing on his front porch interrupted his inner monologue. Making his way to the front door, Ethan pressed his face against the sidelight window and placed a finger to his lips. "Shh. My dad's sleeping."

Cole and Theo kept laughing and barged inside once Ethan cracked the door.

"Where've you been, asshole?" Cole said. "We waited for you at the game?"

"I told you. I had to go to the cemetery with my dad. Did you give Grace my message?"

"Grace, Grace, Grace! Is she the only one you care about?" Theo mocked.

"No. I just wanted her to know why I wouldn't be at the game. Did either of you tell her?"

Theo and Cole exchanged drunken glances and laughed even louder.

"I'll take that as a *no*," Ethan said, annoyed.

"So, what, man? I heard she doesn't want anything to do with you anyway. Get over it," Cole said.

"Screw you," Ethan said. "You two can get out of here now."

"Oh, relax," Theo said. "Don't listen to Cole. He's wasted. We half-expected to see Grace over here tonight with you."

"With me? Why would you think that?"

"Everyone was at the after-party. It was awesome. She's the only girl from the team that didn't show up. Her teammates were worried."

Ethan didn't like the sound of that. He remembered the strange vibe he'd sensed when Grace rushed away from him at the waterfall, and all the times she'd been moody ever since. Now, he was worried, too.

****

Caroline arrived home after ten o'clock, surprised at the absence of any other cars in the driveway. Where was everybody? She had briefly talked with Jordan while he was still at the stadium. The girls won the game, and he and Kyle were waiting to congratulate Grace before going out for chicken wings. The restaurant must have been crowded. They'd probably be back soon.

She opened the back door and bent down at her

knees, waiting in the dark for Tanner to greet her. "Come here, boy," she said. He plodded toward her without barking, his nails clicking on the hardwood floor. All he wanted was a short pat on the head before returning to his dog bed in the corner of the family room. It was past his bedtime.

Caroline walked through the kitchen and flicked on the family room lights, delighted at how immaculate the house looked. The magazines were stacked together on the coffee table. The blankets were folded neatly and placed on the end of the couch. Both remote controls were lined up next to the cable box where they belonged. It was nice to be home. She'd only left this morning, but it felt like she'd been gone for a week.

She slowly climbed the stairs toward the second floor and heard water dripping inside the kids 'bathroom. Grace's soccer uniform hung inside-out from the doorknob, sopping wet and creating a puddle on the floor. She must have gotten caught in a downpour. How often had she told her daughter to hang wet clothes in the shower if she was too lazy to take them downstairs to the laundry room?

Uninterested in going back downstairs either, Caroline grabbed the uniform and wrung it out in the sink before hanging it over the shower head. She peeked inside Grace's room on her way down the hall. She'd tried calling her daughter after she hung up with Jordan but only got her voicemail. She assumed Grace had gone out with the team to celebrate and didn't expect to find her home. But she'd stopped home at some point, so maybe she was still there. Nope. Her bed was made, and her room was empty, although she'd obviously rummaged through her dresser drawers. They were wide open, with clothes busting out from the insides. Whoever straightened the family room should have spent some time tidying the upstairs.

The sound of the garage door opening stopped her from getting too aggravated, and Caroline walked to the top of the stairwell to wait and see who was home.

"Hi, honey!" Jordan called. "Are you in bed already?"

"No, but I was headed there." She walked downstairs to greet him, kissing him on the cheek and breathing in the musty smell of aftershave mixed with damp clothing. "Did you get caught in the rain, too?"

"Only at the start of the game. The weather cleared up quickly, and you should've seen our girl. She was on fire!" Jordan's smile stretched the entire width of his face.

"I'm so bummed I missed it. Can you believe I ran out of gas?"

Jordan gave her a sly grin. "Of course, I can. You're always driving near empty, flirting with disaster, or living on the edge—whatever you want to call it. Maybe that'll teach you a lesson."

"Yes, Dad," she said sarcastically. Then she smiled and playfully whacked him on the shoulder. "How were the wings? And where's Kyle?"

"Wings were awesome. We saved some for you." He handed her a Styrofoam container with hot sauce smeared across the lid. "And Kyle wanted to stop at a party for a bit."

"Whose party?" She peeked inside the container, then walked to the kitchen to wipe off the lid and put it in the refrigerator for tomorrow, rearranging the shelves to make room for the wings.

"A girl from the soccer team. Grace was heading there, too, but she promised not to be late. She looked exhausted."

"She stopped home to change," Caroline said with her head deep inside the fridge. "I'm surprised she didn't just hop into bed."

"She's a teenager, Caroline, who just played in the biggest game of her life. Did you think she'd miss the victory party?"

Caroline shut the refrigerator door and leaned back against it. "No. Not really. I feel so terrible I wasn't there. Do you think she'll forgive me?"

"Maybe not initially. You know how Grace likes to lay the guilt trip on you. But once you sit her down and explain what happened, she'll come around. Don't beat yourself up. There's nothing you can do about it now anyway."

As Caroline used her shoulders to shove away from the refrigerator, a bright yellow sticky note fluttered to the floor. She must have knocked it loose from the front of the fridge. "What's this?" She bent down to pick up the note and read what it said.

Her knees buckled, and she grabbed the countertop to prevent herself from collapsing. "Jordan." She could barely utter his name. "Come see this."

She handed him the paper. No need to look at it any longer to visualize the message scribbled in Grace's handwriting.

"We won, Mom. You shoulda been there. Oh, well. All you care about is people with cancer. Would you even miss me if I were gone?"

Chapter Nineteen

Shooing his drunk friends out of the house wasn't
easy. Cole and Theo refused to leave until Ethan lost his
temper, and then he slammed the door behind them
without thinking.

"What's going on down there?" his dad called
moments later.

"Nothing. Go back to sleep," Ethan hollered.

But within minutes, Dad stood scowling at the
bottom of the stairs wearing the flannel pajama pants
Mom had given him last Christmas. "Everything okay?"

"Yeah. Cole and Theo just stopped by. Sorry about
the noise."

Dad stepped away into the kitchen, dragging the
bottoms of his hard-soled slippers across the floor. When
the doorbell rang, Ethan assumed his friends were back.
"I'll get it."

But as soon as he opened the door, Ethan gasped.
"Kyle! What are you doing here?" He stood frozen in the
doorway with his mouth open, staring at Kyle and
bracing himself for another confrontation.

But Kyle slumped his shoulders and avoided eye
contact. He looked uncomfortable, not threatening.
Splotches of faded green and yellow underlined his eyes,
but his nose appeared normal, fully healed. Gone were
his usual air of confidence and Hollywood swagger.
What was he doing here, and at this time of night?

"Sorry to bother you." Kyle's mouth barely moved as he spoke. His lips remained pressed together without revealing the tiniest glimpse of his perfect teeth. His voice shook as he continued. "Have you seen my sister tonight?"

The mere mention of Grace sent Ethan's heart racing. "No. Why?"

"She's missing," Kyle said. "She came home after the game but took off again, and no one knows where. I thought she might be here."

"I haven't seen her all night, never even made it to the game. My dad and I ate dinner at Fortella's and then—" He stopped himself from rambling when he heard Dad rummaging around in the kitchen pantry, probably searching for a late-night snack.

"Who's here now, Ethan?" Dad entered the front hallway, holding an open box of sugary cereal. Before he laid eyes on Kyle, he dug inside the box. Upon spotting their unlikely visitor, he dropped a few mini marshmallows to the floor. "What's this?" He stepped forward aggressively. "You're the last person I'd expect to see at my front door. Not just now but ever. What the hell are you doing here?"

Kyle adjusted his posture and stood straight as a pin. "Good evening, Mr. Shawver. I'm sorry to bother you. I wouldn't have stopped over, but it's an emergency. My sister Grace is missing, and we wondered whether she came here."

Kyle had obviously rehearsed what he wanted to say, and Ethan enjoyed watching him squirm in front of Dad.

"Your sister isn't welcome here. Neither are you. My son knows that, so I'm not sure why he opened the door for you. Time for you to leave, Mr. Beasley." Dad turned to Ethan. "You best be heading up to bed now, too."

But Ethan didn't budge.

Turning his back toward his dad, he looked at Kyle and said, "Give me a minute to grab a coat. I might know where Grace has gone, but I should come with you."

Ethan kept one step behind Kyle, following him out the front door, onto the porch, and down the steps. When they reached the driveway, Kyle turned and said, "I'll drive. Hop in!"

Kyle's good-as-new Jeep had been left running. The motor hummed, and the headlights illuminated the back end of Mom's minivan as if shining a spotlight on the damage he and his vehicle had caused.

"No thanks. I'll drive myself." Ethan got in the minivan, relieved to find the keys inside. If he'd had to return to the house to retrieve them, he might have changed his mind about joining the search—even to find Grace. He rolled down the window and shouted to Kyle. "Wait! You don't know where we're going."

Kyle, still standing outside the Jeep looking dumbfounded, said, "No shit."

"Go to the soccer field behind the elementary school. The one next to the waterfall."

"I know the one," Kyle snapped. "You think she's there?"

"Just a hunch," Ethan said before turning the key in his ignition and waiting for Kyle to drive away.

As they traveled through town, Ethan glared at the back of Kyle's head in the Jeep in front of him. His neck sat high above the headrest, and his shoulders spanned wide across the driver's seat. Ethan waited for Kyle to remove his gaze from the road, to turn his head to the side, or to glance down at his phone, anything to suggest he was distracted. But nope. Nothing. He never even crossed over the speed limit. By the time they parked in the school lot, the muscles in Ethan's neck ached after straining so hard to keep an eye on Kyle. Had Kyle felt him watching? Judging? Is that why he'd been so careful?

After looping around the parking lot a few times, Kyle got out of his Jeep, and Ethan followed. The brisk night air greeted them. While the lot was dimly lit, the overhead lights at the soccer field were turned off. Ethan stood beside Kyle, staring into the blackness.

"Do you think she could be out there on the field?" Kyle said.

"Could be," said Ethan. "She comes here to practice on her own a lot."

Kyle eyed him suspiciously as if asking, "How the hell do you know?" Then he called out. "Grace! Grace! Are you out there?"

"Shh," Ethan said. "If she doesn't want anyone to find her, you might spook her and cause her to run."

"You got a better idea?" Kyle snapped again. "Seeing you seem to know my sister better than I do."

"As a matter of fact, I do. Have an idea, I mean. Not know your sister better," he stuttered. "Follow me." Ethan walked swiftly, shining his cell phone flashlight on the ground in front of them and scanning the soccer field until he was satisfied she wasn't there. Then he turned his attention to locating the narrow dirt path Grace showed him earlier in the month. The sound of rushing water from the waterfall grew louder as they got closer, and he ducked to avoid low-hanging branches.

"Ouch!" Kyle yelled from behind.

"Watch your step." Ethan snickered.

His heart sank when they neared the small clearing under the willow tree—no sign of Grace. The empty spot where they had watched the water rush over the cliff together haunted him. He should have been more honest with her that afternoon. After she rejected his kiss, he'd been reluctant to tell her his true feelings, how he'd never felt this way about a girl before, and how he was falling for her—big time. Their situation was so complicated. And unfair. Why did it have to be her brother who hit his mom? Of all the kids at school, why Kyle?

Why anyone at all?

Ethan walked to the chain-link fence, looped his fingers over the railing, and stared across the water. Darkness prevented him from seeing too far, but the crash of the falls conjured a clear sensation in his mind—instability, chaos, and volatility— all words describing his life after Mom died. The only calming force he'd had since then was Grace, and even that hadn't lasted very long. He turned to see Kyle's profile leaning against the fence, too. His cell phone light shined on his face as he appeared to be reading a text. He looked worried, petrified, in fact. There was something Kyle wasn't telling him.

"She's not here," Ethan said. "I really thought she would be. What next?"

Kyle's phone light turned off. "I dunno. But my mom's a wreck. She seems to think Grace might hurt herself. She left a note, but my mom won't tell me what it says."

"Grace? No way!" Ethan knew how upset she'd been about everything happening with her family and how she resented her mom for being so unavailable. But it never occurred to him she'd consider harming herself. Despite Kyle's drama, Grace had so much going for her, and she'd never once even hinted at the idea. Ethan had to believe she would have confided in him if doing something so drastic had crossed her mind.

He glanced back into the darkness, searching for an answer. Over the rumble of the waterfall, he thought he heard a voice. Grace's voice. He brushed it off as his imagination, but then he heard it again. "Ethan, is that you?"

Ethan rubbed his eyes, trying to see farther down the fence. A slight shadow faded into focus, and he recognized Grace's silhouette, her long hair blowing in the wind. She stood on the opposite side of the chain-link fence, close to the cliff's edge. Her arms stretched from her sides, making the shape of a *T*. Her head rolled sideways, and she called after him again. "Ethan. You came."

Slowly, Ethan scaled the fence. Holding his breath, he inched toward her without peering over the edge until she was close enough to touch. "Of course, I came, Grace. I care about you. More than you know."

Her hands flew to cross over her chest. She turned around, moving away from the waterfall and into his arms. He inhaled the mist rising above the falls as she melted into his embrace. And for one long and intimate moment, they were the only two people in Shawnee Springs.

****

Caroline had been pacing the family room when Kyle called and told her they'd found Grace. She collapsed into Jordan's arms and couldn't stop her body from trembling. "She's safe," she whispered into the warmth of his chest. "Thank God."

She turned her cheek, resting it against the softness of her husband's shirt and listening to his heartbeat. She flinched when he touched her nose and tipped her face toward his. The stubble covering his chin scraped against her skin like sandpaper. He kissed her gently, letting his mouth linger before parting her lips with his tongue.

Something inside her awakened a feeling that had been dormant far too long. If she hadn't been so eager to talk to Grace, she would have begged him to make love to her right there on the family room floor. For now, she'd settle for a passionate kiss that made her toes curl. It reminded her of how much she loved her husband and how much they'd let slip away.

Reluctantly, she broke free, and Jordan didn't resist. The tenderness in his eyes told her everything was all right. They were going to be okay. "Let's go get our girl," he said softly.

Holding hands, they drove to the school parking lot, where Kyle waited in his Jeep.

"Where is she?" Jordan said after both he and Kyle rolled down their windows. A cold gust of air blew inside the car, and Caroline joined the sides of her collar together to keep warm.

"She's by the waterfall. It's a bit of a walk, but I can show you the way."

"You left her alone?" Caroline leaned across Jordan and stuck her face close to the open window to scowl out at Kyle.

"Relax, Mom. She's not alone."

"What?" Jordan said in an alarming tone. "Who else is out there?"

Suddenly, Caroline noticed the empty minivan parked next to Kyle's Jeep. It looked familiar. She had a good idea who was with Grace.

Kyle said, "Ethan Shawver. But don't worry. She's fine. She called out and asked me to give them some privacy."

"Thank, God you heard her voice. But what's she doing with him?" Jordan turned toward Caroline. "I thought we put an end to that."

"Me too. Let's not jump to conclusions. The important thing is we found her." Caroline paused, twisted around, and searched the backseat for the waterproof blanket they kept handy for sporting events. Plucking it from the floor, she exited the car and wrapped the blanket around herself. "But I think they've had all the private time they need. You two wait here while I go get her."

"Wait, Caroline!" Jordan called after her. "How will you know where she is?"

"I know exactly where she is. There's this spot overlooking the waterfall where I used to go when I was first diagnosed with cancer. I'd take Grace with me sometimes to kick soccer balls on the field while I cleared my head."

She marched through the parking lot to the chain-link fence, using the top railing as a guide until she found the narrow path leading to the top of the waterfall. The rush of the water soothed her. She wondered how much longer the river would flow until winter forced its movement to a standstill, dislodging the memory of selling hot chocolate with Amy Shawver from the back of her brain. A burst of sadness disrupted Caroline's journey until the silhouette of two people sitting near the cliff came into view. Ethan's right arm draped across Grace's shoulders, and her head was tucked in the crook of his neck. Caroline squinted to get a closer look and grew dizzy once she realized they were on the opposite side of the fence. She approached quietly, not wanting to startle them.

What if they fell forward and into the falls? She could hear murmuring but couldn't decipher what they were saying over the rolling water. She wrapped the blanket tighter around her body and waited. In adjusting her feet to lean on the fence, she must have made a noise that echoed in their direction. Grace's head turned toward her first, then Ethan's.

"Mom? Is that you?"

"Hi, honey."

"How long have you been standing there?" Grace sounded angry.

"Not long. I didn't want to interrupt, but we were all worried. Are you okay?"

"I'm fine."

She stared at her daughter's face and squinted again to focus in the dark. Grace's gaze cut through her like a knife, and Caroline suddenly felt like an intruder—invasive and unwanted.

Ethan's voice broke through the awkwardness. "Mrs. Beasley, I'm sorry we didn't call you. Kyle was supposed to tell you that Grace was okay."

"He did. I just needed to see for myself." Caroline wanted to insist Grace leave with her, but she feared scaring her away, even over the edge.

Rising from the ground, Ethan pulled Grace with him. They whispered to one another until Ethan helped her over the fence, then hopped to the other side and kissed her on the cheek. "I better get going," he said. "My dad's probably furious I left the house after he told me to go to bed. I'll see ya around, Grace. Goodbye, Mrs. Beasley."

Grace stood shivering, thankfully back on the right side of the fence. Caroline stepped toward her, expecting her daughter to back away. When she didn't, Caroline extended her arms and invited her inside the blanket. They inched toward one another at the same pace, slowly, cautiously, as if neither wanted to take the final stride toward a full embrace.

But once Grace's tiny shoulders disappeared into the waterproof blanket, Caroline squeezed her tight, forcing a giant breath from her daughter's mouth. Grace's body shook like it was the middle of winter.

Tears streamed from Caroline's eyes, landing in Grace's hair. She inhaled the sweet smell of her daughter's shampoo. Not long ago, she had regularly breathed in that scent while bathing Grace as a child and wrapping her tiny body in a hooded towel. Caroline always had a way of making her daughter smile back then. Reassurance was as easy as telling a story or singing a song. But her tongue tied in knots as she held Grace at the top of the waterfall, trying desperately to determine what her daughter needed most from her mother.

"I love you, Grace. I'm sorry I didn't make it to your game."

Grace's body stiffened inside Caroline's hold, but only for a millisecond before softening again. "I'm sorry too," she whispered. "I didn't mean to scare you. You've been through enough."

"We've all been through enough. That doesn't mean

your feelings aren't important. If I made you feel—"

"Irrelevant?" Graced filled in the blank perfectly.

"Yes, if I made you feel irrelevant, I'm sorry. I worry about you just as much as your brother."

"It doesn't seem that way."

"I know. I need to get better at expressing my feelings. I tend to bottle things up inside, and I know that's unhealthy."

"I do that too," said Grace.

"You must have learned that from me—the master." Caroline grinned and drew Grace closer.

"Sometimes it's easier than letting things out," Grace said. "Like when something hurts so bad you don't want to give it any power for fear of splitting wide open."

Caroline's eyes widened in surprise. "That's a good analogy. Where'd you hear that?"

Without hesitation, Grace said, "Ethan. He knows a lot about pain."

Of course, he does. The agony of losing a parent at a young age is unbearable. She remembered the hurt well. The Shawvers were living through a terrible ordeal, just trying to survive. If Ethan had stuck around, Caroline would have invited him inside their blanket, too.

"Is that why you never talked about your cancer?" Grace continued.

Caroline's heart fluttered, and the hairs on the back of her neck prickled. "What do you mean?"

"I don't remember you ever saying you were afraid when you were sick," she said. "And later, you were more comfortable sharing your story with the world than with us at home. Did you think you were protecting us from the pain? That's what Ethan thinks."

"That Ethan—he sure sounds like a wise one. Maybe he's right, at least partially. I was probably protecting myself in a way, too—like if I gave my feelings any power, they could split me wide open."

The wind kicked up, and the air temperature dropped even further. Caroline kissed Grace gently on the forehead. "Let's go home and get out of the cold."

Although she hadn't felt this warm in years.

****

When Ethan arrived home, he found Dad sitting in the dark. The shadow of his body loomed large over the family room as he stretched out in the recliner.

"You didn't have to wait up." Ethan walked toward the stairs to go to bed.

"Did you find her?" Compassion leaked through his otherwise flat tone of voice.

Ethan paused, exhausted and craving sleep but wanting to unload at the same time. Leaving Grace at the edge of the waterfall wasn't easy. Her relationship with her mom was so volatile, and he wondered how far she would go to grab her attention.

Grace told him about the note she'd left on her fridge. Despite everything else going on inside their family, she needed help. She needed her mom. More than her physical presence, she needed her full attention. It wasn't Ethan's place to spell things out for anyone, but if Mrs. Beasley didn't get the message after tonight, perhaps she never would.

Ethan sat down on the couch across from Dad. "We did. She's safe."

"Was there ever any doubt?" His dad sounded surprised.

Tears welled in Ethan's eyes, and he nodded. Dad

turned on the lamp sitting on the nearby end table. His eyes were red and swollen. He'd obviously been crying, too. Folding his hands in his lap, Dad said, "I'm not sure how you got mixed up with that girl, but if I had to guess, it's because you're your mother's son."

"Meaning?"

"You're drawn to people who are hurting, and you'd try anything to make things better."

Ethan scratched his chin. "You're only half right," he said, quickly remembering when Mom would take him to visit the animal pound. She'd always wanted a dog and typically narrowed in on the ones that appeared sickly and unloved, most likely to be put down first. More than once, they'd come close to adopting a mutt, but they knew Dad wasn't crazy about the idea.

"What's the other half?" Dad said.

"Grace and I were drawn to each other. She's been there for me as much as I've been there for her. Somehow, she understands me."

"But of all the girls in school to pick as your girlfriend, why Grace?"

Ethan's spine straightened. "She's not my girlfriend. Not yet."

"Details. I'll ask again. Why her? Couldn't you see how that would hurt me? Or was that your objective?"

Ethan hadn't seriously considered that before. He never intentionally set out to hurt his father. "No," he stammered. "But this isn't about you."

Dad pressed the power button on the recliner and lowered his legs until his feet rested on the floor. "I expected you to understand how devastating the loss of your mother is for me and how any reminder of that terrible afternoon would keep me from healing."

Unexpected guilt washed over Ethan. He could concede to being somewhat insensitive but remained ambivalent about whether to back down about Grace. "I don't know what to say except that *I'm sorry*—again."

"Thank you." The pain on his dad's face softened. "Can I count on you to keep your distance from the Beasleys from now on? If it matters after the sentencing hearing anyway. She might want nothing to do with you after that."

The subtle warning didn't go unnoticed, but there was no way Dad could comprehend what he and Grace shared. Ethan couldn't make any promises after what they'd gone through together, not just over the last couple of months but at the waterfall tonight. They needed each other. Probably not forever, or even after he moved to California or graduated from high school. But for now, for the near future, he couldn't let go. He wouldn't.

"What if we compromised? I'll keep her away from the house and never mention her name. But you can't keep me from seeing Grace. Please don't ask me to do that. Please."

Dad gave him an odd look, suggesting disgust or disappointment. Either way, his dad didn't appear pleased, and no amount of begging would make a difference. "How will she feel about the statement you're expected to make next week in court? Will she still *understand* you after you tell the judge how her brother ruined your life?"

Ethan sucked in his breath. After a long, slow exhale, he said. "I told you before, I'm not making a statement at the hearing. I don't hear you badgering George to hop on a plane and come here to make one.

303

I'm not doing it either. Period. End of story." His heart pounded, but he didn't take his gaze off Dad while waiting for a response.

His dad rose from the recliner and walked toward the stairwell. Gripping the banister until his knuckles turned white, he leaned over the railing before heading upstairs. "You may not care what I think, but your mother would have been disappointed in your defying me. Do what you like. I'm going to bed."

Ethan wanted to believe he and his father had made progress since Mom died, but at that moment, he felt completely at odds, giving him one more reason to stand behind Grace. He couldn't betray the one and only person who truly knew him. And no matter what was about to happen to Kyle, Ethan refused to play a part.

Unfortunately, Dad didn't share the same sentiment. Whatever Dad was preparing to say at the sentencing hearing, Ethan dreaded it. The Beasley family had been through a lot, too, and Ethan worried whether they could handle much more. He wished Dad would at least go easy on them, but Ethan couldn't shake his doubts.

Chapter Twenty

Filing into the courtroom was anticlimactic. Thankfully, the public attention had died down. Caroline only spotted one reporter on the courthouse steps, and so far, today's proceeding had yet to attract any protestors. As usual, most people had moved on to the next tragedy.

She sat next to Jordan in the back of the room, needing to stay close to the door in case she had to exit abruptly. She was nervous and jittery as if she'd chugged an entire pot of black coffee, and her knees shook uncontrollably despite trying to settle them with her palms.

She glared at Kyle and Valerie, who sat calmly at the defense table facing forward. Thank goodness, her son had agreed to a fresh military haircut for the sentencing. He appeared more handsome than ever, clean-cut, and All-American looking. She hoped the judge would see putting a proper young man like Kyle behind bars as unnecessary, knowing it shouldn't always work that way.

Valerie had changed her hair, too, coloring it platinum blonde and cutting it short. The new look softened her face and took years off her appearance. Earlier that week, Val had called with good news. She'd been participating in a clinical trial, and so far, so good. She was back in remission and feeling better than she had in long time. "Thanks for nudging me to get a second opinion," she'd said to Caroline over the phone. "If I hadn't met this new doctor, I may not have been picked for the trial. And if I hadn't represented Kyle, I may not have reconnected with you and gathered your advice. If you believe in fate, we're the perfect example."

"Yes, we are." An intense feeling of mutual respect accompanied Caroline's response. If Jim hadn't referred Valerie, and Valerie hadn't represented Kyle, this case could have turned out far worse. She appreciated how passionately Valerie represented their son, and how delicately she got through to Kyle on a personal level. No matter what happened today, she'd never doubt Valerie's abilities again and looked forward to getting to know her better after the trial.

Dwight Wingassett stood tall on the other side of the aisle, pacing behind the prosecution table. His bright red hair seemed like the only vivid color in the room, as the remainder of their surroundings matched Caroline's mood—dark and gloomy with an air of dread.

As soon as Judge Gallagher shuffled through the door in the front of the courtroom, everyone sprang to their feet. With the help of the bailiff, the judge settled in her chair. "Please be seated." She fidgeted with the zipper of her black robe.

Dwight was up first, and he approached the bench with the confidence of a lion. With his velvety, baritone voice, he first summarized the facts of the case and then explained the decision to drop the negligent homicide charge. Somehow, he made the dismissal sound like they'd done Kyle a huge favor instead of admitting they never would have been able to make the homicide charge stick. Judge Gallagher looked bored, yawning without attempting to stifle a low sigh.

When it sounded like Dwight was about to wrap things up, he struck off on a tangent about the dangers of not paying attention on the road. "Nowadays, too many people think they need to plug into their devices twenty-four-seven. They might miss out on something if they're not intravenously connected to the rest of the world every moment of the day. God forbid they miss the breaking news about some reality TV star's new clothing line or a pop singer's latest dance moves on TikTok. We must reset this country's priorities and get people back on track and focused on what's truly important. While the law doesn't generally require an ordinary citizen to do what's morally acceptable, to act like a Good Samaritan when someone's in need, New York State is clear about requiring drivers involved in a hit-and-run accident to stop and at least call for help. If Kyle Beasley had obeyed the law, Amy Shawver may still be alive today."

Judge Gallagher interjected. "Move it along, Mr. Wingassett. This isn't a trial. I'm not interested in your closing argument. I understand the parties in this case have reached a plea agreement, so please outline the terms for the record."

"Thank you, Your Honor." Dwight's ability to command the room was impressive. He adjusted his tie and drew his shoulders back before preaching more about the downslide in humanity among today's youth.

"I'm warning you now, Mr. Wingassett. The plea deal. On with it."

"Yes, Your Honor. Of course. The prosecution has agreed to accept the defendant's plea of guilty to the charge of fleeing the scene of an accident in exchange for a lesser sentence. Since the accident involved a fatality—the death of a beloved mother, an upstanding member of her community—the charge could carry up to seven years in prison. In this case, we have agreed to one year, with a driver's license suspension for two, followed by a probation period."

"Thank you," Judge Gallagher said. "Please be seated, Mr. Wingassett. It's your turn, Ms. Saks."

Valerie stood and tugged at the back of her skirt, which bunched around her thighs. "Good morning, Your Honor. My client appreciates the prosecution's willingness to compromise in this case. He is tremendously remorseful for what happened, as he knew the victim personally and understands how tragic her death is for her family and the Shawnee Springs community."

Val spoke eloquently. "Kyle's only explanation for not stopping to help Amy Shawver is that he panicked. He was disoriented and confused, so he sought refuge in the safety of his own home. He's extremely sorry and understands the need for justice. Despite his parents ' wishes, he admits his guilt in hopes of moving forward with his life. Kyle Beasley is a smart young man with a bright future. He'll carry out whatever punishment he's handed and learn from his mistakes. He won't escape culpability, as he'll always have a felony record to remind him of his lapse in judgment. We ask that you consider sparing him any significant prison time, allowing him and his family to put this nightmare behind them to the best of their ability. Thank you, Your Honor." Valerie sat down.

Caroline was pleased. She couldn't have said it better herself. While she still didn't agree with Kyle's decision to accept up to one year in prison, she knew his mind was made up. They could explore getting the felony record sealed later if possible. After revealing he remembered everything about the accident and could picture Amy Shawver's face crashing against his windshield, Kyle somehow needed to relieve himself of his guilt. If serving time was the way to do it, she'd support him—unconditionally. That's what parents do.

Her mind drifted to Grace, who went to school today instead of accompanying them to the courtroom. Her daughter wanted to avoid hearing Ethan speak out against their family first-hand, and Caroline didn't put up a fight. Grace could be too fragile to handle what the boy she'd apparently grown so close to might say. Aware of their situation, Mr. Leandry arranged for Grace's guidance counselor to keep tabs on her throughout the day. If anything seemed off, they would contact Caroline or Jordan right away.

As if Judge Gallagher could read Caroline's thoughts, she called Ethan forward to say a few words. Caroline hadn't noticed him earlier, but he and his dad were seated in the back corner of the courtroom, concealed by a news reporter. Ethan approached the judge with his head hung low, murmuring something unintelligible to anyone behind him, and then he returned to his seat.

What was happening? Why wasn't Ethan making the victim impact statement they'd been dreading?

Judge Gallagher broke the long silence. "For the record, Ethan Shawver has declined his right to speak in front of the defendant today. We'll proceed with his father's statement."

Caroline, overcome with relief at Ethan's apparent change of heart, held her breath as Dan Shawver walked toward the judge's bench then turned to face the back of the courtroom. She grabbed Jordan's hand and braced herself for what would come next. From everything she'd gathered about Dan recently, he was utterly grief-stricken, as expected. His words would undoubtedly be harsh and damning to her son's final sentence. She wanted to stay strong, prevent herself from crying and making a scene. But the moment he uttered his first syllable, Caroline lost it. Like a blown dandelion, her insides exploded, and she couldn't stop the tears from flowing. Burying her face in Jordan's shoulder, she closed her eyes tight and listened to the agony in Dan's voice.

****

Ethan was proud of himself for what he'd done. He'd simultaneously stood up to his dad and shown his concern for Grace and the rest of the Beasley family. He couldn't decipher the blank look on Dad's face when he returned to his seat, but that didn't matter. He'd followed his heart with no regrets.

As his father introduced himself to the people gathered to learn Kyle's fate, he stared down at a folded piece of paper that trembled in his hands. Ethan had seen Dad preparing a statement last night and desperately wanted to ask what it said, but he was afraid of hearing the truth in advance. Whatever Dad decided was beyond Ethan's control; he was entitled to say whatever he needed to ease his pain. If seeing Kyle Beasley behind bars satisfied Dad's need for retribution, let him do his best to make that happen. But in Ethan's heart, Kyle was already paying the ultimate price for his actions. Nothing anyone said or did could hurt worse than what Kyle told himself.

Dad's voice rang out in the courtroom, echoing as if they were all trapped inside a hollow cave. "What happened to my wife Amy was the ultimate tragedy. Losing her is the worst thing that has ever happened to me, my son Ethan, and her other son George. Everyone who knew Amy understood how special she was. All she wanted out of life was to be a good person. She'd give anyone the shirt off her back, most evidenced by her final act of caring when the organs she donated made a difference to others clinging to life when she couldn't."

Dad unfolded the paper still in his hands, stared at it for a few seconds, then crinkled it into a ball. "But what many people don't know about my wife is how she came to be such a kind-hearted person—the type of woman who cared more about others than herself. When I met Amy, she was drinking heavily. Her life was a train wreck. She'd lost custody of her only son George, was estranged from her son's father, and worked as a server at a conference center to keep from becoming homeless. I fell in love with her at first sight. I know that sounds corny, but it's true. There was something about her I couldn't resist. After I proposed and she moved here to Buffalo, I was happier than I've ever been, knowing I'd found my soulmate."

A single tear slid down his cheek, and he wiped it away with the paper ball. Ethan's insides screamed at seeing his dad so visibly shaken. He wanted to stand and interrupt, spare him any more anguish. But he sat in awe of his father's courage while anxiously awaiting the rest of the story.

"Before we married, Amy told me everything about her life in California and how bad it had been, which never deterred me from loving her. How she overcame her past convinced me even more that she was the right woman for me. You might be asking yourself what this has to do with Kyle Beasley and what kind of punishment he should receive. Besides disclosing how much Amy meant to me, the court needs to understand where I'm coming from when I say what I'm about to say. If anyone believes in second chances, it's me. Amy, of all people, understood how poor decisions can change someone's life trajectory, the same way an act of forgiveness can.

As much as I wanted to assign blame for my wife's death, I accept she died from an aneurysm, and there's no predicting whether Kyle's stopping would have made much difference. I also understand that he's a kid—the same age as mine and Amy's son, Ethan. Kids make mistakes, and denying leniency to Kyle Beasley makes no sense. He confessed to what he did, and I can tell how terrible he feels."

Pointing to the defense table, Dad continued, "If that were my son sitting in that chair over there, I'd want people to show some compassion no matter how hard it might be. Nothing's bringing my wife back, and there's no reason to send this young man to prison to make an example out of him. So, please, Your Honor, have mercy on Kyle Beasley and his family."

Ethan had closed his eyes somewhere in the middle of his father's statement. The words Dad uttered could have come from inside Ethan himself or from his mother in heaven. Ethan could feel Mom's presence. She was in the courtroom, watching over them and ensuring they understood the true meaning of compassion. Ethan wished Grace had been there to experience the pure honesty and power of absolution. Hearing about it after the fact would have to do. He opened his eyes at the sound of a sniffle, just in time to see Mrs. Beasley wipe her nose on Mr. Beasley's shoulder and kiss him on the cheek.

"Thank you, Mr. Shawver," Judge Gallagher said. "We appreciate your openness. If you're finished, you may sit down now."

Dad returned to the seat next to Ethan and took his hand. They interlaced fingers as Kyle addressed the court, agreeing to the plea deal and sincerely expressing the genuine remorse he and his father already understood in their hearts.

When Judge Gallagher handed down a sentence of a suspended driver's license for two years, one year's probation, and one hundred hours of community service—with no prison time—he and Dad embraced. Over his dad's shoulder, Ethan watched as Dwight Wingassett gathered his belongings from the prosecutor's table and walked toward Valerie Saks to shake her hand. She was busy hugging Kyle, who then approached his parents and melted into their arms.

Resisting the temptation to speak to the Beasleys, Ethan whispered in his dad's ear. "Let's get out of here. I wanna put flowers on Mom's grave and see what's happening with her headstone."

"Good idea. Then let's grab something to eat downtown at that new Italian place."

"Perfect," Ethan said. "It's definitely time for something new."

****

The morning after Thanksgiving, Caroline led her family through the Buffalo Niagara International Airport terminal, eager to board a flight to New York City. She

usan Poole

had a meeting with her agent about the new book idea that finally crystallized shortly after leading Grace away from the waterfall that terrible night. The same night Caroline herself *split wide open*—in a good way— allowing nothing but emotion to flood inside and fill the gap. She used the meeting with Toby as an excuse for a family trip. "Mandatory family fun," she called it.

Both kids protested when she and Jordan first announced their plans, but none of their excuses had merit. Kyle started his community service job in mid-January, and baseball practice was optional over the long weekend. Since soccer season ended after being knocked out in the second playoff round, Grace could only argue that she didn't want to miss out on her social schedule back home. So, Caroline insisted, and Jordan backed her up. After everything they'd just been through, nothing was more important than getting away together, and there was no better time to visit New York than before Christmas, when the city buzzes with holiday cheer. Neither of her kids had ever been there. "Trust me. You're going to love it," she said.

Arriving at the TSA Security Check, they stopped at the long line of people snaked around rows of black stanchions. Weary-looking travelers removed their shoes, loaded their belongings into gray plastic bins, and waited for space on the conveyor belt. Others readied themselves to align their feet with the white outlines on the floor of the X-ray scanner, raising their hands over their heads and holding their breath. Caroline suddenly remembered what a pain-in-the-ass air travel could be, and it was nice to have Jordan and the kids by her side for a change.

"Anyone hungry?" Caroline asked after they cleared

security. "We've got more than an hour before our flight boards."

"Me! Me!" Grace took off toward the coffee kiosk.

"Wait up!" Kyle hopped to catch up with her.

Caroline watched as the kids laughed and elbowed each other once they got in line. She looked at Jordan, walking alongside her, and said, "We sure are lucky. Things could have ended up a lot differently than they did."

Jordan nodded. "Don't get ahead of yourself. There's plenty more to work through. We've got to get Grace some counseling as soon as we get back. Kyle, too. They've both got a lot to process."

"We do, too," she said. "I think marriage counseling would be good for us."

"Haven't I been saying that for years?"

Her face glowed. "You have. But I'm finally listening." She stopped abruptly in the middle of the terminal and planted a kiss on Jordan's cheek. A female traveler, who must not have been paying attention to where she was walking, crashed her rolling suitcase into the back of Caroline's leg.

"Hey! Watch where—" Caroline caught herself before snapping and turned around to see who ran into her. "I'm sorry. I didn't mean to stop in your path."

The woman behind her grimaced and tugged at the headscarf atop her head. "You could have at least stepped over to the side," she said. But then her face softened. "Wait a second! You're Caroline Beasley. I recognize you from your book jacket."

Caroline smiled and inched toward the wall to escape the rest of the oncoming foot traffic. Jordan and the woman followed. "I am. And what's your name?"

"Jackie. Jackie Stone."

"Nice to meet you, Jackie. This is my husband, Jordan." He nodded as Caroline placed a hand on his arm. "Again, my apologies for stopping so suddenly in your path."

"It's all right. I can't believe I ran into you at the airport. I just finished my second round of chemo. I read your book while sitting in that damn chair getting my infusions. You're an inspiration."

Caroline cringed, wondering what exactly Jackie had taken away from her writing. Had she been inspired because her story was one of overcoming adversity, or because of the warrior-like attitude she was best known for but now semi-regretted? Wanting to set the record straight, she said, "My story is one of many, and I've been rethinking the message I want to send to other cancer patients. I'm working on a new book right now. Can I contact you for input sometime?"

"Of course," Jackie beamed and handed over a business card. "I've got to hurry and catch my flight, but I'm flattered. Thank you. Please call or email me anytime."

Once Jackie disappeared around the corner, Kyle returned with a carrier full of hot drinks.

"Where's your sister?" Jordan said with a hint of panic in his voice.

Kyle snapped his head around, bobbling the cup carrier without spilling a drop. "Huh. She was behind me a second ago."

"There she is," Caroline said with a sigh of relief. "Talking with Ethan Shawver by the restroom."

"Ethan Shawver? What's he doing here?" Jordan said.

"Yeah. Of all people. What are the odds of bumping into him here?" said Kyle.

But running into Ethan was no coincidence. Earlier, Grace told Caroline that Ethan and his father were headed out of town to visit George in California. There'd been some talk Ethan would move there in January, but he'd changed his mind and settled on a short vacation during the school break. Since they were all flying out of the same gate around the same time, he and Grace had arranged to see each other to say goodbye. No one else knew they were still "talking" until now. Caroline wasn't sure how Jordan or Kyle would take it.

Without warning, Caroline felt a tap on her shoulder. She turned to find Dan Shawver standing so close she could smell the coffee on his breath. "I guess there's no keeping those two apart." He tipped his head toward Ethan and Grace.

"We're okay with it if you are." She looked at Jordan for affirmation, and they joined eyes. His unspoken acceptance comforted her.

"I'll come around," Dan said. "Did you have a nice Thanksgiving?"

"We did. What about you?" The moment the words escaped her mouth, she wanted to reel them back in. How insensitive could she be? Of course, he hadn't had a nice Thanksgiving. It was his first one without Amy.

Caroline wanted to disappear in a puff of smoke like a genie or wriggle her nose and vanish like a witch—whichever provided the quickest escape from a very awkward situation.

But Dan answered immediately. "It was nice. Different, but nice. Ethan and I spent our morning baking a pie from one of Amy's recipes, and we took it to my brother's house to share with his family."

Jordan jumped in. "Where are you two headed now?"

"California. Ethan's half-brother lives there, and he offered us a tour of some places he and Amy lived when he was younger. It'll be good for Ethan to learn about the parts of his mom's life he knows nothing about. Good for me, too."

The sadness cutting across Dan's face prompted Caroline to change the subject. "We didn't get a chance to thank you Monday," she said.

"Thank me for what?"

"For what you said at Kyle's sentencing. Without your support, he may have been sitting behind bars instead of boarding a plane with his family. We'll be forever grateful for your kindness."

Dan stammered. "It was the right thing to do. The same way dropping my civil suit is—you'll get formal notice next week. This isn't easy for me. I'm not quite ready to talk about much else."

"We understand," Caroline said. "More than you'll ever realize." She wanted to repeat how sorry she was about Amy's death, but no words sufficed. Instead, she stepped closer and held out her arms, mouthing a simple, "Is it okay?"

Without answering, Dan allowed Caroline to wrap him in a warm embrace. She held him tight as the world continued around them, only loosening a little when her gaze landed on Grace and Ethan as they hugged farewell a few yards away.

Goodbyes are difficult, made easier by the promise of another day. But life doesn't come with a guarantee— of just about anything except the here and now.

As Caroline clung to Dan, she breathed in the moment and vowed never to waste another second angry or disconnected. A vague new theme for her next book took shape.

After boarding the flight to New York City and settling into her window seat, Caroline closed her eyes and began brainstorming more ideas. The thought of sharing a fresh perspective with readers filled her with excitement. She imagined a story that would be messy and unpredictable yet filled with love, joy, and plenty of forgiveness—enough to last a lifetime, no matter what that might mean.

Acknowledgments

Expressing thanks to everyone who helped me reach this point in my publishing journey is insurmountable. So many people. Too little space.

First, I'll be forever grateful to my friend and critique partner extraordinaire, author Brenda Haas. If our paths hadn't crossed at a WFWA conference, this book might still be unpublished and collecting dust alongside my first two novels. Thank you to Najla Mahis and the entire team at The Wild Rose Press. I am humbled by the warm welcome to the Rose Garden and appreciate everything you've done to make my dream a reality.

To Kathy Moore Heine, Dave Vattimo, and Brenda Wittman, I'm thankful for your early interest in my work and for being so generous with your time whenever I asked for feedback. To Michelle Meade, your editorial advice helped shape this story in ways I never could have imagined on my own. To Pat Revzin, while you weren't involved in this project, I'll never forget everything I learned from our years of back-and-forth emails.

To Kathy Fagan. This one is tough. I've never met anyone with whom I connected as easily as I did with you. Your faith and input into this novel made it so much stronger. I'm deeply saddened that you're not here in person to celebrate my debut's launch, but I can feel you cheering me on from heaven.

To Patti Klenk, your friendship and support over the last 25+ years has kept me sane. I couldn't have achieved this milestone without you.

Thank you to my parents for instilling a love of reading and writing from the very first bedtime story you told me. To my brothers for believing in me unconditionally. And to Brett, Kendall, Addy, and Hudson, you are my world. Love you to the moon and back!

A word about the author…

Susan Poole enjoys delving into the moral gray area, developing a passion for exploring both sides of a situation while attending law school at the University of Buffalo. After leading a nonprofit social services agency for almost a decade, a breast cancer diagnosis gave her the courage to finally pursue her lifelong dream of becoming a writer. Susan lives in Cleveland, Ohio, where she and her husband raised their three children and remain empty nesters with two spoiled dogs to keep them company. Out of the Crash is her first novel. susanpooleauthor.com